Bandita Bonita
and
Billy the Kid

The Scourge of New Mexico

Bandita Bonita
and
Billy the Kid

The Scourge of New Mexico

Nicole Maddalo Dixon

SUNSTONE PRESS

SANTA FE

Sunstone books may be purchased for educational, business, or sales promotional use.
For information please write: Special Markets Department, Sunstone Press,
P.O. Box 2321, Santa Fe, New Mexico 87504-2321.

Cover art by Jim Paul

Book design › Vicki Ahl
Body typeface › Aparajita
Printed on acid-free paper
∞
eBook 978-1-61139-472-6

Library of Congress Cataloging-in-Publication Data

Names: Maddalo-Dixon, Nicole, author.
Title: Bandita Bonita and Billy the Kid : the scourge of New Mexico / by
  Nicole Maddalo Dixon.
Description: Santa Fe : Sunstone Press, [2016]
Identifiers: LCCN 2016017535 (print) | LCCN 2016022773 (ebook) | ISBN
  9781632931337 (softcover : acid-free paper) | ISBN 9781611394726
Subjects: LCSH: Women outlaws--Fiction. | Billy, the Kid--Fiction. |
  Outlaws--Fiction. | GSAFD: Biographical fiction. | Western stories. | Love
  stories.
Classification: LCC PS3613.A283466 B365 2016 (print) | LCC PS3613.A283466
  (ebook) | DDC 813/.6--dc23
LC record available at https://lccn.loc.gov/2016017535

SUNSTONE PRESS IS COMMITTED TO MINIMIZING OUR ENVIRONMENTAL IMPACT ON THE PLANET.
THE PAPER USED IN THIS BOOK IS FROM RESPONSIBLY MANAGED FORESTS. OUR PRINTER HAS RECEIVED CHAIN OF CUSTODY (COC)
CERTIFICATION FROM: THE FOREST STEWARDSHIP COUNCIL™ (FSC®), PROGRAMME FOR THE ENDORSEMENT OF FOREST CERTIFICATION™ (PEFC™),
AND THE SUSTAINABLE FORESTRY INITIATIVE® (SFI®).
THE FSC® COUNCIL IS A NON-PROFIT ORGANIZATION, PROMOTING THE ENVIRONMENTALLY APPROPRIATE, SOCIALLY BENEFICIAL AND
ECONOMICALLY VIABLE MANAGEMENT OF THE WORLD'S FORESTS. FSC® CERTIFICATION IS RECOGNIZED INTERNATIONALLY
AS A RIGOROUS ENVIRONMENTAL AND SOCIAL STANDARD FOR RESPONSIBLE FOREST MANAGEMENT.

WWW.SUNSTONEPRESS.COM
SUNSTONE PRESS / POST OFFICE BOX 2321 / SANTA FE, NM 87504-2321 /USA
(505) 988-4418 / ORDERS ONLY (800) 243-5644 / FAX (505) 988-1025

Dedication

To two of the most very important loves of my life:
My nieces, Alexandria Nicole and Samantha Maria

"Dream big and dare to fail."
—Norman Vaughan

Preface

The legend of Billy the Kid is one that has been told over and over again, well before the young boy ever breathed his last.

Before I wrote my first book, *Bandita Bonita: Romancing Billy the Kid*, I intended to simply write a historically accurate, fictional account of Billy, a sort of modern-told biography. There is so much about the Kid we don't know, and my intention was to fill in those gaps by creating an interesting version of the biographical accounts for the reader's disposal. My inspiration for the modern telling of this story had a couple of checkpoints which were as follows: I wouldn't simply pilfer the hard-won research uncovered by revered historians and pass it off as my own work, and I had no intention of telling the same story yet again. Use what I've been taught by those who worked hard to give us his story, yes, but give it my own outlook. His story has been told many times over from the many different perspectives of historians and authors (not to mention in film and song), but it's always the same story with slivers of new information if the reader is lucky. I simply chose to give it my own spin.

I decided I wanted to give my audience an interpretation of who I believed the Kid to be. I didn't want to create another retelling of the same old tale. Interesting though the biographies are, of course (and without the numerous accounts of which I wouldn't have gained the amazing insight I have into William H. Bonney, and for that I will always be grateful for and cherish them), I wanted to breathe new life into his story. I wanted to create an example for a new generation, and so I wrote the events as true as I know them to be as historical fiction for a modern audience. It was, however, very important to me to keep things as accurate as possible. I had a responsibility to Billy's legacy, as all historians do, if I planned to articulate his life.

With the advent of the main protagonist, Lucy Howard (or the titular Bandita), I was able to bring the reader intimately close to Billy in such a way that a male protagonist could not, but I found she presented another aspect of the Victorian time period: The oppression of the female individual.

Lucy represented the restrained yet strong-willed, resolute woman of the century, but she did something other than get close to Billy, and that was to play the part of the foil to Billy's "chilling" outlaw. She drives him absolutely crazy and challenges him repeatedly, but he adores her nevertheless.

Billy was impassioned, could be ruthless if crossed, and possessed the grit to back up his words with a bullet if he had to, but he was also fiercely loyal, had a gratuitous sense of humor, and was a well-groomed (often referred to as a "dandy" in his day), respectful gentleman to the elderly, children, and especially the ladies. His relationship with Lucy grants contention to this last point and allows the reader to explore the romantic tension between male and female, but Lucy also allows humor to flow freely into the story and lets Billy be human in the way he deserves rather than the cold-blooded killer he's become known as through legend.

I had only intended to write one book, but as time would prove, there was so much to this story that an extension only seemed inevitable. In the first half of the first book I had to communicate character development to the reader, and in addition I had to relate the tension that led to the little-big, famous (but oft forgot) war that made Billy who he was—Without that war, there would be no Billy the Kid. And then there was the fact that I had fallen absolutely in love with Lucy and realized that she had much to say, and not just about Billy the Kid and his tribulations, but about her own circumstances. It became my understanding that she would be an integral part of the story on so many levels, whether we're talking about the role of women during the 19th century, or vividly relating Billy's story. She's wildly vocal and has a wonderfully frank sense of sass. She was the perfect match-wit for Billy, and I wanted to discover what this girl was about. I wanted to explore her relationship with him, giving them both the chance to explain who they are to their audience. It was fiction meeting fact, yes, but Lucy is very real in the mind. She is a representation of what many of us women want out of life. The difference is the period of time we live in.

Because this book is not only relative to Billy and the events of his life, but also a portrait of his legend, and because Lucy gets a say, it is an extensive tale, and one I plan to continue telling.

Prologue

July, 1878

The McSween home was burning, illuminated magnificently against the night sky as each of us stood silently thanking God that we had escaped the infernal death trap, and that fate had not seen to it that we were one of the unlucky.

We listened to the triumphant, morose carnival that echoed throughout the black night from the Dolan boys and soldiers alike, shouts and thunderous shots of victory declaring their triumph over the Regulators and our dead who lay at their feet.

Gruesome music came from the strings of a fiddle as it announced our defeat, drifting down to where we stood huddled together, our bodies bitter from the biting dampness of the Bonito as its water soaked our soiled, ragged clothes and caused them to lie heavy against our skin.

Victory continued to strum upon strings playing a morose tune we were forced to hear, but in my grief I felt Billy's arms come around me tightly, protectively, as he buried his face in my neck. He was relieved. He could breathe knowing that I had made it through the squall of gunfire unharmed and was standing here with him now. It surprised me not at all that he must have given no thought to his own entanglement with near-death.

None of us spoke. We only turned to go and get out while we could.

Part I
Fallout

1

September, 1878

We fled to the hills on the outskirts of Lincoln County in order to lay low for a spell. The Regulators did not believe that it was they who had been defeated. As far as it concerned them, it was they who had been victorious despite their severe losses. The head of their faction, McSween, was dead, and there were collateral damages they would need to recoup: horses and other various necessities left behind and burned, or confiscated by Sheriff Peppin.

Tuntall's death was now considered avenged and shut of, but with McSween's death new wounds were torn open and the Regulators' avengement would start anew. It occurred to me that Alex's death was not a simple misfortune, a casualty of war, but a measured insult— an intentional exploit to goad the Regulators into a prolonged fight, a stinging shot of salt in their raw wounds. The Ring wasn't finished with them yet.

Rumor in Lincoln and its surrounding counties and villages claimed that Billy was the most wanted man in all the New Mexico Territory, a convenient, primed scapegoat to make an example of. And so the Dolan men were on the lookout for the Regulators as they were impatient to finish the war and crush them once and for all, but they were unable to locate them as the Regulators went on their way, always one step ahead of Dolan, knowing the terrain and trails better than his faction. They went along replenishing their inventory, ill-gotten and without hindrance.

We passed on through the Mescalero Agency and sought refuge in the small scattered villages and placitas in the surrounding area, landing again in Picacho.

Leaving the hills for this small village sanctuary attracted the boys to its gambling and dance halls and tempted them to act wildly—dancing, drinking, and misbehaving with regular all-around hell-raising which was meant in the interest of celebrating life after our so considered "Great Triumph" and acquaintance with death in Lincoln. In their opinion, it was not the Ring who had been victorious.

I contemptuously wondered if the boys would administer vengeance for every friend who would be lost as a result of this fight. Death was a hazard of this war, and one would think that fact ought to have been accepted. But I knew it was of no use to protest the retaliation they would dole out as retribution at the drop of a hat if they saw fit to do so. They were unstable in this regard. They were arrogant and prideful, vilely pleased with themselves. But I suppose when a man faced death in the way they had, he earned his right to live life a little more boldly. But they were not ignorant to their good fortune at making it through, and I was only too happy to let Billy celebrate by wearing me out in bed.

Billy's cool prevailing head and grace under fire had earned him a place as the newly appointed, illustrious commander of what was left of the Regulators. He was put up alongside me and the others in the home of a sympathizer and friend by the name of Herman Guzman. So busy was Billy with strategic campaigning that I was most likely a mere, fleeting thought to him. I did not take offense as I was confident that this would change once he grew used to his new position and again came to terms with the true horror of our situation.

I had lost my personal effects in the McSween fire, leaving only with my guns and the ruined clothes on my back. I now sat wearing a traditional Mexican china poblana, a loose fitting, low-cut blouse that caused me discomfort as my bosom was exposed for all to see, and so I clung to a shawl that I wrapped tightly about my shoulders. I wore a long, castor skirt that allowed the slip beneath to peek out. I was horrified by the indecency of the clothing, and I wore no shoes. It was comfortable, I could not argue that, but regardless, I did not feel confident or at ease dressed in this manner. I wanted my proper clothes back.

When I told Billy of my need for new clothes, he said, "I know it, Mí Querida. We'll fix that right up soon enough. You'll do all right for now."

"And how should you know? I won't ride to another godforsaken place dressed like this."

Laughing, he replied, "*Santo Dios*! I got it. I'll take care of you. Besides, we'll be staying here for a while yet."

"Oh. So I get to do 'all right' in these clothes for a while, do I?"

"Oye, Princesa! Be thankful these people are kind enough to put clothes on your back!"

I sat on the edge of our bed with my feet propped up by the frame, chastened. My elbows rested on my knees and I cradled my face in my hands and frowned.

"Niña, you know I do believe this is the most I've heard from you in a long while. Why don't we make ourselves a pleasant visit?"

"I don't have much to say to you. And besides, I don't see you making any effort to pry any words loose from me, either."

He looked at me with a curious grin. "Why is it you're so ornery?"

"Are you really so obtuse? How can you not know?"

He frowned at my fussy vocabulary and then slid onto the bed beside me with his arms crossed, one over the other.

"Obtuse?"

"*Dumb.*"

He laughed. "Sí, I should've guessed. I believe I know none of this should put you in a good mood."

"Oh, no?" I said, mocking him.

He sighed lightheartedly as I sulked. I hadn't looked at him since he had come to me and I had no intention of doing so in any event. I could not. My resolve to be angry with him would collapse if I looked at his sweet, pretty face and into his light, cerulean eyes, and I wanted very much to be unhappy with him.

"I see you have plenty of time for your little señioritas."

He smiled, genuinely amused. "Is that why you're behaving like such a little mocosa?"

"I know what that word means, and I don't like it."

He laughed.

"That girl...Adriana. The one you've been playing around with—she's troubling me, always, but that's not all. I'm displeased by your new appointment. Look at you now, captain of your little gang out there, Chief Wandering Eye. And the word is out that you're to blame for that Mescalero business and the murder of that clerk, did you know? You were fingered by name, you and Henry both."

"Yeah, I heard." And taking his chance to get me back for the snide remark I'd made he said, "So what anyway, Little Cries A Lot?"

I gave him a nasty look as he smiled back, pleased with himself.

"My *God*, Billy. You just keep digging yourself in deeper and deeper. You had nothing to do with that mess and still they're pinning you for it. You're now accredited crimes you had nothing to do with. Hasn't all that's happened been enough to prove to you that pushing forward would be unwise? That I was right from the beginning? Surely you can finally see where this is headed by now."

"They're going to do all they can to drown us out like rats, you know that."

"So then I shouldn't mind?"

He sat up and hugged his knees to his chest, resting his head on them.

"Fine," he reached over and took my hand in his. "What is it you need from me, Bonita? You're what I care about. *That* I can fix."

I pulled my hand from his and crossed my arms.

"Forget about that. I'm too proud to let you to placate me—if I need to explain *why* my emotions are so unfit."

He pulled his face into a knot of struggled thought.

"So...am I supposed to figure you don't want me to pay you attention because it's what you want me to want on my own instead of doing it because you say so?"

I was impressed by how well he understood me. He was no fool.

"Something like that," I spat.

"Well, I *do* want it on my own. I want to talk with you, querida bebé."

He reached out to me again, but I sulkily shrugged away from him.

"No, you don't have the time," I conceded sadly. "I know that, even if I don't like it."

"I always have the time for you. Anything you want from me, you just ask me."

"I want new clothes."

He laughed. "Yeah, you said so. I told you, I'll take care of it."

"Well, when? I don't feel very self-assured dressed like this. And I haven't any shoes."

"I'll get you shoes. Just tolerate the rest a few more days, all right?"

"If you say so," I answered, trying to sound bitter.

He got up from the bed, stood up straight and stretched, and hooked his thumbs into his gun belt.

"Good God, Niña. *My*, but you can be *mean*." He then looked at me impishly, "You trying to make me want you? Because I gotta tell ya, the more ornery you get the more interested *I* get."

I rolled my eyes. "How is it you can make jokes at a time like this?"

"What else should I do? You want me to sit around miserable as you? *Esto es lo que es*. What's happened is done and it can't be undone. I'd rather set my mind to the work that's ahead of us—that's what I'm about."

"Don't you understand? There doesn't have to *be* any more work to be done. All of this concern you have with this...*conflict*. You must forget how very well I know you. I can see how you're all in high spirits over this ugly business and still out for blood—you just don't want to let it go. How is it that it doesn't affect you like it does me?"

He was thoughtful a moment. "It angers me, but I accept it. I accept what it means, what has to be done. I understand why it bothers you. I wouldn't expect you to react any other way. And I'm sorry you're feeling low, but you'll come back around. If I need to spend time by your side, I will."

He sat back down on the bed next to me and put his arm around me affectionately.

"I do miss you," he whispered, moving to place his face against mine. "And as for Adriana, don't worry two pence about her, okay? Ignore her."

"I do, but she makes an effort to stare me down. I can't walk past her without her stopping to take stock of me."

"Well, she's touchy. I don't pay her as much mind as you seem to think. You want I should talk to her?"

"Oh, ain't *you* such a prize, always saving the day!" I scoffed. "No, leave it as it is."

"Whatever you want, poquita cariña."

∞∞∞∞∞∞

Outside the solace of the villages that harbored us, gossip ran wild that the Regulators were causing trouble around the territory. Some of this was true, but some was catastrophically false. An Indian agent by the name of Godfroy claimed that the Kid intended to kill him, and a former Lincoln County Sheriff, Saturnino Baca, accused Charlie and Jim French of threatening his life by burning down his home. This was all nonsense. The Regulators were indeed bringing an undesirable amount of attention to themselves with their raucous, careless celebrating and reckless undertakings of collecting stolen property, but they in no way went directly from such a scandalous conflict in Lincoln to threatening anyone's life, especially if it should serve no direct purpose. I was long weary, and I was disgusted by those who were in so much need of attention that they sought to gain it by making out as if the celebrated Regulators had it out for them. Anybody with a thimbleful of common sense would have guessed that the Regulators couldn't concern themselves with such petty grievances: the pathetic few who wanted to garner attention by playing that they held some importance with the notorious gang.

2

September, 1878

We made plans to ride to Chisum's ranch along the Pecos driving stolen heads of cattle from the Mescalero Agency.

Before the excursion, Billy put together a spruce getup for himself that made him look both fine and well-trimmed, as was his preference, and he had me outfitted as grandly as possible in the little placita that gave us refuge. I had gotten the smallest pair of boys riding trousers that could be found. They were corded and fit me nearly well, but they needed a small amount of tailoring so as to fit and show off my figure in a way that should please the menfolk now that I wore sporting britches instead of skirts, but the style of the pants were cut low and put me in such a state as they came to rest directly at my navel. But, around the waist, there were bandolero style cartridge loops for shotgun shells and this made up for my unease as I liked the look of it. Though I didn't yet know how to fire a shotgun, I was pleased with the effect as I had to wear my gun belt loose to accommodate the bandolero loops so that my belt slung unevenly about my hips.

Billy also had tailored for me a new suede jacket, and though it was not as fine or as soft as the expensive kid suede jackets I had lost, it still fit me almost as nicely and managed to help compliment my figure along with the trousers. He also had me furnished with a new pair of spurs and gave me a present of a bowie knife with a sheath that I could strap to my thigh.

"Any maldito idiota gives you trouble, mi niña, you cut that pedazo de mierda left to right,"—he slid his right forefinger from the left side of his throat to the right—"you understand me, my love?"

He smiled playfully as he said this, and I nodded enthusiastically. Billy was being fairly playful, but I knew he meant the words he spoke and it frightened me a little. But I understood. He wanted my safety at all costs.

When we reached Chisum's ranch Billy spent some of his time with Sallie, and I couldn't blame him as my mood was sour and she embodied all of the elements that passed for a lady. Unlike last year, it was I who now felt awkward because of our difference in appearance—the tables had turned, and I could no longer exhibit grandeur over her, at least not outwardly. My refinement was relinquished as she was, by comparison, much finer than I considering my circumstances. She was well-groomed, though I always made it a point to maintain myself despite my predicament. Still, this time, it was she who seemed a lady to the manor born.

Unlike that afternoon when Billy first kissed me here on this very land and it was I who had chagrined and embarrassed Sallie, now it was I who felt I had been put in my place without so much as one word from her, though I knew this was my own imagination. Superiority existed within, but my self-assuredness had been weakened due to the coarse trials I had suffered.

Sallie reacted with trepidation toward me at first because, at first sight, I seemed to possess an ostensibly hard-bitten demeanor which, of course, did nothing for my self-esteem as a lady. And didn't Billy just buy her thoughtful little presents and chocolate candy, making me feel more the worse for wear? *The little cad.* I disliked his behavior with her and kept my distance from them both. I was so focused on my own jealousy that I had forgotten just how deep still waters ran with Billy and me, and being reminded of this calmed me. Billy cared not for how I appeared on the outside. He loved me for who I was and what I meant to him.

Walking about the property with only my thoughts to keep me company I heard my name called. I turned to see Sallie walking toward me in the yard. Unease enshrouded my common sense as she approached, and my composure unexpectedly failed me. It never would have occurred to me that I should falter in the presence of another woman. My etiquette, once impeccable, was fostered to inhibit such a thing, yet my heart raced with alarm. Warmth flushed my cheeks, my anxiety flaring irrepressibly in the moment. I was not accustomed to this reaction as I had never had to burden myself with the uneasiness brought on by fair innocence, but these days, my circumstances being what they were, my emotions were fickle at best.

"I see you've managed to fit in after all," she opined, seeming to gaze upon me reproachfully.

I could not tell if her comment was intended as a cruel slight or merely an innocent observation based on a conversation we'd shared the day I had come to visit in December of last year. I confided in her, then, that I had wished for an agreeable existence in Lincoln despite my legacy, hopeful that I'd be able to mend the differences between east and west and make friends with ease. Was it only my newly infected imagination that she appeared to put on airs?

Course and direct, I asked, "What is it I should think you mean, Sallie?"

"Well, just look at you now. And you have dressed the part grandly! And you were so worried, having to mind the gap between yourself and the people of the territory. It would seem you are a natural after all, fitting in as seamlessly as a stitch would have it."

I sensed, indeed, a hint of assertive spitefulness concealed in her words, but the edge of contradiction had cut its way in, allowing me to perceive a moral confliction within her. Her ill-behavior nurtured doubt, and I could feel her discomfort as she struggled to demean me as I had done her when last we met. She had plans to make me suffer, but her kindly nature had trouble coping with such a vexing performance.

With my spirit rising to the occasion and taking full advantage of her visible guilt, I feigned ignorance and replied, "Yes, Sallie. I shouldn't be surprised at all that you have managed to recognize my newly established character"—I smiled sweetly—"Well..."—I looked down and bore an insincere, awkward expression—"I suppose I didn't have much of a choice when it came to disposing of my finery, what with Brady on the hunt for me after his vicious murdering of my John. My attire must be practical if I am to be hidden away in such a place to survive, as you would know. Blending in is vital, or so I've been told."

Her face softened a bit at hearing this, her lips parting as though they meant to impart a few kind words, perhaps feeling sorry for me and wanting to settle things between us, her guilt instructing her to set things right and treat me with kindness.

But with a rapidity that would have shamed a bolt of lightning, her demeanor altered. She realized, a second too slow, that I had only been toying with her.

Setting her shoulders straight and stiffening her jaw, she said, "Yes, that must have been quite a chore—a real culture shock for you, to have to fend for yourself and run for your life, thriving like a desert rat among men—"

She stopped suddenly, growing quiet and abashed.

"Careful, Sallie. Billy's one of them desert rats thriving like such."

The catty bitch! It was clear that she was unable to figure out the game she and I were playing, the decency of her western breeding superseding the desire to prick with eastern thorns. She cleared her throat as if to pretend her last, horrid words had not been spoken—as if I were to ignore or forget her response had ever occurred.

"So I've heard," she replied, and with a look of concern she fabricated worry. "But by now you are most certainly out of danger and safe."

Through squinted eyes I peered at her and wondered, *was she really so simple?*

Did she honestly believe her shift in tone had fooled me into forgetting she had made that dreadful remark? Well, it was no matter. I had grown bored anyway.

"One can never truly tell, Sallie. I'm now a marked woman, riding with the Regulators and standing right there beside them during that awful skirmish in Lincoln. I have been made an enemy."

She observed me silently, looking me up and down and taking stock of my person. She must have indeed thought herself grander than I when at first we began to speak, but she had missed her mark in trying to intimidate me. I felt sorry for her. If my controversial appearance is what it took for her to feel as though she were above me, then truly, it served only to prove that I was much more sophisticated than she, for she obviously clung to the superficial belief that I was fallen by the clothes I wore, and if my outward appearance should cause me to fall so low in her eyes for her to feel she had finally beaten me, then let her have her simple happiness for she was none the wiser. It was the mind and the tongue that did the bidding of superiority, and at this she could not beat me.

"Besides, Sallie," I continued, "I am having the greatest adventure of my life. I cannot tell you how exhilarating everything has been. It's as though I've only just been born and am seeing everything for the first time in my life."

Her eyes grew wide. "So you mean to tell me you enjoy the horrors you must face every day?"

"Of course not! There is the occasional predicament. That is true. But I am well protected enough. But what I mean to tell you is that you cannot imagine that freedom *truly* exists. Wars have been fought for it and men have died in its name for centuries, and it is often talked about by blustering, arrogant politicians who are masters among men. But it was always just a word to me—a word that meant nothing that I once only read about in books, but it's real. It's real, and it is out there."

I stretched my arm out in dramatic pose and pointed as I tried to indicate the idea. Her eyes followed but seemed mired by the boundaries of the yard despite the wide open space before her. She did not understand—the idea was incomprehensible to her.

My enthusiasm felled her attempt at making me feel small yet again. I had beaten her at her own game once more. *I will always win.*

I went on, declaring, "At night, one has never seen such beautiful skies in all their life! The stars come out so bright that they seem as though a million little diamonds. And if I choose, I can return home anytime I like, but I'm all too fond of my life here, things that I have experienced because of Billy and want to keep experiencing with him. To spend all my time with him, no matter the circumstances. Without a thought, I would endure *hell* just to be with him!" *And I have*, I thought. "Billy is liberation to me."

Believing Billy was her ticket in bringing me to heel, she said, "I see. Speaking of Willie...he had bought me gifts of chocolate and a tobacco pouch."

I seethed but countered, "And so did you enjoy them, then? I suggested he pick them out." I didn't, of course, but how should she know? "As you are friends, I thought he should not come empty-handed, and I told him so. It is also my understanding that he had thoughtfully written you a letter just before the troops burned Alex's home right to the ground."

Letting her know I was aware of this intimate action removed any pleasure she might have had in telling me otherwise.

"Yes," she answered. She was looking down, defeated by my knowledge of what she had counted as a private, affectionate gesture on Billy's behalf. "he did write."

Suddenly, there was a measure within me that ran warm with emotion for Billy, so I told her, "He is a good man, and he considers you a dear friend, Sallie. No matter what degrading rumors you might hear of him, you must ignore them. It is the Santa Fe Ring's sole purpose to destroy the credibility of the Regulators, and Billy's most definitely, when the Regulators are only trying to reinstate fairness to the people of the territory. Billy has made himself a first-rate enemy of them. They would be happy to catch-as-catch-can."

She nodded her head so slightly I might have only imagined it. And Billy! Giving her presents of chocolate and Indian pouches. *Indeed*!

"Oh, and look here!" I instructed, showing her the finger of my left hand which boasted the ring Billy had given me. "This ring is the only thing Billy has left of his mother, and it is I above all whom he felt should have it—better than any other gift a man could give!"

I made this my final point to let her know I was done with all of this, and for good measure I made a great show of beaming down at the precious little symbol, and she looked upon it, appreciating its significance.

"Can you imagine what I must mean to him? For him to give me such a treasured gift?"

At this, Sallie retreated. The game was now up and I was victorious once again.

Fortunately, we did not stay long, though unfortunately, we headed back to Fort Sumner were Paulita was. With the exception of Josiah and Charlie who stayed on at Chisum's taking jobs on his ranch, the rest of the Regulators had come with us to Sumner and Billy made them a big celebration. Again, just as I had in the little villages, I kept to my room and ignored the little baile.

As I sat in my room at the Maxwell house I peered into the mirror and reflected back on the conversation I held with Sallie. I wondered about my vanity and what she had supposed of me based on my appearance. Had my pride gone, along with my social graces and sensibilities? Or did it only lie resting beneath a disguise of western disposition.

Billy left the revelers to be with me. When he entered my room he stepped behind me without a word and leaned down to place his arms around my shoulders and affectionately brushed his lips against my neck as he often liked to do. He gently pulled me up from my chair and placed his arms about my waist, enfolding me, before taking me to my bed. He laid me down and then lay down beside me. He kept his arms around me for a long time until he fell asleep next to me. Before he drifted off I asked him why he'd come, leaving the excitement of the celebration. He yawned quietly and answered, saying that he preferred to be with me.

"You're my best niña pequeña in the whole world. It ain't any fun with you hiding away."

We left Sumner for the settlement of Puerto de Luna. After a short argument with Billy as to whether or not I should stay behind in Sumner, I won out and left with him for the "Gateway to the Moon" along with Tom, Jimmy, Minxie, Fred, John Middleton, and Henry Brown. Billy never could win these arguments with me because he knew he hadn't any cards to play. He couldn't force me to stay put unless he locked me away, and that he could never do. Sometimes I felt guilty knowing that it made him anxious to have me along, but what else could I do? I went where Billy went, and I wanted to go with my friends.

Puerto de Luna was so named because of a narrow gap in the hills to the east that revealed the moon as it cut its path across the sky. New Mexico had so many beautiful landscapes that I was often astounded by its beauty whenever I found myself camped out in God's country. In Puerto de Luna alone the stars were so bright and lively. They twinkled and winked and seemed prideful of their beauty. I could hardly make out the constellations as the stars were so plentiful and close that they crowded my eyes, and Billy would often play a game with me out in the dark before turning in, pointing out Cassiopeia or Orion. He pointed out Sirius of Canis Major and how it follows Orion the Hunter, telling me how it was the brightest star in the sky, and that it should make him think of me when he'd see it. Then he told me of its companion star and how maybe they could stand for us both, and I smiled at him for this. But then I wondered aloud if maybe he ought to be Orion the Hunter, with my star following his. He smiled at me, outshining any old star as I imagined I could see the little points of light twinkle in his eyes. By the dying fire he glowed, and the night sky behind him seemed to rotate around him so that he was ethereal. Finally, I leaned against him as we looked to the heavens before bed.

A celebration was held in honor of the Regulators that lasted two nights and this time I easily joined in. But we had become tremendously nomadic and soon departed from Puerto de Luna, heading for Anton Chico, a tough town by most accounts. When we arrived we discovered that a posse, led by a man named Desiderio Romero, sheriff of San Miguel County, was waiting for us. When Billy had heard Romero and his posse had been asking questions about us, he insisted that we have a look.

"Billy, let it go. I don't know why it is you go about looking for trouble," I said.

"Mi niña querida, there are times when I got no choice. *Uno no puede alejarse de destino de uno*. And when it rains, open your umbrella," he laughed, knowing full well I understood barely a word, his disposition full of good humor.

"Why do you play such games and enjoy them so much? Quit pretending it's your duty to confront the hangman and let's just run out and lose him."

"Niña!"

His brow furrowed so deeply that his blue eyes went dark as they stared at me in disbelief. He looked at me accusingly, in shock that I would dare suggest he turn tail and run as though he didn't know this was a favorite suggestion of mine.

"Now isn't the time to hide behind my mama's skirt. Sometimes you hafta make a stand—show 'em what you're about and that you mean business. Girl, don't you tell me that after everything you know you could think any different."

I thought a moment.

"Well...what about if you ran like a hen instead of die like a rooster?"

He looked at me crossways a moment, cocking his head and again furrowing his brow, but this time only slightly. He placed his hands on his hips and wore a look of confusion before nearly splitting his sides with laughter. He put his arm around me and pulled me to him as he wound down with a chuckle.

"Lucy," he laughed, "sometimes it's better to keep your mouth shut and look pretty than open it and look stupid."

I smiled in spite of myself and let him walk with his arm around me.

"It's true!" I declared. "I've heard your people say it."

"*My* people?"

"Yes, *your* people. The Mexicans.

"I believe you mean to say, "*Es preferible que la gente dice 'aqui huyó una gallina' en lugar de 'aqui murió un gallo'*"

"*What?*"

"It's better that people say 'here fled a hen' than to have them say 'here died a rooster'."

I lifted my chin and thought on that, understanding.

He stopped walking and turned me to him. Holding my face in his hands he put his to mine. "You are so precious to me. ¿Comprendes?"

I nodded, my nose rubbing against his, and he kissed me lightly on the lips before letting go and taking my hand, leading me along the street.

"Don't never let anybody tell you different, no matter what they think they know of me."

We went to the saloon where it was said the posse frequented, and there we found them. Eight large Mexican men. Billy, his swagger overpowering his self-preservation, approached Romero and dared him to do what it was he had intended. He dared him to take the Regulators. I was instructed to stand out of the way but I ignored this and crept closer still. Though he was properly backed up by the rest of the boys, his nerve disturbed me. I was used to him tempting fate sometimes with that hot-blooded Irish temper of his, but what a severe sense of disquiet this brought on for me. Why he insisted on putting himself out in the open was beyond me—it frustrated me to the quick. He was truly set on being dangerously prideful, though I must tell the truth and admit that this induced a spark in me. But oh! How it worried me.

Billy squinted cockily at Romero.

"Word around has it out that you're looking for us War Boys. The Regulators are here"—he waved absently in the boys' direction—"what d'you propose to do with us now?"

Romero became distressed, nervous. I stood in a state of awe. Romero and his men were terrified of the Lincoln County Regulators. *Ha*! It was the first time I realized the power and influence they held. Romero, when faced with the very throng of men he had pursued and mouthed off about, declaring that he would capture and bring them down, now proclaimed fearfully that he hadn't any warrants, and he and his men beat it out of that saloon without so much as a backward glance after Billy told them to leave town. Billy and the boys laughed over their remarkable bullying and Romero's braggadocio.

It was in Anton Chico, a stone's throw from wild Las Vegas, that the Coe cousins decided they would quit the Regulators. They and I pleaded with Billy to go along with them to Colorado but he refused, only shaking their hands in parting and telling them he planned to stick around and steal himself a living.

Anton is also where I had my first run-in with the infamous band of female outlaws, the Painted Ladies. They were the dirtiest bunch of women I'd ever seen. Scantily clad and unwashed, yet I was drawn to them. They were rough-and-tumble and they lived by their own set of rules with no men standing over their shoulders as I had.

I spent an inordinate amount of time with these women as they were impressed with me just the same, made no secret of wanting me along for the ride. Harper Dealy, the gang's mistress, made several attempts to recruit me, and I heard constant grumbling from Billy about my participation in hanging about with such a band of women. He frowned upon my association with them. I, however, snubbed his concerns and decided to do as I pleased. Still, he would often come and haul me away from them, and I would go willingly to appease him only to rejoin the group of girls when he wasn't looking.

A savage girl who rode with them, an Apache named Hateya, preferring to be called by the white-sounding name of Hattie, was beautiful, and I found her brilliant. She had tawny skin and hair so black it boasted a bluish sheen, and there was a mean-streak in her that could span a mile wide. She held it hard against the Whiteman as he progressed over her people and added to their desecration, but no ill will was harbored by her toward me as she was quite friendly.

There was also Maya Essex, whom I befriended quickly. She came from a background similar to my own. She was not an heiress by any means, but her family had wealth. When I asked her why she came out west she told me she wanted the freedom a girl could only get in a place such as this. However, freedom for us girls out here was a funny thing. Despite being rewarded an unrestricted fare, we were still second class citizens and held a minimal chance of securing means of survival that did not involve our God-given talents, hence, she rode as a Lady in Waiting. The brand of freedom out here for a woman came with a hefty price as Billy had warned, and these women were still beholden to the Godamned Bastards for male protection, handing over a percentage of income to them—it was no secret that the Painted Ladies were traveling prostitutes, making their money on the fly. This of course pleased Billy even less when it came to my associating with them. Every day spent in Anton with these women meant fresh reproof from Billy.

"Niña," he'd say, "I don't care for your bothering with those whores. You're making it much harder on me and it gives me another reason to wish you'd go on back east."

"Well, forgive me if I am making things too difficult for you, Billy," I remarked snidely. "Anyway, I only talk with them—they entertain me. I'm always surrounded by boys. Surely you can understand. It's nice to have women to talk to."

"*Women*?" he cackled. "They're not *women*, not in my book, little sister—not in anyone's book! Not only are they bad for news, but they make a living on their backs. They're a bad bunch of trouble and I don't want you waltzing around with them."

"Oh, Billy...you are not the boss of me. And I get so tired of having only boys to keep company with. I'm not about to run off with them, either. It's nice to have some female companionship. And besides, they're not so bad. They're quite nice, whether you find them troublesome or not. If they are bad news it's only because they need to be. I believe we all know a thing or two about that. After all, there are those who think the lot of you is trouble."

Billy conceded, "Yeah, I realize that. Still, I would feel a lot better if you'd distance yourself all the same. We may not be angels, but we ain't about what they are, and we spend much of our time making sure you don't wind up a bed-fagot."

"Oh?" I asked, flippantly. "Haven't you all dragged me into plenty of contention? You've had me sleep in brothels, but you have a bee in your bonnet about my conversatin' with those girls?"

Despite himself, he snickered a bit before replying, "Bonita, what you say is true, but don't we see to it that you're fed and clothed and cared for without your compromising any of your dignity or virtue? You're never made to make a nickel offa what God give ya. Them girls, they ain't interested in keeping you unless they can get you to turn a buck on your back."

I knew he had a point, and so I promised that I wouldn't talk to them so much, and he agreed to the compromise, allowing me to spend some time with them for my own sanity. If any other man had given me grief, disapproving of my friendship with those girls, I would have none of it and I would turn mean. But Billy, my dearest boy, was permitted anything as far as I was concerned. I would listen to his council and try to make him happy. I knew he cared for and loved me, and he only wanted to shield me from as much wickedness as he possibly could, though he and I both knew this to be a naïve ideology as I had already been fully exposed to and established in the ways of being wicked.

Celebrations were thrown, one held every night in Anton, and I spent most of my time with the Ladies rather than the remaining Regulators. I drank and became giddy with them. One of the girls going by the name of Marcia Hancock offered and shared some laudanum with me during one of the dances. The drug dulled my senses and relaxed me, and my inhibitions turned loose. It was powerful stuff and gave me a euphoric feeling of drifting along. Little trails seemed to follow in the wake of moving objects and more so, it took away what anxieties I held. Eventually, I had come to treasure a bottle of my own, dosing myself when I felt moody or skittish, carefully hiding it from Billy and the others.

As was now our way, the Regulators once again picked up to leave Anton and head back to Lincoln with a plan to raid the Fritz ranch of horseflesh, intending to trade along the Texas Panhandle in Tascosa. I thought of the money I had just sitting there in White Oaks, dreaming of being able to use it to settle down and have an ordinary existence. I still said nothing of it to Billy. That money was meant as a nest-egg, not as a means for running this way and that across New Mexico.

But as we drifted along, I wondered if that dream were foolish, the idea of making roots even while we moved from place to place, never staying long enough anywhere. I couldn't truly imagine it, and I wondered if it were even possible to become settled again. We travelled so often—long, grueling trails, eating from cans and sleeping out under the open sky—that it would sometimes startle me to think that I had once been tethered and stable. My old life seemed surreal and this new, wandering existence natural. Had I once been grounded? It seemed it was something I had only misremembered.

Once Billy and the boys stole us horses and a large stock of cattle from the Fritz ranch, we drove them onward to the Panhandle. It was a demanding, arduous task, fifteen horses and one-hundred and fifty head of cattle. I had to ride drag, as always. *"I don't want you run over by any stampeding, ya hear me?"* Billy would squawk. I'd nod, bored of his usual bossiness. But once we made our arrival, we stayed in Tascosa a while, and there I had the most fun yet.

It was a rough-and-tumble town—a sordid place, really, which we took full advantage of. We stayed on at the Exchange Hotel after trading off our stock and joined in on yet another celebration being held. Celebrations were held every night with women kicking up their heels and skirts with no concern for modesty. Everywhere we went there seemed a constant revelry, merriment in conflict with my infrequent feelings of insecurity. I spent a lot of my time in brothels, wanting to get my hands on any feminine necessities I might be in need of. In every town this was a task of priority for me, and speaking with the prostitutes educated me on the tricks of the trade, learning how to please a man though I had not asked outright for any revelations regarding the profession's secrets, instead learning them accidentally from spilled conversation.

A Madame by the name of Lily Rose took a liking to me and allowed me to explore around, encouraging me to ask all sorts of daring questions. At first I was awkwardly polite, but Lily played with my womanly gifts, all the while praising my graceful features. She insisted on coloring my face with make-up that had been lined up along her dressing table, and though I did not quite recognize myself when she had finished, I felt as though I were quite the work of art, marveling at her skillfulness. I had never had my face done up before with rouges and ruby lipsticks that had been set off by kohl lined, darkened lashes highlighted with tint that placed my lids in shadow. I envied these women their freedom to paint themselves up like a Rembrandt despite my having looked down upon them once upon a time, a contemptuous display of self-pride in my previous life. Fine ladies such as I was did not mark their faces so.

Billy and I hired a room at a hotel and, forgetting how it was I must have looked after a visit with Madame Lily, he found me sitting on the bed deep in thought with my face painted up one night when he entered our room. He came toward me and took a good hard look at my face.

"What in the hell is that all over your face?"

"Madame Lily Rose did it. She applied some color. It was a curiosity for her to do so, and I obliged."

"You look like a goddamned whore!"

Not expecting such a cruel response and feeling nipped as a result, I snapped back, "Aren't I? *Yours*?"

Stung, he looked at me as though he wanted to slap me for saying such a thing. At this angry sight of him, I quickly stood from the bed and fled as swiftly as my little feet could carry me to the other side of the room and away from him. I faced the wall and crossed my arms as I tried to seem brave, though I knew the jig was up where bravery was concerned.

"Lucy! Scrub that filth off your face!" he demanded.

"You are not the boss of me!"

"Lucy, don't try me..."

"I thought you liked your women like this. At least I find you like it sometimes. Why should it be so terrible on me?"

He ignored my petty insult and said, "Because it ain't you. You look like a goddamned harlot."

"You like harlots!"

He walked over to me and grabbed me by the arm, spinning me around to face him.

"I'm losing patience with you. Go wash that goddamned tint off your face or you can go to hell."

"What should it matter to you anyway? You ignore me, always. I was only having fun and passing the time."

"Bonita, what you just spat about me ain't true and you know it ain't."

"What's not true?"

"I don't ignore you."

"Is that so? What I know is you're off and running with every other girl in these towns except me. They are exotic, just as you like them, and I am not. How can I compete with them?"

"I am not off and runnin', quit saying that! And you don't need to compete—

they're the ones who compete with *you*, and they can't. I explained all of this to you already. I stay away from you as much as I can help it—"

"Staying away doesn't make a bit of difference because I'm not going back to New York, no how."

He sat down quietly on the bed and said nothing.

"Susan is still my guardian. I wrote her a letter and implored her not to give me up to my father."

Since Alex's death, the process for turning my guardianship back over to my father was made that much more difficult, and so my being handed over to him did not happen as planned back in August. Now it was Susan's duty to contend with this state of affairs, and so it was not much of a worrisome issue for me.

"So now there is not much of an excuse for you to keep yourself away from me," I pointed out.

Still, he said nothing.

"Why do you give them gifts, Billy?"

He looked at me, confused.

"The other girls? Why do you give them little gifts?"

"You know the reason for that."

I put my head down, disheartened. "So they know you're interested."

"It don't mean anything."

Sad, I whispered, "It does to me."

He sat quietly a moment more, and before getting up from the bed he said, "Wash that stuff off your face. I don't want to see you like that again."

With that, he left the room, slamming the door behind him.

After he'd gone I went through my things and took out my bottle of laudanum. I took a short pull and put it back, making sure I hid it but good. I washed my face, dried it, and changed into Billy's old shirt before climbing into bed and pleasantly drifting off to sleep.

3

September, 1878

Word got out that Susan McSween was to be assassinated by men in the employ of the Dolan party. Catching on to this, Susan pulled off a magnificent trick by dressing herself as a Mexican laborer's wife and boarding a mail stage, making her way to Las Vegas to join her sister. This served both her and me well, as not only would her life be spared but, as my guardian, it would make things all the more difficult for my father to regain control of me without her being readily available.

Other news told of a brutal pack who called themselves the Rustlers, a gang of hard cases made up of Peppin's ragtag fringe delinquents. They were the men who remained by his side in New Mexico to serve out his greedy politics. They descended on Lincoln like a plague, stealing cattle, plying in horse trade, and pulling off regular, all-around hell-raising by robbing stores and breaking into the homes of the citizens. To my womanly mind, the worst of their offenses was the rape of two millworkers' wives, each member of the gang taking their turn. The women were held as hostages until one of them had mercifully escaped sometime in the early morning hours. This news devastated me, though I found a spark of solace in being comforted by Billy who was vicariously apologetic as he held me, attempting to make up for the horrible cruelty his gender had caused mine by lavishing me with his kindness.

See? He seemed to say as he wrapped his arms around me, his warm breath on my neck, *I can love you.*

Marauders and brutes, the Rustlers were pimps and butchers alike. And hanging their hats with the lot of them were none other than Finnegan Flynn, Ru Bach, and Engle Brauer.

Another of them, a man by the name of Collier, murdered the son of a farmer while the rest of them stole the man's horses even as they taunted the despairing, brokenhearted father, proclaiming they were "devils just come from hell." Whatever the Regulators may have been, whittled down as they were to mere rustlers themselves, I'd bet Lincoln would have preferred the refuse of their company over the hell that befallen them just on their heels.

While the "devils" were burning things down, Billy forbade me to leave his sight. I was to stay by his side or the side of any one of the remaining Regulators, never to approach strange men or walk myself alone.

I had come across the wretched sight of Jimmy as he sat on a bench outside the local Dry Goods. I sat and spoke with him, and he told me that he was sorry he ever helped Finny get away.

"Now there's them two other women—"

"That's nothing to do with you," I interrupted.

"I could have done him in."

I agreed but said nothing.

"It doesn't surprise me that he's in with a pack of real miserable bastards now," he lamented.

I looked down and nodded at this.

"If you come across him, Lucy, you go the other way. He'd take you on the principle that it would piss the Kid off something awful. Instead of just going for him hisself, he'll hurt him by going after you. If that happens, I'll kill him myself."

I put my hand on his shoulder. "Don't worry, Jimmy. I'll watch out for myself. Besides, Billy already warned me not to go wandering off, and I always listen to what he tells me—it all frightens me just the same. Something I don't get, though."

"What's that?"

"By what you just said, Finny's smart enough not to attempt going after Billy directly, but me dying by Finny's hand would mean his own death by Billy's anyway. What could he be thinking by going for me just to get back at the Kid? Could he be that arrogant, or foolish?"

Jimmy laughed. "You bet he is! Both of those things."

Jimmy grew solemn and said, "It's because he loves you."

I looked at him strangely a moment and asked, "Who, Billy?"

"Who else? You know, I can't blame him for pestering you so much about going back home."

He looked at me with worry, knowing how much I loathed the constant haranguing of my going back. But my affection for Jimmy and appreciation of his well-intentioned contemplation gave me the desire to overlook his statement and put him at ease.

"I know it, Jimmy."

I smiled at him and he smiled back.

Some nights later yet another baile was given by a man named Don Pedro Romero who came from a very prominent Hispanic family. Anyone who took part in the dance was obligated to check their firearms at the General Store, and after we had all done so we joined the celebration, enjoying ourselves full to the hilt. Billy spent much of the evening dancing with me despite the Hispanic girls who coquettishly hoped to steal glances from him and gain his attentions. *A fat lotta good luck to them*, I thought.

There in the Panhandle, Billy had met a young man by the name of Henry Hoyt, a young doctor who was in town working as a cowhand. He had decided to do some travelling before settling down to practice his trade. The two got on very well and liked each other immediately at the outset. The thing about Billy was this: he could make fond friends with just about anyone, so well-liked and charming was he. He was always quick with a laugh and always smiling and making jokes. He was the proud owner of a disposition that was always pleasant when he hadn't any cause to be angry.

As it happened, Billy and Henry, ensconced in a conversation of interest, had decided to carry on outside in order to enjoy the warm night and get some fresh air. Jimmy and I partnered up and were having the time of our lives when a sudden commotion interrupted the fun. When I and everyone else turned to look, the place growing quiet as the band quit playing and the couples quit dancing, there was Billy, lying in the center of the floor, sprawled out and face down, flat on his belly. Tom, Minxie, Fred and Henry surrounded him on guard thinking trouble had arrived and that Billy had run into the house to take cover. The four of them pulled firearms. Where they had gotten them I could not say, but I stood there watching all of this in awe when Billy stood and dusted himself off, calling off the guards. Don Pedro took all five of them aside, and I stood there by the group of them listening to the story as Billy explained that he and Hoyt were racing one another to see who was fastest when Billy, refusing to slow down, reached and tripped over the door's threshold, sending him flying across the room. This might have been fine and well enough, but because the others had brought out guns, which were strictly forbidden, they were nonetheless told to leave the premises despite their obvious regret and apologetic soliloquies. I crossed my arms and stood there staring at them reproachfully for ruining such a fine time.

In Sumner, Billy and I were in our room reading the papers and their reports from the surrounding counties. Because of the atrocities and lawlessness in Lincoln County as of late, which had been attributed to the Rustlers, though it had all began with the war back in February, Governor Lew Wallace had been called in to oversee the troublesome causes. He decreed a Proclamation of Amnesty for all of those who had participated in the late Lincoln County War, and this meant that all men involved would be forgiven so long as they lay their arms aside. At first, Billy's hopes soared, but it soon became clear that those who had received a Federal Indictment would not be pardoned, which meant that Billy was doubly taxed as the blame was placed squarely on him for the killing of Sheriff Brady and Buckshot Roberts.

"I ain't been rightly reckoned as the killer of either of those men," he exclaimed. "I wasn't there alone, neither. I know sure as hell I didn't kill myself Roberts. And Brady, I couldn't rightly say for sure I had done so, either. Hell, why's it me they're set on hanging their grievances on?"

"You've made quite a name for yourself—you're the obvious choice to make an example of. I've warned you, but you've gone right ahead and stuck your own neck right out there on the chopping block anyway. And now the people look to you to do what they themselves cannot. Who better to punish? All would see what becomes of a man who stands against the law, crooked law or not, and a man who rallies the masses against it at that."

"There ain't never been a law or politician that weren't crooked."

"Maybe now you can take it as a sign that you should leave New Mexico. It won't be long before all our friends are gone."

"I ain't leaving my home. Besides, they've got a new Sheriff up there in Lincoln. Maybe with all this Rustler business I won't be much of a thought."

"Oh no, Billy. You've done it now—you're front and center, the real prize. If you think those Rustlers are gonna wipe your slate clean and make everybody forget what went down with you in Lincoln, you got another thing coming. Ain't nobody gonna forget what you did, and Lew Wallace likes to get things done. He was sent here to clean Lincoln up of the likes of you, and he'll do just that."

"What *I* did? Whose side you on, anyway?

"Yours. Just telling it like it is, anyway."

"Then it looks like I have my work cut out for me."

"Meaning what?"

"Meaning I want my name cleared. I have just as much right as any one of them other boys to have my life given back to me. I don't need to swing for any of their crimes just as they won't be swinging for any of mine."

Billy's nerves were fraught with tension. He tried to hide it, to conceal the regret he felt behind anger, the one emotion he allowed himself to show. But I saw, albeit fleetingly, the young boy I remembered him to be when we first met—scared and lost.

Sitting in a chair placed before a writing desk he stared blankly, and I watched as he ran his hands through his hair in frustration before locking them together at the base of his skull. I went to him and sat on his lap, placing my arms around him and holding on tightly. At my warmth, he gave in to worry and tucked his head by my chin instinctively, trembling as he wept a little. I placed my lips next to his ear and spoke softly to him, telling him how much I loved him in an attempt to soothe him, running my fingers through his hair until he calmed well enough. We sat together like that until just after dusk.

ooooooooooooooo

On the bed we lay on our backs, our arms folded beneath our heads, elbows splayed out. I begged Billy to let us please celebrate the Day of the Dead.

"After such a long tour of dying, shouldn't we experience a celebration of life?" I asked.

"It's a private celebration held in the Mexican communities. It's not some sideshow for Easterners," he teased.

"But Billy, you *are* a part of the Mexican community. We all are, now. Can't we go? I want to see it. We can paint our faces up like banshees and spooks—"

"*Calaveras.*"

"What?"

"Skulls. Not *spooks*. And a banshee is a shrieking woman spirit hounding the living to warn that death is coming." He gave a short yawn and said, "Mexicans use skulls for something positive—to remind us that death is only the next step to rebirth." He became quiet, thinking a moment. "On second thought, you can do yourself up like a banshee if the mood strikes you. I think the role might fit you fine."

I plucked at his arm playfully and begged again, "Wouldn't it just be so much fun to do it?"

"It ain't supposed to be *fun*...not in the way you mean, anyway. It should be taken very seriously."

"Then wouldn't it be just so very *serious* to do it?" I grinned.

He smiled back at me. "You really wanna see Día de los Muertos?"

I nodded emphatically and he responded, "Well, all right then..."

We helped each another paint our faces with white and black greasepaint, giving us each an ethereal quality that was both charming and subdued. Over the curve of my maquillage blanched lips, Billy had done his best to draw the illusion of bare teeth, and on my cheeks he painted flowers with yellow petals while I, in turn, bored into the pits of Jimmy's eyes with black paint and grafted wispy, delicate black swirling lines that grew from the corners of his mouth. The men all took part in this celebratory task to please me as well after I had begged them into it. Wary at first and uninterested, they each took to this responsibility with amusement after all. Ultimately, we each enjoyed the masquerade.

We all wore traditional mariachi costumes with wide brimmed, velvet sombreros, silver embroidery snaking dazzlingly across the brims of our hats and our jackets. I refused to dress like the women, preferring instead to stand united with the boys, blending in and keeping in step with my newly adopted identity. The Mexican tradition stated that the more color the better, so we wore colorful silk sashes across our persons, and I found and strung a long, flowing bright red ribbon around the crown of my hat while we all wore bright red kerchiefs around our necks.

I could say that we all looked remarkable, all done up the way we were: dead men walking. But the masks of the Sumner patrons outdid us tenfold. Their various tints blended seamlessly and were so outwardly skillful that it was astounding. The women had beautifully painted faces that fused vivid color together alongside the rendering of Death's face. It was clear that this was their history, their tradition.

Nevertheless, we melded alongside the denizens effortlessly, dancing and carousing, laughing at regular intervals and enjoying one another's company and the fact that, for tonight, we were free. The celebration reminded us, for the time, that death would not be the end, and this made for a cheerful evening amongst us all. It was as though our past and future endeavors were of no consequence as death, if it should soon find us, would only be the beginning. We celebrated the lives of the dear friends we had lost and let the evening lift the weight of their deaths off of our backs. It was pleasant for me to think that, no matter how I chose to live my life in the present, there was some greater purpose to be found should my current, errant ways find me lain below the earth.

I shared in the free flowing mezcal with Jimmy while the others held drinks of their own. Even Billy, who drank so very rarely, threw down a shot or two. We were all feeling fine, as though we were anything but the desperados we'd become. We were free, devoid of guilt and perfectly innocent of being in the pinch of the game. Not since last year in Picacho had I seen Billy somewhat inebriated, though still, he was only slightly so. I used this to my advantage to maneuver myself into his graces (as if I had to work at this), outdoing any other girl who might have gained on him otherwise. When he asked me to sit at the piano with the band and sing I obliged and belted out a rendition of Red River Valley, my favorite song and verse here, plying out its melody on the old, faintly out of tune piano. Billy stood, smiling that particular smile he reserved only for me, pleased as he watched, knowing I played and sang for only him. I was his pet, and he ignored everyone and everything else, swelling with pride at the learned gift of his querida niña. When I was through, I stood and turned to the picker and, in the best way I knew how in Spanish, asked him to play for Billy his favorite song: Turkey in the Straw. *"Por favor,"* I pleaded. *"para mí la Turquía..."* The musician nodded and soon the strands I had become so familiar with began as he plucked out Billy's tune. Billy took me along with him and danced with me. We stumbled off balance a bit for the liquor, but managed to get all the way through the song, laughing hysterically at how our tipsiness had made fools of us both.

I danced with all the boys and we had such a remarkable time. I could not have imagined a little over a year ago the life I was now living. It suddenly became plain to me to thank my lucky stars that I was put on that train westbound for New Mexico.

Spinning arm-in-arm in time to the music with Billy in a dos-á -dos, I heard a terrific "pop" and turned to see a magnificent display of color explode in the sky, lighting up the old fort and its patrons. Without much thought, I immediately let go of Billy, leaving him behind as I ran toward the light show that lit up the dark with its intense brilliance. I could hear him calling for me, but all too late as I was caught up within the crowds gathering to watch the fireworks burst over our heads, the throngs of people closing in on me as I weaved my way around them.

When I had reached the front line of the mob I looked up into the night at the lights, extraordinarily aware of their magnificent radiance upon the faces in the crowd even as they stunned my own eyes. I had never seen such a grand sight, the complete blackness of the firmament a proper backdrop against the dazzling exhibition making it into something unforgettable. I would have thought it a miracle of the heavens had I not known that the glory of these lights were something man-made, but that did not stop them from being an enchanting spectacle. Until now, I would not have believed that the splendor of the Southwestern stars could have been outshone so easily.

I felt a hand take mine and I looked back, wide-eyed, to find Billy there, smiling at me, Jimmy, Josiah, and Tom standing with him, all looking up as well, faces lit up by the sky and temporarily unadulterated from the ugliness of corruption they had come to know so well as they expressed a childlike exuberance. We were, for a brief moment, innocents caught in the loving embrace of death while it stood captivatedly still and bright all around us.

4

November – December. 1878

Finnegan Flynn was caught for the murder of the half Chinaman, Gavin Greenfield, last April in Patricio. Chavez, who, last spring, was constable and headed up the posse to find Flynn, received word from Patricio that he was in a holding cell awaiting trial after being captured in Vegas while drunkenly terrorizing another Chinaman in his shop over not wanting to pay the cost of bullets. He shot the proprietor and his wife dead simply for not "handing them cartridges over", said a witness, as Flynn found himself indigent for the price of whores and poor gambling skills. His Selman Rustler cohorts had abandoned him to avoid being ratted out by Flynn and to wreak more havoc of their own in other parts unknown at present.

I was summoned at the behest of Chavez to go to Patricio and testify as I was witness to the murder of Greenfield there and the one to finger Finny as the killer. Happily, I gathered my things and set out with Chavez and the boys, anxious to arrive and exercise more finger-pointing in order to have Finnegan Flynn hanged but good.

Upon reaching our destination, I found I had a week to prepare my testimony and thought of nothing other than how best to articulate that Mr. Flynn was no more than a detriment to the whole of society and a no-good, dirty-rotten scoundrel, most definitely sent up by the devil himself. I spent my days and nights in our room at the boarding house plotting out my words carefully, devising a mantra-like verse meant to inflict maximum damage, a near divine character assassination. I treated this responsibility of mine seriously, as if it were my destiny and sole purpose in life—I wanted to end him. I wanted desperately to watch that bastard swing. I was preparing to lie before the law and God in order to fortify the truth, painting a portrait of the inhuman monster Finn was: A rancorous fiend who subsisted on lies, deceit, and the blood of innocents. But, to my chagrin, there weren't any horrible fabrications I could tell that would outdo what Finny had already done. But, no matter—I meant to employ every effort I could muster to ensure that that evil, hideous creature paid with the blackened sludge that ran within his veins, his own polluted blood as payment for the blood of others which he had shed, his life for the lives of those whom he had destroyed.

I would enter that courtroom playing every part of the ruined lady, sacrificing my pride in an attempt to garner sympathy as a fail-safe to the truth. *Your honor*, I would tearfully declare, pointing damningly at Finn, *that man violated me.* What difference did it make if he had not actually done so? I would merely be substituting my voice for his victims, speaking for those women whom he had defiled since they could not do so for themselves. And who's not to say he wouldn't have done it to me if given a proper chance, anyway?

"Don't you say such a *thing*!" Billy demanded. "Don't you *dare* go up there and *lie*!"

"Why? Would it be considered bad behavior? Is the *Kid* giving *me* advice on how to properly behave?" I replied.

He looked at me with resentment, his vivid blue eyes thorns prodding me with contempt as they darkened.

"Is it what you'd want for me? Someone to tell lies?" he asked, distressed.

"If the shoe fits!"

His eyes blinked back something horrible and my arrogance faltered. An ominous specter infiltrated the room, suffocating me. It was exactly what they were doing to him, to Billy—lies to doom him. After making such an erroneous statement and error in judgment in saying such a thing against him, it didn't seem enough to proclaim that I was sorry—that I hadn't meant what I'd said.

Instead, I stamped my foot and asked, "Why must I always compare you to others? Finny deserves nothing less than to die, and by any means necessary. You aren't like him!" I exclaimed this in a pathetic attempt to repair my poorly chosen retort.

"You think that matters at all? *You* know I ain't like that, *they* don't. As far as they're concerned, they'll think me just like him right before they hang me!"

I backed up and slumped down along the wall to the floor, coming to rest cross-legged and hiding my face within my hands. Finny was the worst sort of man, if one could refer to him as a man. It seemed wrong not to lie if it rid the world of such a demon. I told Billy this, that I didn't know what else I could do but my very best to seal his fate.

"You won't need to lie for anything. His crimes will speak for themselves. Nothing else needs to be said."

"What do I do? If I walk in there like this and say what I know, if I look the part of what I am now, how will they believe me based on my appearance? I cannot live if justice evades him simply because they find my own circumstances convenient to disrepute me."

I began to weep for how my hands were tied. I could not go against Billy—I couldn't make myself, not when the action I meant to take hit him so close to home. I understood this but, still, I wondered, should I choose Billy over the threat of Finny walking free if I could not manage to convince the court of his guilt with the truth? If I could make Billy understand me, would he still want me to choose him over the lives that might be lost if this was exactly the scenario that played out, if Finny went free? If I could do my worst to try and keep Finny from breathing any more air than he was worth, couldn't Billy understand and sanction it?

Billy came and sat on the floor next to me, taking my hands away from my face and wiping away the tears that had fallen. In a small, uncertain voice I asked him again, "What do I do?"

At that moment my breath caught and I dropped my head in despair. He lifted it back up and placed his face close to mine, saying nothing. He stayed that way with me for a while, and that was all he needed to do. He would not make a liar out of me for anything in the world.

∞∞∞∞∞∞∞∞∞∞∞∞

It was evident that Finnegan Flynn had plenty of friends to rally him, and there they were, acting as witnesses, his peers, and what excellent witnesses they were, nodding and laughing in the gallery during the proceedings, encouraging Finn whenever he dispensed a wicked joke upon the stand. Only out here in the wild where law was backward could a crooked man have the luxury of being tried by his very own allies.

Regulator sympathizer, José G. Trujillo, sat as justice of the peace, but he also sat exhausted from what appeared to be a pointless endeavor thanks to the antics employed by Finny's supporters as they carelessly and incorrigibly presided over his fate, entirely uncaring of all that he had done. Trujillo could get nowhere and I could stand it no longer. They had called me to the stand where my testimony was discounted by Finny's council who cited that I could not possibly be a decent enough witness as I had stood indoors and by far too many yards away when Finny allegedly killed Mr. Greenfield last April, and I was unduly further discredited as I was a woman, given over to emotion and hysterics. And, infuriatingly adding insult to injury, undermining and overestimated by me was the witness James Moffey, who shocked me by testifying that he could not say with any degree of certainty that Finn had murdered

Mr. Greenfield. He explained to the court that he did not actually see Finny shoot the man. This was the truth, neither of us actually *saw* Finny shoot Mr. Greenfield, but Jimmy knew damned well that Finny was indeed guilty of the murder. Why he didn't slam a nail in Finny's coffin by admitting that Finny had bragged of this act I could only guess was out of some sort of twisted loyalty he must have held for their long history together. As Jimmy testified he smartly refused to look at me, though I prayed he would so that he could witness the hatred I felt for him in that moment as I stared daggers at him. And though instructed by Billy to tell what I knew, which was that I did not see it happen, that I only saw Finny standing over the body shouting, I knew that even if I had done what I had wanted and lied through my teeth, it would have been futile as I was torn apart by the defense for being an devious outlaw in my own right, and in fairly subtle terms deemed a whore anyway, the general consensus being that a whore had no value and could not be trusted.

As they disrespected me upon the stand I looked to Billy and he looked back, somewhat upset and sympathetic, but still relatively unmoved as their accusations were of no surprise to him and thoroughly expected. All that mattered to him was that I told my truth despite every fiber of my being screaming at me to *lie, lie, lie!* Lie and say that I had seen the entire event play out which, ironically, would have made me exactly what they argued me to be: a dirty liar. Either way, my character would be beaten to the quick, but happily so if I could make Finny swing. Finny's cohorts, who claimed to have been with him in Vegas, reported that he could not have shot the Chinaman and his wife as he was not in Vegas at the time. They laughed as they told this lie as if considering Finny a murderer were a ridiculous notion. Finny laughed along with them, smug and arrogant. He looked at me viciously, daring me to understand that he had me marked—his look was profound and I felt a shiver to my very core that he had it out for me for sure now.

I knew now that Finny was going to get away and, with my anger blistering inside, I could not help myself and I disrupted the court, standing up and pointing at the accused, yelling, "You are a no good, low-down, dirty scum-sucking, back-shooting, lizard, Finny Flynn. You murdered that Chinaman in Patricio, and I'd bet my life that you killed that Chinaman and his wife in Vegas!"

The court roared furiously at my disrespectful outburst and Trujillo banged his gavel, calling for order. Over this noise, Finny sneered and ordered me to take my seat, shouting, "Shut-up and sit down, Bonney Junior!"

Billy grabbed my arm and pulled me down into my seat, after which I heard

Trujillo state that if I or anyone else disrupted proceedings again we would be tossed out.

I sat, enraged. I had seen Finn with my own two eyes giving that Patrician man grief and standing over his corpse, gun in hand. I was there! Yet they would not hear me out. I folded my arms, seething with contempt and listening to the blood pulsing in my ears. When the courtroom finally settled down Finny went back to lying on the stand.

"Your Honor," he started, "I promise you I never seen either Chinaman or that wife before. I don't know who could'a done such an awful thing, but as for that dead man right here in Patricio, you might want to take a look at the girl right there," he pointed to me. "Y'all know she was there, and clearly she's desperate to have the finger pointed here. That's a mark of guilt had I ever seen one."

Such audacity! He cackled up there to himself and his friends joined in. I couldn't take it, and Billy knew it would be of no use to hold on and attempt to keep me seated. Instead, he raised his hand and covered his eyes in sufferance of me, a sentiment that plagued him often, and sat looking defeated, knowing he couldn't hold me back and keep me quiet. He sighed overdramatically as I stood again and made a terrific show of heated tumult, stamping my heels to the floor in an angry tantrum, spurs jangling furiously. Before I could open my mouth the men around me, apart from Billy, were ready and also stood up, happily prepared to deal with me as Trujillo set to banging his gavel again and ordered them to throw me out. I had caused a real commotion as ripples of disjointed chatter went around the room, outdone only by the jeers encouraging my removal and the sound of intermittent clapping. It was an incredible production, I must say. And with my thoughts being so angrily occupied it was all but a blur to me as two burly men dragged me through the court by both of my arms, though I managed to catch a glimpse of Billy looking back at me with an amused smirk on this face. I tried to scream above the din at Finny before they put me out like a dog, but my shouting was feeble compared to the gruff voices of angry men and my words sank beneath their bellowing.

The courtroom was so packed that the doors were forced to stand open and men spilled out onto the portico. As I was hauled through the confusion in the courthouse I could just barely make my way to peer over my shoulder and around the large men, who herded me along and all but blocked my view, to find Finny gleefully sitting there upon the stand, smug over my calamity. Once they had thrown me out I crossed my arms in disgust, kicked at the ground with the toe of my boot, and walked away. A white man being tried for the murder of a minority was good fodder for entertainment in a town like this, everyone flocking to hear a good tale concerning the slaughter of one by another. But in the end, nobody really cared about the death of a Chinaman.

In my room I sulked and put drops of laudanum down my throat. If I hadn't dosed myself I might have killed Jimmy flat-out for what he'd done. Billy had stayed to watch the rest of that miserable Greek comedy play out and, afterward, he left me alone knowing how agitated I was. There would have been nothing he could do to console me, and I'm sure he realized that I would have been significantly unpleasant to keep company with. And if I had to guess, I'd put my money on the fact that he pointedly and very wisely instructed Jimmy to copper his bets and keep his distance as I had not heard from him, either.

The next morning, after emerging from my room, Jimmy met me on the street as I made my way to have breakfast. I tried to effectively snub him, but he would have none of that. Instead, he insisted that I allow him to explain.

"Explain what?" I asked spitefully. "Why you stood behind that murdering, coward rapist after admitting to me your own disgust of him? Or why you stabbed me in the back by doing so?"

"Lucy, I know I should have done all that I could to prove his guilt, but I couldn't make myself."

"Then I see you have cowardice in common with him. Now I understand, finally, how you two could have remained friends for so long."

"It isn't fair for you to say that to me. You of all people ought to know how it feels."

"Me? Of all people? How so?"

"Billy, that's how so. What wouldn't you do for him—"

"Blow it out your fucking ear, Jimmy! Quit using Billy as an example to explain and excuse your bad behavior and garner sympathy out of me, the two are not the same. And anyway, it was *Finn* on trial, not Billy. If Billy were the sort of evil person that disgusting excuse for a human being is I wouldn't want to know him in the first place, so leave him out of it! I love Billy because he inhabits all of the humanity that Finn lacks."

Jimmy stood quietly a moment before telling me he was sorry to have let me down. Without responding I pushed past him, categorically uninterested. I had grown tired of his excuses and regrets. Apologies of this sort were as idle hands. They did no good. He'd already done the devil's work, committing the damage by doing nothing. It was no accident that Finny was walking free, and Jimmy deliberately implemented himself in resolving that fact as he alone might have changed the outcome of the court's deliberation. I was sure he held the key to putting Finny away for good.

After I had walked more than a few feet from him I turned and yelled at him to never speak to me again.

"Well?"

"Well *what*?"

"Did he apologize?"

"Yes. Why?"

Billy winced and anxiously sucked air through his teeth. "I told him not to bother."

"This is a Regulator town!" I exclaimed abruptly, thrown by the court siding with an outsider and against me.

"And?"

"How could Trujillo of all people cut me off at the knees like that and let Finn walk away?"

Casually, Billy said, "Looks like ol' Finny has gotten himself a few more friends these days."

"What should that have to do with anything?"

"You were there, you saw it. It were them friends of his let him walk. There was nothing Trujillo could do. The witnesses were stacked in Finn's favor. Whether or not the people of this town side with you don't matter. It weren't for them to be up there claiming he was innocent."

"I realize that. Finny and his *so-called* witnesses!"

We had just eaten supper at the Kavanagh's and stood leaning against the house as this conversation between us played out. Five minutes had passed quietly as neither of us spoke, the sound of horses, human traffic, and wagon wheels out on the street filling the short silence.

"Don't be so angry with him, Niña. He ain't so bad. It's not his fault he got mixed up with that idjit."

I gave him a look of peculiarity, wondering if he must be full of it. Then I concluded that he must have been thinking of himself and how he had his own history of getting caught up with hard cases in order to be able to say such a thing to me, so I spoke up.

"Don't imagine you'd have done the same."

"Don't know that I wouldn't have. Influence is a funny thing, and loyalty gets in the way."

"You forget. I know for a fact that you abandon loyalty where lowlifes such as Finny are concerned. I know you wouldn't have done what Jimmy did."

He smiled sadly but appreciatively at my naiveté, that I could believe in him so faithfully.

"It can be complicated, sweetheart."

"You wouldn't have!" I insisted loudly, looking directly into his eyes before walking away from him and going back inside the house.

I ran into Maya Essex and let her talk me into visiting the Oriental side of town and its opium den. I had never been, but the foul mood I had been in as of late confiscated my common sense. I was still angry with Jimmy and the fact that Finnegan Flynn was still out there living another day to ruin someone else's, and all of this on the heels of my inability to sort out the still very raw events of the past year. All that had happened during the war left me sullen when I'd think on it. I felt helpless, for what could anyone do to quell my distress? And so I turned to "Johnny Poppies."

I found myself tired of hoping against hope to be saved by a man who only dragged me down with his warped sense of honor, and always with the excuse that there was bloody payback to be tendered.

In a soporific miasma by sundown, I had been jerked forcibly from a chaise I lounged on and smacked across my face in an attempt to rouse me from my stupor. After this unpleasant gesture was dealt me, I made out the blurry vision of Josiah before me as he dragged me through the place and out its door. The remaining light outside still managed to hurt my eyes and I walked offbeat and slowly. I kept losing my standing as my weakened knees repeatedly buckled, and so Josiah picked me up and carried me the rest of the way to the Old Ruidoso. When we reached the building I was set back down on my feet, promptly lost my balance, and stumbled before being able to right myself. I was in no condition to notice who it was that stood around me, nor was I aware of what was happening when Billy viciously grabbed me by the arms and shook me violently in an attempt to bring me around. All of this manhandling caused me a tremendous amount of discomfort as it attacked my easy state of repose. It was all so rudely irritating. Unresponsive and clouded, I feebly tried to fight back and push him away but, even if I had had all of my faculties and strength about me,

I still would not have been able to fight him off. Being horribly jostled about in my condition was so very unpleasant and, in my hazy state, things had been made even more disagreeable as I was again lifted from my feet and thrown into a trough of cold December water to sober me. I screamed and kicked while Billy held me down, nearly drowning me before pulling me up for air and then plunging me back under again. He would hold me there so long that I thought he truly meant to sink me, and as I kicked and fought my energy waned quickly, causing my held breath to give out faster than it ought to have otherwise.

He yanked me back up, shaking me something awful again out of anger, attempting to wake me. I managed to strike out and claw at his face before he smacked me to render me useless and again plunged me back down beneath the water. I kicked with all my might when he finally let up, pulling me up and over the side of the trough, letting me fall carelessly to the hard-packed, frozen ground.

Lying there in a pool of muddy, cold water, I retched so violently from all the exertion that the muscles of my belly cramped and burned, my stomach feeling as if it would tear open as the bile mercilessly flooded out of me. I was then left there to wither in my sorry state as I gasped powerfully for breath. When I had caught enough wind, Billy brutally picked me up and cruelly threw me into our room, locking the door behind me and making me a prisoner. I fell to the floor, happy to be left alone though I was wet and shivering. I couldn't think straight. I hadn't even the sense, or the energy, to crawl to the lit stove and lie before it or remove my drenched, icy clothing to exchange it for something warm and dry. Instead, I only lay where I fell, too exhausted to move.

My punishment had not yet ended with the next morning. I had contracted a terrible cold and an aching head which was joined by a sore and swollen throat and, after falling asleep on the hard floor in my wet clothes, I had woken up on my right side to discover an excruciating agony in my hip and a hard ache in my shoulder that whipped across my back, disallowing me to move my arm and neck painlessly. I had also inherited stiff and sore muscles throughout the rest of my body.

Bleary eyed and ill, I coped with my discomfort while I crawling at a near slither toward the bed, managing with difficulty to pull myself up onto it. I lay there in a fetal position, desiring only not to move anymore. I could smell the damp filth that had settled into my clothing, making me feel all the more unpleasant.

It was not long after this ordinarily small achievement, made extraordinary by my current condition, when Billy entered the room, his usually pleasant voice piercing as he lectured me on my behavior, presenting to me the bottle of laudanum that I had been hiding. Slowly and with some effort, I raised my deeply sore arms so I could bring my hands to my ears in an attempt to try and stop the torture he was pressing upon my aching head, but he would be undeterred and unsympathetic by my deteriorated state. My head pounded as Billy's angry voice seemed earsplitting as it merged with the screaming pain in my head. I plead with God to make him stop through the mercy of humanity, but God would not budge. I could not understand the words he was shouting. I could not understand anything but the agony.

After exhausting himself he finally took pity on me and carefully removed my dirty clothing, sweeping his fingers gently over my skin and tenderly minding my physical discomfort. He redressed me cautiously in my nightshirt and placed me under the covers, stoking the heat in the stove before going for the doctor.

I had a fever and had developed a cough, and through witnessing my misery, Billy finally seemed to break down and gain compassion, lying in bed and staying with me for the rest of the day. As I turned away from him and tried to sleep, he lay bolstered but close against my body, his right hand resting on my hip as he read to himself with his other hand, worried and guilt-ridden over my deprived health.

Restless, I drifted in and out of a dreamless unconsciousness. Billy would rub my back to try and soothe me as my body fussed about. Though I did not want to look at him out of some peculiar combination of fear, anger, and shame, I did not make any attempt to move away from him or in any way give him the impression that I wanted him to leave me alone. I could not blame him for being so upset with me for what I'd done, going to that opium den and hiding the laudanum. I knew that he had only reacted out of fear. I knew that he was rightfully angrier with me than I with him, but I couldn't realize the self-doubt he felt at treating me with such brutality. Before he had come to try and fix things with me after locking me in our room for the night, he had gone off alone to sit and brood over what he'd done.

oooooooooooooooo

"Will you leave me *be*?"

Jimmy stood and looked down at Billy, who sat hiding on the floor of the livery stable, his head hung low. Jimmy ignored him and sat down alongside him.

"Billy, what you did..."

Billy raised his head to Jimmy, his eyes warning the well-meaning boy to watch his words. Jimmy's breath caught and he second-guessed himself, the Colts strapped to Billy's waist drawing his nervous attention before he dared himself to go on.

He won't shoot me over this, he reasoned.

"It was—"

"What do you know about it?"

Billy's tone was downright malicious, but Jimmy knew better, that Billy would only bark and not bite. And, he knew, once he understood Jimmy had come as a friend, Billy would back down.

"I know plenty more than you might think," Jimmy replied, defensive.

"Is that so?"

"Yeah, it's so." Jimmy's voice grew subdued. "I never coulda done a'thing like that, what you did—"

"And I suppose that makes you a better man than me?"

Billy's agitation was becoming ever more apparent. He was defensive, and Jimmy realized that he needed to make his point quickly.

"Why exactly is it you're here?" Billy demanded. "You intend to make me feel worse than I already do?"

"No. In fact, I intend just the opposite. I wouldn't a'had the courage to do that."

"So, what's your point? It takes a big man to beat up on a woman?"

"No...it takes a big man to do what needs doing, even if it means using a strong hand against a woman."

Snorting derisively, Billy said, "Shit...d'you know how stupid you sound, Moffey?"

"No, I mean it, Bill. I couldn't of brought myself to do that to her. I couldn't of risked her hating me, despite being angry enough to want to throttle and beat sense into her myself. She'll kill herself if she's allowed to go down that road. Talking to a person about it doesn't get the job done, I know. You were the right man for the job that way. She won't never hate you for nothing."

"Yeah, well, right about now she hates you, anyway."

Billy couldn't keep the bite out of his voice, making his remark meaner than he had meant to. He began to understand that Jimmy was on his side, but that didn't make him feel any better about what he had done. He was cruel beyond words to the one person who meant everything to him, the one person he wouldn't have wanted to hurt for anything in the world.

Jimmy was quiet a moment, and then said, "I lost my ma that way."

Being of a mind to quickly respond nastily to anything Jimmy might have to say, Billy pointedly caught his next words at this unexpected, heartfelt confession, and felt a hitch in his throat, immediately regretting having previously spoken to the boy with such spite. After waiting a few moments he said, "I'm sorry for that."

"Yeah, so am I." Jimmy chuckled awkwardly. "My pa, he left us. He took up with some other woman—left us poverty-stricken. And my ma, she just about fell apart, and I could only watch it happen. Once a body gets into that poison and gets to back out of reality for a little while, well, that's a hold that won't let go. That grip only gets tighter. It only gets worse."

Billy nodded, appreciative of Jimmy's comprehension and loss. Letting his guard down, an attribute he'd never shown Jimmy before now, he said, "I don't know how to keep her safe. I don't know what to do with her. I can't make her do anything."

"Yeah," Jimmy agreed. "I get that. She really digs in her heels."

Billy laughed at that before returning to a sullen and regretful disposition.

"I shouldn't have done that to her."

"Hell yes you should have!" Jimmy said. "Maybe that goddamned dummy will think twice next time."

"I found a bottle on her. Did you know she'd been doing that stuff?"

"No. If I had I would'a told ya about it."

Billy nodded. "Yeah, guess you might of." Shaking his head he added, "How come I didn't know? I should have *known*. I'm so goddamned caught up in all this game bullshit, I can't seem to make anything right for the trees."

"How's that you mean?"

"If it weren't for me and the hole I gone and dug myself into, none of these things would happen to her. How can I pay attention to her? I ought to pay attention to her. I don't want her to leave me, but mostly I'm just so desperate for her to go just so I know she'll be okay."

"Don't never mind about all that, Bill. She's smart as a whip. She ain't no fool. She does these things to herself. And that girl that took her, that painted lady gal—they ain't, not any of 'em, any good for her. I see you direct her. We all do. She rebels. It ain't you, it's her. Hell, you're right—you can't make her do anything. You never influenced her poorly, not deliberately. You only tried to set her right out here all along and you know it. I see it, that if she don't get her own way she burns it down."

"I can't say as I blame her for that."

"Why's that?"

"Because she's had to do things everybody else's way all her life."

Billy put his hands to his head and repeated, "I shouldn't of done what I did to her."

Jimmy put his hand on Billy's shoulder. "Any fool can see you love her, Billy. We all know you'd never put a hand on her out of anger just for the sake of doing so. I know there ain't a thing anybody can say to make you feel better about it, at least not any one of us."

When Billy didn't reply, Jimmy said, "Talk to her. If I had with her what you do...I see now that you love her as much as she says you do. I'd thought I loved her more, that I was more devoted, but," Jimmy shook his head. "I see now why you are the way you are—to protect her. I wouldn't have had the guts to put her in her place like that for her own good." Jimmy blushed, his face falling with sadness. "I might of just stood by and watched rather than risk her hatred. What you both have...she'll set you right. Just go to her."

Jimmy left a beat of silence before opening his mouth again.

"But Billy..."

Billy looked up, preparing to hang onto the words Jimmy would say next, waiting to hear any other words of encouragement that might help him fix what he'd done, but what Jimmy would say, though it was advice indeed, sounded more as if it were a threat.

"Don't underestimate Lucy. She has every intention of staying here, no matter what happens. You may know her better than anyone, better than me, but I know her well enough. I pay attention where you take her for granted. I know without a doubt that there is nothing even *you* can do, *nothing* that will drive her out. Be careful of how you push her."

ooooooooooooooo

I sat in bed waiting for Billy to bring my breakfast. It had been three days since he put me in this predicament and I was feeling much better. A knock came at the door and, calling to answer it, I discovered that it was Jimmy on the other side.

"Go away!" I yelled.

Disregarding my command, he opened the door slightly and peered in.

"Can I come in?"

"Are you hard of hearing?"

"No."

"You must be."

He came in and closed the door behind him. Cautiously, he sat down in a chair that had been placed beside the bed.

"What can I do to make you forgive me?"

Curious, I bitterly asked, "Why do you need my forgiveness so bad?"

Stoically, he replied, "You make me see how ashamed I oughta be."

I frowned at him. "I am sure it is not my forgiveness you'll be needing."

"How do you mean?"

"I'm sure at this very moment your little friend is corrupting an innocent who deserves your apology for making that so."

Now it was he who frowned.

With the purest intention of honesty I asked, "Why are you such a cur, Jimmy?"

"Pardon?"

"Don't act wounded. You do the wrong things and then make excuses for them. It's indecent and dishonorable. In fact, you truly get on my nerves sometimes."

Despite my being angry he laughed at me, amused. "You really don't have trouble saying what's on your mind, do you?"

I sat quietly, and then, "No. Why should I? I've been through too much to worry about how the truth should affect your feelings, and to that end, with all that's been done, how could I stand by and watch such a charade as yours and just let it go? You're the trouble out here. You're what's wrong with this place."

"Yeah? How's that?"

"You let the bad happen. You've balked about Finny, complained how horrible he is and how you wish you'd have done something about it, and then, when you have the opportunity of a lifetime, you cannot rise to the occasion. And worse, you excuse him and then cry over your mistake. I won't forgive you because I can't. Knowing the things he has done and what he might do yet because of you will not let me, so don't bother asking anymore."

5

February, 1879

Billy sent his old adversary, Jesse Evans, a letter stating that he would like to put their differences aside and end the fighting between what remained of the Regulators and the Dolan gang. As a result of this, we found ourselves sunk low behind a corral wall in Lincoln directly opposite Jesse's men who were concealed by a corral wall of their own on the other side of the street. Billy and Evans antagonized one another, aggressively hashing things out despite Billy's charitably extended olive branch. Myself, Josiah, Minxie, Jimmy, Tom, a man named Joe Bowers, and another named Jose Salazar, sat waiting for the outcome of the argument, a predicament of which I began to feel we had unwisely gotten ourselves into.

Upon hearing that the Regulators were in town, the citizens had made themselves scarce, or they refused to get involved as nobody, save for the craziest of fools, was keen to tangle with our gang, and it didn't help at all that Evans and his gang were in town adding to the trouble.

Understandably, each side was skeptical of the other. Jesse Evans hollered that he'd kill Billy where he stood, declaring that he was "impossible to treat with," and expressing obstinately that he should kill him there and then and be done with him. Billy countered that he did not care to fight, but if they should come at him he'd whip the whole damned bunch of them. I became nervous as was my way, but ultimately both sides grew weary and, with the help of a man by the name of Edgar Walz who rode with Evans, Billy and Jesse resolved the issue.

Eventually, Billy and Jesse shook hands and a pact of peace was drawn up between both bands which, in its most basic form, cited that neither party was to give any member of either gang up, that they would aid each other in resisting arrest and escape if need be, would kill no members for any deeds previously acted out, and that neither party was to offer evidence during trial if any member of either gang should be summoned as a witness. The wages for breaking any of these advices was outright death, and I was reminded of the silly contract signed by Tom and Huck after witnessing a murder, so I couldn't help but roll my eyes at the absurdity. They were as children, making their little rules and setting up their principles just like the children in Mark Twain's tale.

When I had stepped out from behind the wall with the others, Jesse Evans took notice of me, smiled, tipped his hat, and offered me his compliments.

"You must be the infamous Lucky Lu I've heard so much about."

I nodded slightly at his correct realization and he beamed at me.

"Well, ain't you just as pretty as they say?"

I was surprised at how I blushed. I took note that there was nothing in his tone or countenance that was overtly threatening as he spoke to me. In fact, his words seemed sincere and charmingly innocent, but though I was not able to help the coloring of my cheeks, I made sure not to smile openly at him, keeping my inclination toward his flirtatiousness in check as best I could, though admittedly, I found the boy to be pleasantly appealing. Perhaps it was the way this notoriously vicious boy seemed tame and sweet-natured by my presence that drew me to him. Knowing how volatile and dangerous Jesse Evans was known to be caused me some excitement when he smiled affectionately at me, but nonetheless, I refused to let on how he had thrilled me. I could see that Billy was entirely put out by Evans' engaging conduct toward me, but not wanting to stir things up he let it go, deciding instead to keep a wary eye on my interaction with the vile outlaw.

"Well, with all this ugly business out of the way then, why don't you come walk alongside me for a spell and let me buy you a drink?" Jesse said.

"I don't partake in drink unless there's an appropriate celebration," I replied.

"Ah, but sweetheart, this *is* an appropriate celebration. If you can't drink to peace, what can you drink to? But all right, darlin'. Fine, whatever you want, just so long as you come along with me." He gave me a charming grin.

Cautiously drawn to him, I took his arm when he offered it and walked by his side. Billy sniffed derisively as we made our way past him, keeping endearingly close as I lent Jesse my company.

We walked along the Lincoln streets, the Dolan boys becoming extravagantly drunk as they and their former enemies got on with one another, celebrating the cease-fire and their laying aside of arms.

Stopping in McCullum's Oyster House which neighbored the sad, burnt out remains of the McSweens' once proud home, Jesse plead with me to drink just one shot of whiskey with him in a toast of harmony. I looked at Billy for approval which he gave with a slight nod.

"All right, I will have one drink with you in the spirit of peace."

Jesse grinned. "There ya go, darlin'." Pleased, he demanded the shots, ordering the barkeep to keep the drinks "pure", ominously warning "None of that grainy varnish", and threatening to shoot the barkeep where he stood if he so much as got sneaky. When we were served our whiskey, Jesse had me hold my glass high and rang it with his own.

"To peace with the prettiest little gal I've ever had the pleasure of keepin' company with."

He winked at me, and again, I blushed, unable to help it, and this time I gave a smile as I downed the dram, coughing as it burned my throat. Jesse laughed breezily at my small hardship and stared thoughtfully at my face, studying me. He remained a perfect gentleman. Not once did he place his hands on me, and he was protective, threatening any drunken, rowdy man who managed to get a little too close.

"So, you really with that little peckerwood?" he asked in jest, jerking his head toward Billy. Billy snorted and rolled his eyes, feigning irritation.

"What can I say?" Billy started. "The girl's crazy about me."

"That true sweetheart?" Jesse asked. "Don't break my heart and say it's so."

I said nothing. I only looked at Billy and smiled, only too happy to show my adoration of him and let them all see the plain, intense luster of my eyes as they glanced in his direction.

"You don't talk so much, do you sugar?" asked Jesse.

"Oh, she talks a blue streak," Billy declared. "Appreciate her reserve while you got it."

Both men laughed at this, and as the day wore on I became more and more comfortable with the situation that had started out so worrisome. Billy began to relax while I stood with Jesse, and he began to defer his attention elsewhere as his tension eased, holding casual conversations with others, though he continued to glance in my direction and keep watch. Jesse continued to dote on me and remain patiently respectful.

"You know, if I'da known you was with Tunstall, I'da gone looking for employment under him myself. I admit, I'd been wondering about you all this time and you haven't disappointed me one bit. You really are just the prettiest little thing."

One of the men from Jesse's gang drunkenly bumped me and Jesse viciously pushed him away into a table where the man promptly toppled glasses and such as he lost his balance. Jesse asked me if I was okay and I nodded and flushed yet again as he made a point of defending me from any infraction no matter how minor. But in witnessing his stark aggression I could imagine, charming though he seemed he could be, that the murderous intent he was famous for lurked not far beneath the surface.

"Bonney's the luckiest fuckin' little bastard, ain't he? Pardon my tongue, sugar. I never woulda thought I'd say such a thing, but I wish I could swap places with the sonofabitch right now."

I laughed at this and Jesse was pleased with how he had amused me, my laughter piquing Billy's curiosity, warranting another sideways glance from him while he spoke with Jimmy, Tom, and another man I did not know.

The men moved along the street, their behavior ever more riotous as they caroused from one place to another, loading up on drinks and presenting a sloppy sort of gaiety, the Evans/Dolan boys becoming drunker and drunker and more belligerent as they celebrated to excess. Jesse continued to fuss over me, keeping me by his side as we moved place-to-place, with Billy, Minxie, and Jimmy always remaining close by. As the day wore on, however, the drunken Evans boys grew exceedingly bellicose and troublesome, which was of no surprise as their infamously grievous, reckless behavior had forewarned they might, liquor being of no help.

As we wandered along I saw Phyllis Dillinger coming out of Dolan's store. She looked up just in time to see me staring at her and just as quickly put her head down and began moving along at a fast pace. Hurriedly, I walked over, wanting to seize this opportunity and worry her.

"Phyllis!" I called.

She continued on, pretending she hadn't heard me. I began to skip to bridge the gap between us quicker, and as I was successful in this I pounced in front of her.

"Phyllis!" I said again, forging excitement. "How have you been? It's been a long while, has it not?"

Fretfully, she answered that indeed, it had been.

"You and I have much to catch up on, I would imagine. I'm sorry I haven't been around to feed your appetite for gossip, but I've been busy, you see..."

I cocked my head toward the boys for her benefit and noticed them watching me. Billy was smirking, amused more by my ridiculous behavior than by my toying with the poor girl which he would have frowned upon. Perhaps now she knew how it felt to be pestered by an unwanted visitor.

"Have you a comment, as per usual, on my state of dress, Phyllis? You don't seem your usual, blurty self."

"No," she said, nervous.

"No?" I asked sarcastically, cockily pivoting my head to the side as though I were suspicious of her. "Are you *not* typically impressed, then? Oh, I do know that my fashions are not what they used to be, but I am very desert chic, I can assure you of that."

Staring down at her shoes she simply nodded, quietly.

Quickly growing bored by my little caper, I excused myself from her presence, saying, "Well, it was nice catching up with you, Phyllis. I do hope we meet again. I know how much you do so love to feel important by my association. Good day, then."

I doffed my hat to her as a man might and walked off to where the boys stood, turning to watch Phyllis hurriedly scuttle off and making myself a good laugh of it. We then continued on our way.

Susan McSween's lawyer, a man by the name of Huston Chapman, came walking up the street toward us, having the misfortune of meeting our group along the way.

Susan had hired Chapman to bring justice to J.J. Dolan and his gang of killers for the death of Alex. Bad blood, which typically ran considerably deep between Dolan and those who opposed him and his associates, circulated throughout his band of hired killers over the lawyer's meddling. Considering the magnitude of the suffering he caused, it was now strange but interesting to note that Dolan was in fact present here, and he, Evans, and an Evans man by the name of Billy Campbell, created trouble for the lawyer, stopping him in the middle of the street and intimidating him for their own amusement. Billy, Minxie, Jimmy, and me bore witness to the horror as it unfolded.

Campbell had caused trouble for a man named Juan Patron earlier in the day. Patron, a probate clerk in Lincoln who was no stranger to the hell we all knew so well from the beginning, had a gun pulled on him by Campbell when the Evans gang drunkenly stormed his home for more drink. Campbell now drew on Chapman and demanded that the lawyer state who he was and his case for being in Lincoln. Chapman, clearly annoyed and in pain from an obvious ailment of the face, irritably gave his name and explained that he was visiting on business. Campbell then demanded that Chapman dance, an indignity which Chapman proudly declined, snapping that he hadn't any intention of lowering himself to dance for a drunken mob and stubbornly refusing to be bullied by crooks such as the lot of us. Understanding Chapman's position, but knowing how dangerous his predicament was, I prayed silently that he would simply comply before he was sorry he did not, and as I anticipated, Campbell refused to let up, angrily insisting that Chapman watch the tone of his lip service. Chapman, vexed, responded that he was not afraid of us, and demanded to know if Campbell was Mr. Dolan. Jesse spitefully answered for Campbell, saying that he was not Dolan, but that Chapman was in fact talking to a "damned good friend of his."

A bout of true violence finally broke directly after this when Dolan and Campbell, angered by Chapman's defiance, fired their guns near simultaneously upon the ill-fated man. Chapman, understandably in a state of shock, declared that he had been killed before falling to the ground after the fatal shots had rung out and struck him, his clothes set alight from the flash of gunpowder. I instinctively looked at Billy without a second's hesitation. My heart seized when I saw that worry that had besieged his eyes.

"I swore to God and Dudley I'd kill him, and now I've done it," Campbell shouted merrily.

As Chapman's body lay ablaze, the awful stench of his burning flesh pervaded my nostrils. So soon, the new pact had been put into effect as the men attempted to create a diversion by having Chapman blamed for his own death, intending to stage his corpse to look as though he had drawn his own weapon and had been shot dead by Campbell in an act of self-defense.

We went back to McCullum's where Evans and Campbell and the others in their gang began to further drink as they plotted out the false circumstances of Chapman's death. While there, Campbell, drunk and full of swagger, happily proclaimed that he would now go off to Fort Stanton to murder Susan McSween's cattle detective. A shiver went through me as I called to mind how they must have talked of me this way when they planned of ending my own life in February of last year when Billy and the boys took me away from what may have been a certain, disagreeable fate for me. My head reeled with an endless hate of this war and Dolan's proclamations of the worthlessness of innocent lives so long as they stood on what the Dolan gang perceived as the wrong side. John and Alex were dead, Dolan's purported competition out of the way, and that was not enough? Now they would get those who crusaded to right the wrongs and bring the dirty, corrupt frontrunners of the Ring to justice.

Over oysters and whiskey, Dolan handed Walz a pistol and ordered him to place it in Chapman's lifeless hand so that the dead man's corpse would look the guilty part. Walz, who struck me as a wise, level-headed man from the beginning when he cooled the egos of Billy and Jesse, declined to do any such thing, after which Billy spoke up and said, "I'll do it!"

I looked at him, wide-eyed and in disbelief. My dewed eyes met his, silently pleading with him to do no such thing.

"Dolan...give it here," said Billy.

After Dolan handed the gun over, Minxie, Jimmy, myself, and Billy left McCullum's and went to find Tom who was down at the Ellis store and house. We passed by the still smoldering, acrid body of Chapman without stopping so much as have another look. To my great relief, Billy went right on by despite his promise to Dolan, having absolutely no intention of placing that gun in the murdered man's hand. Wanting only to slip away from Dolan and Campbell and their volatile mood without further incident, he offered to partake in their charade under the pretense of involving himself in their foul scandal. He was in no way concerned with falsifying that depraved gang's innocence.

Once we caught up with Tom we took off running, Billy wanting to get as far away from the ugly scene as fast as he possibly could. But what we could not have guessed then was that the damage was already done. Billy, only wanting to put to rest the animosity that lie between our gang and Dolan's by implementing a treaty that would further reduce the troubles in Lincoln and its surrounding communities, put us in a bad situation as it became well-known that we, Billy especially, were in Lincoln when the trouble occurred. Good intentions were unknown and meant nothing. This new trouble only pushed Lew Wallace even further into furious action after hearing of Chapman's murder—another death that would wrongly be pinned on Billy. The irony was that Billy's gesture of going to Lincoln was well-meant, an act of goodwill. But as a result it gave others, *important* others, others who held the future of his life in their ignorant hands, the misdirected confirmation that Billy was nothing but a malevolent brigand and must be crushed like a bug. It would seem, then, that there was indeed some dark specter shadowing Billy just as he had surmised not too long before. No matter what he did, no matter where he turned, misfortune awaited.

6

February, 1879

We hightailed it out of Lincoln and headed straight for Patricio. When we arrived, Billy, though he retained his wits, was in a real quandary and didn't know the first thing to do. I said nothing to him, knowing that anything I'd have to say would only serve to exacerbate the situation as my first instinct, as always, was to cry "Run!" This always incensed him, especially when he was preoccupied with frying bigger fish, and I knew from experience to just let him suss it all out on his own—he'd calm down and come to a conclusion.

We were holed up at the Kavanagh's, sitting around on their small back porch after dinner, the men spitballing ideas off one another. Knowing my thoughts would be unsolicited, I grew frustrated as I sat and listened to them discuss their next move. Withdrawing from the group of them, I walked off into town alone to find some peace and do some much needed and considerable thinking of my own. They were so caught up in their discussion that none of them noticed when I slipped away.

Approaching The Keeper's Inn, I ran into a man I didn't quite recognize, but who seemed to know me.

"Hidee," he said.

I looked up, nervous, trying to keep my distance and assess the situation.

"I know you," he said.

"Yeah?" I muttered.

"Yeah, sure. You're Little Billy."

"Pardon?"

"You know, Little Billy. Or, uh..."—he snapped his fingers as his mind grasped for purchase—"Lucky Lu. That's it, right?"

I only stood and looked at him.

"And I'm Georgia Folsom."

"Georgia Folsom?"

"Damn right! Though my friends know me as Geo. Can ya truly say you don't remember me?"

"Well, sir, I can't rightly say I *do* remember you."

"I know Harper Dealy and them other girls."

My mind began to work. Harper Dealy, the ringleader of the Painted Ladies.

"Oh," I began. "I don't think you and I must have met formally then."

"Maybe so, I can see how you might misremember me. But you're big talk in a town, hard to get around."

"Is that a fact, then?"

"Yeah, it's so. Billy's girl—riding with the Regulators and all that. You're somethin' all right."

I couldn't keep myself from laughing at that.

"Is that what they say? I'm Billy's girl, and a Regulator to boot?"

"Well, sure. Ain't it so?"

I nodded slightly. "I suppose you can count on that as a fact, at least some of it. How's it you know Harper?" I asked, very curious.

"I'm with the Bastards. We keep up with them Ladies from time to time, you know how it is."

Yes, I knew how it was. Pimps, they were. The hard-bitten Ladies often took exception to turning over a share of their earnings and the occasional fracas broke out between the two gangs.

I took stock of Georgia. He was tall and lean, and I could see by his exposed neck that he was sinewy. The shadows of the fading, dusky light pooled within the hollows of his cheeks, giving him a gaunt but pleasant look.

"Well, Mr. Folsom, it's nice to formally meet you, then."

I stuck my hand out and he took it, pressing it hard.

"So I got the right girl, don't I?"

I nodded. "I think so, though I'm not so sure I oughta admit it."

"Naw...no harm here, I promise you. Just the same, what're you doing walking about out here all by your lonesome?"

"Gathering my thoughts."

"Ah, yeah, me too. You wanna come inside and gather our thoughts together?"

I thought about it and, looking behind me idly as if I might see any of the boys spying, despite knowing they would not be, I turned back to Georgia and agreed to step inside with him.

He seemed pleasant and harmless enough. However, out here, those two qualities could still manage to count out deadly, so I can't exactly say that my trust was in place all the same.

Inside the saloon, Georgia talked me into having a few tosses of whiskey. At first I relented, but he won me over. It didn't take much to break down my sobriety and in no time at all I was having the time of my life.

Once they noticed I was gone, the boys found me atop the bar at the Keeper's Inn leading the crowd in a rendition of song, my arms stretched out and guns in hand as I flailed them about in time to the tune the piano was doling out. The men in the place swung their pints and glasses of whisky about while the women danced to the music, singing along merrily as I cavorted about leading them, lacking any of my natural poise and grace, I'm sure. I placed my fists down on my hips, my guns jutting out sassily, and sang:

For my military knowledge, though I'm plucky and adventury
Has only been brought down to the beginning of the century
But still, in matters vegetable, animal, and mineral
I am the very model of a modern Major-General

The boys were amused by the spectacle I caused, glancing at one another and smiling awkwardly, but nonetheless charmed.

Billy and Tom walked up to the bar. Billy held his arms up to me so he could help me down.

"Oh, but Billy...I'm having such fun!"

"I know it, baby girl, but come down here with me now."

When I complied, collective moans of disappointment were roused throughout the saloon.

Sassed with drink I said, "Billy, see that man over there?" I pointed to a man who lifted his mug in acknowledgement.

"He taught me that song. It's from a new play, The Pirates of—*The Pirates of...* well, never mind. He's from New York and it's a new play from there, and what fun!

"And Billy," I shouted loudly. "lookit here!" I pointed to Georgia Folsom. "This's my new friend Georgia, but he goes by Geo."

Geo raised his hat in greeting, but Billy only gave him a hard stare.

"I met him jus' outside and he invited me in ff'—for a drink."

"And where should Lucy know you from?" Billy asked Geo.

"Lucy? Know me?"

"That's what I asked, ain't no need to repeat the question. What's it your name is? Geo?"

"That's right. Geo. Short for Georgia. I know Lucy from the Painted Ladies. I ride with—"

"The Bastards," Billy said, finishing Geo's sentence. He was less than pleased. "You know who I am, Georgia?"

"Well..." Georgia looked from Lucy to Tom, to the others who surrounded them. "Well, you must be the Kid, I'd have to reckon."

"You'd reckon correctly. You responsible for this?" Billy pointed to me.

"Come again?"

"Are you *responsible* for this?"

Georgia held up his hands in defense. "I can't rightly understand what it is that's got you."

"Is my girl cockeyed 'cause a'you?"

"He offer'd me a drink—yes he did," I said, proud of myself. "Said I should have some with him."

"Georgia, it goes round here that Lucy's with me, and strange men know the first rule of being careful with her lest they have the misfortune of meeting me, you understand my meaning?"

Georgia nodded quickly, eyes wide with understanding and a mind to get going as fast as his feet would carry him.

"You go on now, and you remember what I said. I don't want her having no part of those Ladies, and I guarantee you that it sure as shit goes for the Bastards. I know all about you boys. Nothing but pimps, the lot of ya. Now you go on and git. Next time you run into her, you remember this conversation."

"Yessir, Mr. Kid, I will."

Billy laughed at that and let the frightened boy go. The rest of the boys laughed as Georgia went on his way fretfully before Billy turned his attention to me.

"You know somethin' Niña, you get into nothing but trouble when you're let off on your own."

I nodded and it felt comical. My head felt heavy. My eyes seemed wide and slick, and while I didn't fully comprehend Billy, I realized this instance called for me to agree with whatever it was he was saying.

7

March, 1879

Billy confided in me what he intended to do. After the death of Huston Chapman, the screws were put to Lew Wallace, tauter than ever, as the powers that be demanded he do something about the violence in Lincoln and do it now. It was in all of the papers. There were a handful of men whom the Governor wished arrested, and Billy, as Kid Antrim, was at the top of his list. Billy's going back into Lincoln with the good intention of soliciting a peaceful resolution from his enemies had only gotten him further wedged into trouble. Still, he tried to remain optimistic.

So, when I learned from Billy what he planned to do, l lashed out.

"What exactly do you think writing to Lew Wallace will do for you? What do you think you'll get out of it?"

"I hope to get out of it what I got before—with John, I mean."

"And what on Earth was that?"

Pleased with himself he responded, "A warm bed to sleep in, roof over my head, honest work and pay..." he then looked at me coyly and winked. "You..."

He looked down and then shook his head slightly, sighing. "I don't know...a second chance? I need to try for it."

I looked at him, stone-faced. "Could you really be so foolish?"

Looking at me he said, "By turning myself in to John and talking things through with him, things worked out."

"But he took pity on you. And he decided he had a use for you. Otherwise, you might have wound up convicted and sentenced, and you wouldn't be standing here with me now going over what to do with Wallace because you'd be six feet under for horse thievery and God knows what else. And then there's the fact that you weren't the force you are now. You were a nobody—a sorry sight of a boy who John was willing to allow a second chance to go straight. Some dumb kid. You were nowhere near the man you've become. You were merely some street urchin, a petty, thieving nomad. Now you're a murderer, and of important persons at that. And Wallace should like to make an example of you for what you've done."

He blew this off and referred instead to the conviction of horse thievery that John never attempted.

"Well, that isn't what happened, is it? No example had been made of me, and don't tell me that John weren't looking to do so, neither."

"No, because John took pity on you. *Pity*, Billy! Y'got lucky! Are you even listening to me? What exactly is it you expect to get out of Lew Wallace aside from a public hanging?"

He looked away from me, his eyes static on some unseen fixture as he appeared lost in thought, like a small child trying to remember a recitation. Billy spoke out into the empty space of the room saying, "I figure if I turn myself in, like how I'd done with John, I might redeem myself, and I might just get pardoned—my name cleared."

He looked at me and I grew ever more serious.

"Oh! Hang John, you damned fool! I can see now that that whole circumstance has ill-prepared you and made you irrational. John used you to get to the others who stole his horses—I told you this! *You* were the key to getting what he wanted! It was as though he were killing a snake by cutting off its head—you were a means to an end. And now, where in the end did it get *you*, Billy?"

"I don't know, where? I'm stumped."

"Here, Billy. Right *here*! In a foolish predicament. You stood up for a man who used you, and now the problems of your past have come home to roost tenfold! You are worse off now than you were then!"

"Still got you though," he quipped, smugly. "Besides, there was the war—"

"War! Don't talk at me of that war! It was what all of you made and none of your business."

"Like hell. Didn't I owe it to him for what he done for me?"

I wanted to throttle him now.

"You hardly knew him, and he hardly knew you. You were *nothing* to him. Don't you recall my telling you exactly how he thought of you all, all of his precious hired hands? You were all as a pack of philistines to him, remember when I told you that? That's all. Uneducated ruffians and thugs. And to make matters worse, you know full well that the men who employed you in Lincoln broke every promise they made you, *including* John, and more promises will be broken with Wallace, you can believe that. And can you tell me you still feel the way you do knowing this?"

He turned away from me to make his excuse.

"Yeah, well...maybe things would'a worked out for me if things hadn't a'gone the way they did."

"But they had, and you got involved with it all! If you hadn't, things might have been different, indeed! Of course they might have! And with Wallace, you can bet for certain that things will go badly, still."

"Well, maybe if I give him what he wants—"

"Give him what he wants?" I asked incredulously. "Your head on a silver platter? Cause that's what he wants—your neck broke!" I laughed "So if you go to him you can *bet* you'll be giving him what he wants. And after that incident with Chapman, the pressure is on for Wallace to get things done, and get things done he will! And he'll want to end you!"

At those last words, Billy betrayed his stoicism with his desperations, and his words were of a pleading nature. "I can tell him what happened to Chapman! I can turn over the bastards who did it! Maybe he'll excuse me for that. If I do that, like the way I went to John, and tell him I know who did it and where to find them, and that I had nothing to do with it, maybe he'll take pity on me, too."

He looked at me with such hope.

"No. Oh Billy, *no!*"

The hopeful look on his face hadn't waivered.

"Billy, please. I'm begging you to listen to me. Am I not the one person here whom you can trust? The one person who would never lie fresh to your face? Wallace has no use for you, and there'll be no pity from him. And horse thievery and murder are two very different crimes. And the murder of Brady, a law man, crooked or not, forces Wallace to hold someone accountable, and it's you he's aiming for. Chapman's death caused the citizens of Lincoln to goose him further into action. The only thing he needs from you is your seizure and eventually your head in order to prove he's doing what he was sent for—to get the trouble of you and the rest of them out of the way,"—impassioned, I placed my hand to my heart and expelled a gust of breath—"and with you he'll get a windfall because that's all he really needs. You! It'll be a bonus for him to hang several others as well once you spill the names you intend to"—I held up a finger in gesture of a point—"but mark me! You alone will be used as a scapegoat and that'll do just fine. He'll never need to worry about finding the others. You alone will set him a high score. He'll set an example by you. He's pinning all the trouble on you and your innocence, though you are far from virtue anyhow, and the matter is immaterial. Hanging you, alone or with company, will serve the purpose of a cautionary tale: no man outwits the law. That is the difference between then and now. John made a use for you *alive!* Wallace won't have a use for you without your death.

He doesn't have any use for or give a damn about you aside from getting names and your life as a parting shot."

I wasn't finished with my sermon just yet, but I quit my speech for only a moment in order to take stock of him and make sure he was paying close attention. He was leaning toward me like a child who was conscientious, his eyes focused and astute (those beautiful, cerulean eyes of his beamed with regard). He was listening intently and, satisfied, I went on, though somewhat acerbically. "And I know you're aware that you've been labeled the major instigator in this trouble, and that's as far as Wallace or anyone else is concerned. It doesn't matter whether or not you had anything to do with it. It doesn't matter if there were a pack of you firing bullets. *You* were *there*!"

How many ways could I drive my point home, I wondered.

"Well, I might as well try," was his simple response.

"And fail!" I retorted.

I was disappointed by that lackluster remark of his. In spite of how I preached my point to him, it was as though water off a duck's back.

"What you might as well do is *run*. I *know* Lew Wallace—he has sat at my father's table! All he's interested in is cleaning up the mess he was sent here to take care of. He is an egotistical and well-respected political soldier of affluence, and a lawyer to boot! You ought to know how he'll trick you based on that advice alone. You can rot for all he cares—he doesn't give one goddamned shit about you, and you'll do fine to heed my words on that! Once you give him what he wants your purpose will be served. He's His Excellency, not some proprietary cattleman who could use an extra hand. John saw a young boy who had potential. With Lew, you're a murdering detriment to society who's well beneath him! He'll use you up— chew you up, spit you out, and go about his business. My God, the name you've made for yourself! All of the trouble you've been in, you're in a hell of a lot deeper than the nobody you were when you came to John after stealing a few horses. You're in it now, boy!"

"Nobody?" he looked at me oddly, pretending offense.

"You know precisely what I mean! You were just a boy, then—no past to speak of, not really. A clean slate awaited you!"

Fashionably cavalier as ever he said, "Nobody asked you, anyway."

I fumed at this remark.

"Nobody *asked* me? Conveniently, nobody *ever* asks me. And worse still, nobody bothers to *listen* to me. If you had only taken my advice—"

"I'm not discussing this with you anymore. Your advice was—"

"—Right?" I asked indignantly.

Wanting to answer me angrily, his bottom lip quivered, his eyes tapering down to angry slits as they hastened to a darkened, watery blue. I could see his emotions play out across his face, the muscles beneath the skin rippling, attempting to find purchase—fighting for dominance of his expression as he considered how to respond. To my surprise, he settled upon defeat, running his fingers through his hair and scratching at the back of his head in frustration, letting out an exhausted sigh.

"Yeah, maybe. Yeah, your advice was right, it would seem. But that don't change the situation and do me any good now, does it?"

"So let's change the situation *now*," I pled. "Wallace doesn't care about you, Billy. No matter what you say to him, no matter what you write, or what you promise, or what information you have that he needs, he'll only treat with you to get you to give yourself over to the enemy. You'll make a hero out of him and in return he'll grant you cold as a scoundrel. He'll ensure you are the villain. And what about that ridiculous pact you made Evans and the Dolan boys? Won't both sides have it in for you now—the law and crooks alike, for treason?"

He looked at me forlornly for a moment. Then he said, "You've seen what those crooks are like. I don't want any parts of them—I was only ever out for me. I only agreed to that pact to protect *us*. That man, Chapman...he wasn't doing nothing but minding his own business and they killed him for it, for his daring to make legal troubles for Dolan. Dolan has been doing things that way for a long time now and getting away with it. If I do nothing, I'm the same as them."

I understood him, and I cannot deny that I appreciated this, but still I pointed out, "Dolan has Wallace in his pocket."

He looked at me then quickly looked away, not wanting me to see the fear in his eyes. I decided then that my job was to stand by him if this was what he felt he needed to do to make himself right. It was clear I would not win out. I would try my best not to argue with him anymore.

Billy sat at the writing desk in our room, working on a letter to Lew Wallace as I lay belly down on the bed reading a nickel-dime about Billy and me with my feet in the air, ankles crossed and swaying to and fro as though I were a child.

"I will never know where they come up with these ridiculous lies," I said.

Billy gave a muttered, inaudible vague response as he sat in the chair with his head bent, his pencil sensuously placed between his lips and his eyes focused on the blank piece of paper in front him as he considered how to word his letter.

I looked at him, finding him lost in utter concentration as he wondered how he should write someone as noteworthy as *Mr.* Governor Lew Wallace, as he liked to say.

"Need any help?" I offered.

A few seconds passed before he grunted in response as he was completely ensconced within his thoughts, tapping that pencil against his teeth now, his focus ever-present on that paper.

"Do you *need* any help? With your letter?" I asked again.

Absorbed in his task, he made another imperceptible sound before saying, "No. Thanks."

My mind drifted as I observed him, forgetting his foolhardiness as I admired the look of him, tilting my head in consideration of his person. I noted the sinew of his taught, tanned neck as it stretched, bent over the desk, and the delicate outline of his pretty face. I imagined his sun-brushed cheeks, his large doe-like eyes with their long, dark lashes and vivid blue irises, cerulean that could change to azure or lapis as they acclimated to the brilliance and position of the sun. If the skies were clouded for rain they would remain subdued cobalt. I knew them well, those eyes. They enslaved me to him. Whenever he stood close enough to speak to me, even if it were to profess his undying affection, I could barely hear his words, for those beautiful, God-given orbs of brilliance captivated me. I'd find any excuse to look into them, asking him questions I didn't care to know the answer to just so I'd have a reason to look into his eyes.

His lithe body with his lean, sinewy lines gave him an easy, unfettered agile grace. How he embodied such youthful beauty! I wondered: Did other women feel about him the same as I? Did they see his beauty as I did and appreciate him just the same? Or did they see his beauty and charm as a gratuity to his estado bandido? *No,* I thought. *They've always looked after him.*

I would then wonder if he experienced them the same way in which he experienced me: lost and rapt. I didn't believe he did because, when he was with me, it was as though he had come home from a long, undesirable absence. I felt love in his touch or a look, and when we'd lie together, he'd become so captivated with me that often I could not gain his attention. He was lost in me. A woman could tell these things in a man. It was almost as though I was alone except for the worshiping warmth of his body next to mine. I was not lonely for having him there with me, I only had to wait for his appreciation to wear off before he could give me his undivided attention again.

I spent most of my waking hours imagining the two of us lying in bed together, and I blamed his magnetic exquisiteness for tricking me into giving him my virginity. Yet, when I thought on this and remembered that first time, I was nothing if not consciously willing, and I wished I could give it to him again and again so I could continue to please him in the way I had when I first yielded to the temptation of him.

And that sweet, darling boy *did* love me so. Realizing that, I knew it was impossible for him to think of other women the same way he thought of me. He looked at me differently—I could discern this in a crowd of other girls. He touched me differently, and he treated me differently, much to the chagrin of other girls. No matter who the señiorita du jour he flirted with, his attentions toward me were unopposed if I wished it to be so.

Thinking about these things caused me to accidentally give voice to a thought I often quietly entertained, as Billy always told me I'd be on the first train back to New York if I dared mention it. I spoke the words without realizing I had said them.

"I could be very happy living out in the middle of nowhere with you. Just you, and me, and children. *Lots* of children!"

I was mortified and suddenly nervous, wondering if he had heard. But, he hadn't been paying much attention to me thus far, so why should he unexpectedly do so now? I was comforted by this notion for only a moment before it became clear he'd heard every word.

Still concentrating resolutely on his work, he didn't look at me when he said, "Well, Bonita, that makes me the luckiest man in the world."

In light of how distracted his previous responses were, not to mention his usual opposing views to such a thought of mine, this lucid reply surprised me as I noted how effortlessly and quickly he had articulated it, causing me to forget my nerves and conduct a response of my own.

"Yeah? How so?"

"Because I have your love, and that's all I want from you."

Again, an answer with such conviction. He spoke these words so fluently and without a moment's pause that they caused a swelling in the place of my heart. His answer was so genuine that I could not help but feel anything other than affection for him.

I was so very suddenly overwhelmed with absolute love for him that I sprung up from the bed and sat firmly upon his lap, throwing my arms around his neck tightly, holding onto to him for what seemed like dear life. For the first time in an hour his fraught emotions over this business with Lew Wallace gave way and he allowed himself to notice me as he slipped his own arms around my waist.

"What is it, Niña?" he asked sweetly, kissing my neck before turning his eyes back to his letter.

I smiled and leaned in, kissing him on the corner of his mouth, his head was still turned away and situated on that piece of paper.

"That must be the most liberated, unbelievably honest thing you have ever said to me!"

Finally, he looked directly at me and blinked, putting his pencil down, his eyes tensed in a profound, concerted stare as he said with sincerity, "Now that just *can't* be true."

"Oh, but Billy! It is! Those words came so easily from your lips in the very same way as the words I hadn't meant to say came so easily from mine!" They'd tumbled from his mouth with an instinctive fever, without thought!

"I'm certain I've said plenty of honest things to you since we've known one another."

"And you have"—I smiled—"but those words were spoken so sincerely as your mind was concentrated elsewhere. I fear you'll never tell me you love me in such a way again!"

He smiled, though his brow furrowed in curiosity. "Well, what else could you have expected?"

"Well, tell me how it is you know I love you so much, then. I want to be sure you can trust I love you as effortlessly as you do me."

He thought a moment, biting at his lower lip and piercing the ceiling with squinted, thoughtful eyes. "Well, firstly," he began. "I guess it's because of what you said, as I already explained. You wanna give me babies, and though we men don't harp on that much, you can believe me when I tell you providing a man his legacy is... well, it's something. And maybe it's because a gal like you wants me in spite of all the better men you could have otherwise. I can't figure that out, but to be honest, I don't wanna question it—I think on it as a fact. You've stuck by me through hell and back."

He looked at me with softened blue eyes and a tender smile.

"You're a man's true love, Niña. How could I not be so lucky? You're the one good thing ever that's happened to me."

He smiled at me once again before reaching back for his pencil and getting back to his work as though this conversation had never taken place. His lack of pretense in the matter made the entirety of all he had said all the more authentic. Satisfied and happy, I stood up and went back over to the bed to read some more when I heard him say, "Te quiero, Bonita."

○○○○○○○○○○○○○○

"Can I read your letter?"

Habitually, he tapped the pencil against his teeth and looked at me thoughtfully as he tentatively considered my request, knowing my remarkable education would enable me to find fault with his words, and that I'd have a thing or two to say. Resisting his better judgment, he relented and agreed I could look it over. I leapt from the bed and eagerly pushed him out of his chair so that I could sit down and read what William H. Bonney, the alleged Scourge of New Mexico, would communicate in writing to the great Governor Lew Wallace. Billy now sat on the edge of the bed looking at me expectantly.

Dear Sir I have heard that You will give one thousand $dollars for my body which as I can understand it means alive as a Witness. I know it is as a witness against those that Murdered Mr. Chapman. if it was so as that I could appear at Court I could give the desired information, but I have indictments against me for things that happened in the late Lincoln County War and am afraid to give up because my Enemies would kill me. the day Mr. Chapman was murdered I was In Lincoln, at the request of good Citizens to meet Mr. J. J. Dolan to meet as Friends, as to be able to lay aside our arms and go to Work. I was present When Mr. Chapman was murdered and know who did it and if it were not for those indictments I would have made it clear before now. If it is in your power to Annuly those indictments I hope you will do so so to give me a chance to explain. Please send me an annser telling me what you can do You can send annser by bearer I have no Wish to fight any more indeed I have not raised an arm since Your proclamation. As to my Character I refer to any of the Citizens, for the majority of them are my Friends and have been helping me all they could. I am called Kid Antrim but Antrim is my stepfathers name. Waiting for an annser I remain Your Obedient Servant,

W .H .Bonney

"One thousand dollars? My word, where did you come up with such a number?"

"I don't know. Around..."

I looked at him with disbelief.

"Oh, Bill...Come now."

He frowned and ignored my comment.

As always his grammar, misspellings, improper capitalization, and misguided punctuation categorically caused me frustration. But yet, even more so, it caused me such strong feelings of fondness for him. I found this attribute of his charming, if pitiable, ignorant though it was. After all, not many people in these parts could read, let alone write, and the boy did try after all. I found his lack of pretense in both writing and character refreshing and endearing, and his innocence in these matters caused me to giggle softly with such tender regard.

I must have been staring at his letter with a peculiar look upon my face as I thought on these things because he became quite impatient, saying eagerly, "What!"

Forgetful that he was attentively watching me read his letter, I quickly glanced at him.

"It's nothing," I said, honestly.

"But you laughed."

"Did I?"

"You did."

I thought a moment, wondering if there was a way out of this, to make him believe that he'd been mistaken. I decided it would be impossible, as I suppose it *was* rather obvious, so I tried using it to my advantage and attempted to persuade him to let me help dictate his letter. After all, it was going to the Governor, and I did not want Billy to appear simple when he was anything but.

"Okay, it's...you write well," I stuttered. "I promise you."

Suspicion shadowed his face.

"What I mean to say—you make your point quite fine..."

I went quiet and searched his face, finding it expectant as he waited for me to begin criticizing his letter.

"Well, it's just that..." I looked to him again and studied his sweet, impatient face. Looking into that brilliant face made things difficult for me as I decided the best course of action was to be brutally frank.

"Your letter is inapt. It's peppered with poor capitalization, incorrect punctuation, misspellings, and is a bit..."

I looked at him for a few seconds, trying to get a read on his mood, when he exclaimed, "Jesus Christ! *What else?*"

"Well, it's just...you're writing to the Governor. I mean, the misspellings alone are unacceptable. And you wrote 'do so *so* to', and I feel you meant to write 'do so *as* to', or 'do so *in order* to'... Overall, it just seems *a bit* rather unsuitable to be received by such a stately audience."

He stood up from the bed and swiped the letter from me.

"That's the thanks I get for letting you read it," he muttered.

"What else could I be if not a help to you? Would you rather I lied and cared less whether you make a fool of yourself or not? It's just like I told you, he'll see you as nothing more than some desperado, desert rat—"

"So? I don't find him much more than a rat, either."

I had to agree with him on that point.

"You're writing to an educated man. Don't misunderstand me. I'm impressed with your proposal and the way you stay focused. It's coherent, truly, it is. But won't you please let me help you fashion the letter in a more polished manner?"

He grew impatient with me.

"No, this is *my* letter, Lu."

"I know that—"

"—I'm sure he's not expecting some...some *conversating* done up with prettified words!"

I nodded and sighed, feeling guilty over my judgment of him. I had only meant to help. Now I looked to fix my mistake.

"I know you're right. I just thought maybe I could help you piece it together better, and then perhaps he would be amazed with your talent for diction."

He looked at me, staring me down, and said, "So you would make my letter be a lie. And when he met me and my talk didn't agree with my writing, what then?"

I threw my arms up. "You know what? Never mind. It's written remarkably well for a man Wallace might otherwise expect to be undereducated. I think it will surprise him nonetheless. I just thought, perhaps, with my help, you might throw him further off guard at the first. But you're right, it's your letter. And anyway, you are so very clever that when he meets you he won't be able to help but know you are, for sure."

He grinned at me, evidence that my back-paddling was first rate. Desiring to drive home my concession by laying it on even thicker I said, "And I must say, I *am* impressed by how well you can write, Billy."

I gave him the most charming smile I could manage under the circumstances, but thought, *Oh! How I wish he would not send that letter!*

He came at me and wrapped me up in his arms.

"What would I do without you?"

Still in his embrace, I looked up at him, smiled, and facetiously said, "Be forever lost?"

He tilted his head, kissed me on my forehead, and hugged me tight before releasing me.

Please, I thought, *don't let me go.* But he did let go, just before he smiled and winked at me.

Disappointed, I stood where his arms had liberated me and sulked at the floor. Allowing a moment to collect myself, when I felt I could bear my sadness, I asked him one last time if he was sure he wanted to pursue this gamble with Wallace. Soberly, he assured me that he did, and I knew I had to let it go at that, lest I should cross his patience. I knew I could not change his mind, and if *I* could not, no one could, and so all was lost then. I wished I could impress upon him that I felt it better to love a coward than mourn a dead man who had stood by his principles.

Did he love me more than all of this? He claimed, once, that it was because of his love for me that he chose to be a man who'd stand up and fight. Was it the same now? Would he say that he could not be with me without fighting for a clear, honest name? With every fiber of my being I believed that this were true, and so I learned not to ask him where it was I stood in all of this—what it was I meant to him. All he had to do was hold me and look at me with those eyes of his and I'd know. He loved me as desperately as I loved him.

8

March, 1879

On the 15th of March, Billy received his coveted response from Wallace. In his letter, Wallace promised the existential riches Billy was after, claiming he had the authority to exempt Billy from his current miseries and absolve him of any crimes, clearing his name. He would ensure Billy's safe return to Lincoln so that his life could be spared. This buoyed Billy's spirits but only served to heighten my misgivings as it didn't change anything I'd warned Billy about—that the governor would say what he would to gain Billy's trust. What would His Excellency not promise to gain the testimony of such a prestigious witness? He would want to dangle him before all of Lincoln like an exclamation point to his command. Billy would be the answer to the question: *See what Governor Lew Wallace is capable of when called to task?*

It should be known that the truth is this: For all of his high and mighty political standing, Wallace would be rendered impotent without Billy's initiative. In a million years he never would have captured Billy without Billy's reaching out and agreeing to go to him like a lamb to a slaughter. Wallace was granted the advantage, not by his own self-absorbed belief in his influential shrewdness and authoritative prowess, or even by the grace of God. It was only by the grace of the Kid that Wallace pulled off what the residents of Lincoln called for. Billy kept Wallace from been rendered a failure and a fool, and that selfish confidence of the governor's would have been deservedly deflated had Billy decided against the meeting and chose instead not to meet in Lincoln.

"He says I am to meet him at nine o'clock next Monday night, here..."

He pointed to the section of the letter where the information concerning their clandestine rendezvous was to take place: old Squire Wilson's place.

My worry evident, I said, "But you must go back into Lincoln in order to do this, Billy."

"Where else?" he said. "Lincoln's where Wallace is at."

The expression on his face suggested that he thought me daft as opposed to troubled and disturbed. We looked at one another with inequitable expressions, both experiencing different emotions based on his position.

"He says I'm to meet him at Squire Wilson's because it's the best place to keep my presence secret."

"He also says you're to go alone, Billy. I don't like it—I want to come with you."

I could not keep the sound of desperation from my voice, and he put his arms around me in an attempt to calm and reassure me.

"He also says that if you can trust Jesse Evans, you can trust him," I pointed out.

"So?"

"Do you really fail to see the folly in that? It's bewildering because it's you who's *less* trustworthy than Jesse because it's *you* who broke that ridiculous pact. *Oh!* The irony is that you don't see yourself as one of them, Jesse Evans and his gang, but they stay true to their word, unlike yourself. So that makes you so much worse than they!

Wallace cannot be trusted anyhow, as I've told you. I told you, he will turn on you as soon as look at you. And it's that pitiable resolution of yours that makes you feel you can trust Wallace. That puts you in cahoots with him. That he claims you can trust him if you can trust some brigand like Jesse—the brigand who, I may remind you, is not currently stabbing *you* in the back. You are as dogs conspiring, you and Wallace, the *real* enemy."

I'd stung him with these words, and my saying them put him in a foul mood, indeed. He did not like that I had made him out as a cowardly cheat, nor did he care for how my perception of the circumstances made him feel uneasy. I had darkened his ray of hope.

"My God! The circles you talk in! You don't know that Jesse Evans wouldn't do the same to me. I'm *positive* he would if it meant saving his own neck, just like he's done to me before!"

"True enough, but you were no better than enemies then, and your foolish pact didn't exist—"

"—No better than *enemies*? We were as brothers! At least we's supposed to have been! But he left me to the dogs! Or have you conveniently misremembered?"

Billy was right—it was Evans who abandoned him and left Billy stranded to get caught with John's horses. Fortunately, John took no charge against Billy, going easy and giving him a living instead.

"Fine, what you say counts for something—it's true enough. But at present, I can say with one hundred percent certainty that it's *you* turning on *him*. And whatever happened before, it worked out for the best for you, and you agreed to that stupid treaty! I always figured you for a better man than he. Was I wrong? Tell me."

"I know what it is you're doing, little girl! I ain't as stupid as all that! You're tryin' to get me to think twice after I've made up my mind already, but all you doing is creepin' up my goddamned nerves!"

Soon after, Billy left for Lincoln to meet with Lew Wallace, and I was made to stay behind, having nothing to do but wait.

Billy had let Wallace see his face. Once a mere ghost to the man, Wallace would now know him on sight, a true detriment to the most wanted of outlaws. One of the great many things going for people like us, those who walked outside the lines, was this: it was hard to point fingers when you didn't know who you were pointing at.

When he returned I worried him about the details, chewing at him like a pup. He told me the meeting was quick and to the point, that they had come to the agreement that both he and Tom would turn state's evidence in exchange for Wallace's pardon. With some hesitation he told me he'd learned Jesse Evans and Billy Campbell had been caught and held for the murder of Huston Chapman, but that they had escaped their prison at Fort Stanton. I was horrified as I knew what this meant should the two killers find Billy out in this game, and Billy, uneasy at this news on his own, had to put aside his own distress in order to settle mine.

Because of the crimp Evans and Campbell had effectively put into his plan, Billy was prompted to send another written communication by bearer to Wallace informing him of this poor turn of events, explaining that he was troubled, afraid he'd be caught up and waylaid by Evans and Campbell. If the two had discovered his covert proposition of making a wager with Wallace that included naming names and turning them in, Billy was as good as dead.

Receiving word back from Wallace, there was an offer to stage an arrest of Billy and Tom in order to fool eyewitnesses and any potential enemies so that the true reason behind the visit with Wallace would appear anything but dishonorable to thieves like us. These circumstances, under which Billy and Tom would appear unfortunate and caught up in a bad twist, would help deceive Evans and Campbell should they find out so that they could not suspect that Billy was a turncoat about to give them up. Yet still, it was but a small relief for such an enormous gamble.

"Billy, you have lost your mind! For all of this tomfoolery, in the end, a court of law will still find you out and you'll hang! Or worse, your enemies will come for you first when they find out you *lied* after you swore to protect your 'outlaws in arms'. And only God or the Devil knows what they'd do to you!" My nerves were reduced to tatters, and again I reminded him that I could trust none of this.

"I know it, that I swore that oath in Lincoln," he agreed. "But I would have said just about anything to keep things straight. And how could I know that Wallace would offer up this deal to me? I'll take any opportunity I can get to put my life back, and I sure as hell don't care about keeping a pact among thieves that means nothing to me and protects the men who'd keep me down as the killer of that lawyer. That pact only serves them, anyway, and not me, cause I don't plan on getting into any more trouble like they do. I want to go straight—I've wanted to go straight, only they won't seem to let me. But maybe this is my chance. I only said and did what I had to do at the time to survive. I agreed to their pact so I could hold the peace. Outside a'that, it meant nothing to me."

Hearing these words, his explanation, restored some of my faith in him when it came to this predicament, but still, I was utterly selfish over him. It didn't matter how badly I felt about it, Chapman was dead and gone, and there was nothing anybody could ever do about it now, unless one considers Billy's misguided attempt at setting things right with Wallace. But I knew Billy's hope would crumble soon enough, and that was one of the cruelest punishments a man could ever know. So I was caught between fighting back the feelings that would ruin such hope, and putting on a brave face and attitude that would allow him to hold on to it. I told myself that it didn't matter much anyhow, that he wouldn't let me take it away no matter how hard I tried to make him see reason. He'd believe what he wanted to—that he'd be redeemed.

"I want my life back," he said, "and this is how I want you. I'll make my life deserving of you. And I want you to stop throwing up that ridiculous deal to me. The trouble with you is you can't never let go of anything, even when it's been explained repeatedly. I've had enough of this talk, and I won't hear anything more of it."

I broke down at that last sentence and my tears spilled over. The whole ordeal grew more and more nerve-racking, and it seemed obvious to me that only Wallace stood to make out on this deal. Once he had what he needed from Billy, he would merrily go on his way as a hero and leave Billy to rot in a prison until it was time for him to hang. Billy was so desperate to get out of this life that his wits were failing him and he was willingly laying himself into a trap. He was risking *everything* while Wallace had nothing to lose. I insisted he let me go with him and Tom if he were going to paint himself into a corner.

He argued over allowing me to go along, so I cried uncontrollably, knowing this would break him down and cause him to relent. Billy never could stand the sight of me with tears. It was a cruel trick, but a necessary one in my opinion.

It was decided that Lew Wallace would send men to Patricio to arrest Billy and Tom, but Billy warned him to send men he could trust, that he was not afraid of dying, but that he did not want to "die like a dog" should one of the men sent to "bring him to justice" turn on him while he was unarmed.

After further rounds of exhaustive arguing, Billy finally gave in and agreed that I could go to Lincoln when they took him. Using what I could to my advantage, I reminded him that there was nothing he could do to keep me from following if I so chose. And just like he would, I'd do whatever I could by whatever means necessary to get my way, even if it meant using his fears against him.

I knew Lew Wallace. That arrogant sonofabitch had dined with my family, in my home, and he knew my father well. They had known each other during the war, administering a high respect for one another, and were republican comrades. Wallace was well aware of my father's means and connections, and I knew that by going to Lincoln with Billy and Tom I would out myself, too, but I considered Billy's welfare much more important than that of my own. After all, a life of luxury awaited me if I were waylaid, not a noose. And Billy was the incendiary match whose light the rest of us followed. He was a born leader, and this made him so undeniably important—and dangerous. Me, I was a dime a dozen, special only because I was born with the right pedigree. But Billy? *He* was a natural, and saving his neck was of the utmost importance during these perverse times. He was a revolutionary, and he was just the champion needed by the trampled and bruised.

I tried to consider other options—striking a deal with Wallace by giving myself up, allowing him to send me back to New York with the absolute assurance that Billy would be given his pardon and get his life back. My proposal would grant Lew Wallace favor with my father as he could take responsibility for my safe return home, and this would be no small thing because, though a man of Wallace's stature would not be in need of my father's influence, having a man like him in his debt would be an enticing gratuity. In addition, he would make a large sum of money for my return, and what man with a mind for business would balk at something like that? I would sacrifice my own freedom for Billy's. It was my hope that the governor might consider leniency towards Billy because Billy had cared for me so unequivocally and had kept me safe from the vices of this war and out of danger. But, I could only hope because, the reality was, no matter who I was or to which family I was born, Billy was just too big of a fish to catch and fry, and with my making the trip with Billy, Wallace could get us both in one fell swoop, so I was forced to realize that I did not, after all, hold much of a bargaining chip.

9

March 1879
The Shade of Richard Brewer

By the time Sheriff Kimbrell and his men arrived we had to make a late start of things, and so on our way into Lincoln we stopped to make camp, cooking two rabbit carcasses that had been hunted down for sport by two of the posse men.

Jimmy went with us to Lincoln so that I would have him to keep company with while the two unchained "prisoners," Billy and Tom, were being detained. In addition to the feast of New Mexican desert rabbit, Kimbrell's posse had been more than adequately supplied for such a relatively short trip, but there was a large enough crowd of us, and experienced cowboys who knew even the easiest of terrain could be unpredictable were always well prepared for an excursion.

A banquet was cooked up, consisting of cured deer meat in greasy skillets, roasted potatoes, jerky, and plenty of bacon and gravy for biscuits. Cornbread and canned fruit were offered, and little cakes and candy were available for something sweet while tins full of coffee were heated, though only the few who would remain awake drank it down while the rest of us drank ginger beer or water. It was a real blowout, and one that I had never seen despite my pilgrimages made out on the trails with the men, though they could only ever do the best they could, understandably, to keep us stocked with provisions.

All four of us captives were relieved of our guns to make it all the more convincing in case any wandering eyes should spy our party, but I was allowed my Winchester so I could play at hunting for small game with some of the men in order to pass the time. Making a commotion in unsettled territory was not considered wise as it could give away a party's position to undesirables and, certainly, leaving a lit fire to sit by did no favors, either. But there were plenty enough of us, and well-armed, too! And we were not necessarily in a riotous area, just between Patricio and Lincoln.

Billy was given permission teach me how to fire a shotgun, and interested in learning, I said "yes," obliging him the opportunity to teach me something new.

Taking me to a place that was not too far but secluded enough, he handed me the firearm, an 8 gauge, and showed me how to hold it properly.

"Hold it like you do your Winchester," he explained. "But be careful...it weighs a little more and it's got one hell of a kick!"

Billy took it back and loaded it, handing it to me again. I held it aloft, heavy as it was, pointing it in the direction Billy showed me as he stood behind me, supporting my body with the weight of his own to help protect me from losing my balance when the recoil hit.

Wandering off, we were, for all intents and purposes, alone, and so Billy took full advantage of this, sliding his hands down around my waist and kissing me on the neck. Teasingly, I laughed and elbowed him in the side, telling him to "quit it" and help me concentrate, which he of course chose to ignore for a time.

Finally, his hands still about my waist, he spoke erotically into my ear, sending lustful pulses through me that made me blush.

Leaning in close he said, "That's it, baby. you got it. Just hold steady and pull the trigger. Keep your aim straight ahead."

His warm breath in my ear made my knees weak, but I held strong and sighted the barrel. I felt Billy standing solidly behind me, remaining quiet as he watched how I would fare, and I did my best to block his seductive behavior and concentrate.

I fired once and was punched in the shoulder with the stock, causing me to yelp in pain. Billy laughed as I whined and rubbed my bruised arm.

"You want to try again?"

"Hell no!" was my reply.

"Aw, come on, now...you know how it is. You gotta learn, and these things take some gettin' used to. I want you to practice firing this shotgun, and that's what we're going to do until we hafta go back."

Hesitantly, I nodded in understanding, and he gave me that Cheshire grin of his.

So once again I stood, aiming and ready to fire, Billy behind me trying to hold me as still as he could. I was a little more nervous this time around, knowing the kickback was going to abuse me. But all the same I pulled the trigger to please Billy because he was right—I needed to learn. The recoil did as expected and knocked me back into Billy. I cried out yet again in pain, and he chuckled, though quietly this time, and he placed his arms around me and lovingly kissed my neck again for being such a good sport. Sympathetically, he cautiously asked if I wanted to go ahead and try again. I gave him an emphatic "No!" He laughed and took the gun from me, telling me he'd teach me further another time, and I understood because, despite my whining, I should learn how to use a shotgun properly, and from Billy's own words—he was proud that I at least knew what to expect should I ever need to pick one up and fire it.

"But remember," he said. "you got a lot more learning to do. We're only finished for now because I figure you've had enough, and you gave me your word that you'll let me finish teaching you, which I take seriously."

At the very least, I figured, those "bandolero" pants I have would make a lot more sense on me now.

The group of us was amiable and in good enough spirits which made for a fun night despite my current, usual high anxiety over our present matter. All of the men talked animatedly, and a good many of them sat with Billy and Tom, laughing heartily as Billy made his jokes and stories. Every so often he would look at me and pay me attention with a wink while Jimmy and I played cards until it was suggested we bed down so as to get an early start in the morning.

Billy rolled out our bedding and, closely sidling up next to him, my back to him as he placed his arm around me, I was permitted to keep my Winchester by me as I often did when forced to sleep out in the wide open wilderness, its presence always calming me. Allowing me to keep my rifle did not present a problem since Billy did not pose a threat, being there willingly of his own accord in order to make his pact with the governor.

I felt at odds as I settled in. I was thoroughly exhausted and my heavy eyes dropped easily enough, but my mind was restless. Maybe this was because of the extraordinarily stark emotional turmoil that had consumed me as of late, or perhaps it was due to the exhaustive trials of riding through the rough desert, an undertaking that was commonly strenuous as it could often be coarse and difficult, especially when one factored in the weather. I believed it must have been the former, as the latter would have put me out but good! But perhaps it was in fact a combination of both these matters because, though I dreamt under some semblance of sleep, it was anything but peaceful.

I had been looking up at the tranquil night sky when I must have seamlessly slipped into unconsciousness. It was as though I hadn't closed my eyes at all. My mind's eye could still see the darkened firmament with its glittering stars that seemed only a grasps breadth away beyond the warm glow of the campfire's embers, and I believed that I could still hear the men who kept watch over our party as their faint voices rose and fell mellifluously. These things had seemed to stream unbroken through my mind as though I were fully awake. There didn't appear to be any somnolent interruption between wakeful cognizance and the oblivion of slumber.

And so, under the guise of wakefulness, I listened as the men said peculiar things—conversations that were strange and illogical to me as things often are under the tutelage of sleep. I could still feel the warmth of Billy lying against me as though I were aware, the weight of his arm over me and his belly expanding and pressing against my back as he breathed. I imagined recalling a fabricated discussion that we alter our direction, that we not go into Lincoln after all, instead changing our minds and deciding to head off to California where the gold diggers had gone. Some intuitive part of me that kept tabs on conscious facts understood this as nonsensical. Yet still, I believed in it. After all, are we not at the mercy of our own mind when we are left to its devices? The mind will lead you where it wants, and has the ability to distract you from its deception even as you have the good sense to question it.

My somnolent imagination made me wonder over abandoning the purpose of our intended visit to Lincoln, and the peculiarity of why it was suddenly no longer important to Billy for us to go there after all of the frustration and bickering between us.

My mind was working at this when out of the blackness came a human figure even darker than the night that surrounded it. It was silent as it came toward me, and I noted that a person ought to make noise as they walked over God's natural elements such as rocks and twigs and other things that get underfoot. The vision of this human form was surreal and otherworldly—I thought this even as I believed I was truly witnessing it—and in the final moments of seeing that shape, the darkness seemed to slip aside as though the thing were passing through shadow into light. And when the face revealed itself to me, I saw that it was Richard. The left side of his face was ruined and bloodied, a splintered maw where Roberts' bullet had torn through the eye-socket. But I recognized him all the same.

Startled, my eyes came open and I sat up, lifting my Winchester as the rifle had never left my grip. Getting quickly to my feet I stumbled, my mind unable to function under its self-induced chaos. I floundered in my bleariness, made worse as my sight was dim and indistinct. Confused and frightened by the ghost of my fallen friend, I frantically lifted the rifle should it continue coming for me. *What did it want!* I wondered. Was it here to tap its icy finger upon my shoulder and take me to the other side? I was vaguely aware of Billy sitting up watching me, and of my spooking the others as I fumbled around in the dark out of fear. I fell over a log and hit the ground which sent a shock of pain through my left arm, jarring me fully awake and causing my rifle to discharge, the round shattering the bones of one of the horses. It whinnied something awful as it went down, and I lay there motionless, wisely afraid to move after the alarm I had set off among a gang of heavily armed men, and simultaneously worrying that I had fractured my arm. Men surrounded me with their weapons drawn until their confusion subsided and it became clear that the matter had to do with my being strung out and nothing more.

I, however, was certain of what I had seen. Jimmy, lifting me carefully and tenderly, helped lead me back toward my bed as my Winchester was cautiously taken from me. Terrified, I whispered the name, "Richard," repeating it over and over again in fear. Billy reached for me and Jimmy gently helped guide me down to him before kneeling beside us on the ground and placing his hand tenderly upon my shoulder. Billy put his arms tightly around me and was understandably fraught with concern.

"What about Richard?" Billy asked.

A gunshot rang out and I realized that they must have put the poor horse down. *Yes, there was an awful neighing off in the dark, wasn't there?* The curiosity of whose horse it was crossed my mind as I put my hand to my muddled head.

"What *about* Richard?" he asked again.

I stared at him blankly and he wrapped his hands around my arms, shaking me as gently as he could while trying to be firm.

"Lucy..."

Blinking frightfully, I continued only to stare before becoming aware of everything: of the others looking at me with fear, of Jimmy's eyes probing me, searching for some sign of madness. I looked around at all of them, my eyes scanning the crowd before looking back to Billy, sentient.

"Oh," I whispered with shock. "Oh, *Billy*..."

I placed my hands on his shoulders and clutched them intensely as we sat looking at one another. He gently put his hands to my face, his eyes imploring me to tell him what happened.

"I saw him!" I said.

"Saw *who*, darlin'?"

"Richard! I *saw* him!"

"No, honey, you didn't. You were only dreaming—"

"No! It was *him*. He was *real*! He meant something by it—it brought news of something bad, I just know it. I feel it!" *It*, I had said, a fiendish specter of a once beloved, deceased friend.

"Darlin'..."

"His face, Billy...you didn't see his *face*! He wasn't peaceful! The dead don't look peaceful when they're full of torment!"

Billy pulled me close to him, stroking my hair as I lay my face pitifully against his shoulder.

He had trouble allowing himself to sleep the rest of the night, and I was simply unable to, so we laid there next to one another, our faces so close to one another's, silent and uneasy.

The next morning, as we rode toward Lincoln, I was quiet, still haunted by the ravaged specter of Richard. Though the sun was bright and warming, I shivered, my world cloaked in an eerie dimness privy only to me. The world felt akilter. I had a novel feeling of dread to increase my sense of despair, and I was convinced that if I turned to look behind me I would find Richard there, dogging me closely in warning as we rode on, that ghastly wound of his mocking me.

Billy and Jimmy would look at me and exchange worried glances, but I hardly noticed this as I was too caught up in trying to understand the prophecy that had been presented to me in such a familiar form. My mind, with its taxed nerves, wouldn't allow me to believe it had only been my imagination conceptualizing and trying to relieve me of the demons I carried. I was convinced we were headed for a bad end.

10

March 1879

      The illusory captives were held in Juan Patron's store while Jimmy and I stayed on at the Wortley. The word was still out for me despite the monetary retraction regarding my capture and my status as a New Mexican resident. Tricks were still bid for among the wasters and good-for-nothings who planned to waylay me and give up my whereabouts in the hopes it would still garner a sizeable reward, but nobody would actually touch me as my association with the Regulators terrified and kept the gumps at bay. The hope of my seizure was nothing but a lot of exercised talk. Lincoln County's Sheriff Kimbrell either naively or intentionally refused to recognize me in any of this mess, regardless. But, however he may have felt about my business in the matter, it would not have made one bit of difference—I could not be taken from New Mexico without the reckoning of proper channels, and there could be no excuse to hold me on charges as I was never officially considered a part of any criminal dealings, nor was I considered of any consequence to that effect. And with Susan McSween inaccessible to handover my residency, Kimbrell would do nothing. He was well-known for taking the path of least resistance and could not be bothered with the extra hassle of tracking the good widow down.

      As for my safety, my legacy was all the protection I needed and had in spades. In any case, with Brady dead and J.J. Dolan keeping his head down and level, I was cut loose from any form of murderous retaliation. The only ones out for me now were those looking to use me as leverage in order to wrangle the Kid out or to give my position away to my family in hopes of a reward.

      Meanwhile, Billy and Tom were merrily living it up in their prisoners quarters, playing cards and having every creature comfort made available to them. They ate well—better than they sometimes had as free men—and had the run of the place. They were treated as kings, almost every wish of theirs fulfilled, and I was able to visit whenever I wanted and spend as much time with them as I pleased, which was often.

      At every turn I tried to speak with Billy about his meeting with Wallace, breaking the promise I made to myself to try my best to quit arguing about it with him, but he often waved me off in that cavalier way of his. His being treated so royally lessened his concern over any conference on the matter, I'm sure.

To pacify me, and because he was put off his guard by his lax arrangements, Billy granted me permission to go along with him and meet with His Excellency.

"Elucia Howard..." Lew said delectably, rolling my name over his tongue like a cube of sugar, regarding my appearance as he sat in his expensive, silk-bound Louis XIV chair, just as pleased as the cat that ate the canary to have me in his clutches. Having both the Kid and his exclusively wanted, eastern society girl, so easily collected, was simply too delicious and fortunate for Wallace to ignore. Now he could deliver us both and kill two birds with one stone, all the better to be the hero of Lincoln.

"Or should I fashionably refer to you by your newly, modishly bestowed epithet of Lucky Lu?"

I rolled my eyes and smirked, unfazed by that smug arrogance of his.

"If only your father could see you now. How proud he would be." Wallace smirked.

I laughed silently at his little psychological game. I looked at Billy who had his head down, eyes trained modestly on the hat in his lap.

"I dare beg, what's so funny, Miss Howard?"

"Well Lew," I began. "if I gave a damn about my father's pride as it's concerned me, I wouldn't be here before you now—I'd be in New York."

A soft twitter escaped from Billy. Wallace only sat back in his chair and coolly steepled his fingers, undaunted by our misconduct.

Billy cleared his throat. "Sir?"

Wallace gave his attention. "Yes, Mr. Bonney."

"You promised that I would have a pardon if I made a witness for you, is that still our deal?"

"Yes, Mr. Bonney, of course. Do you have cause to think any differently?"

As usual, I could not keep my mouth shut.

"I'd like it much better if you could give Billy some written documentation to sign, Lew."

Wallace regarded me with dispassion, though I could still see he was piqued by my using his Christian name so informally.

"You haven't any trust in me, Miss Howard. Is that it?"

"No Lew, I do not. I also do not have any trust in the fact that you will procure amnesty for Billy."

Wallace tsked. "I'm surprised by that audacious little attitude of yours. New Mexico has not done you any favors. What would your father say?"

"It's done me all the good in the world, and my father can take solace in remembering that it was he who sent me here. Anyway, we're not here to discuss my disposition."

Wallace sighed arrogantly, as though he were both mildly inconvenienced and unimpressed.

He continued, "I have influence here over Rynerson." He looked at Billy. "That's the D.A. here in Lincoln."

"He knows who the D.A. is," I barked. "And your...*influence* with him is no guarantee, isn't that correct, Lew? Rynerson is no friend to Billy. He's part of the Santa Fe Ring, and *Dolan* is a personal friend of his. Rynerson would have Billy hanged to save Dolan's neck—a neck that should be snapped if only for sport. Perhaps you may fool Billy, but you may not fool me."

"Well, Miss Howard, it's the best chance I have at making good on my promises to your friend, Mr. Bonney, here."

"Okay, then. Fine. But be honest with him on that score. Don't make promises you can't, or won't, keep on your own. Don't use the word 'influence' to him, Lew."

Wallace looked directly at Billy and addressed him. "Mr. Bonney?"

"Yessir?"

"Are you still committed to this parlay of ours?"

"Well..." Billy looked uncertainly at me and made a small clearing in his throat. "it seems it's the best way for me. I'm in, sir."

I rolled my eyes. I considered our position and grew somber.

"Lew?" I asked.

"Elucia?" he responded.

"I know Lincoln has been suffering. Is there any way to make better this arrangement by my promising that if Billy is given his freedom, if his name is cleared, I will go home willingly and have my father contribute a healthy sum of money to this town? I'll see to it that he pays a hefty reward to each of you as well for my safe return. Should Rynerson not consider that?"

Wallace sat back in his chair, studying me.

"I'll raise the issue," he smiled.

Out of the corner of my eye I saw Billy looking at me. I turned to look at him full-on and met his gaze, finding his eyes glassy and water-blue with confusion.

I reiterated, "If you can give Billy what he deserves, then I promise to see to it that Lincoln's coffers are fattened. These people are relying on you to put an end to all of this, and that ought to help secure the legacy you're so hell-bent on."

Wallace continued to smile and study me, and I then said, "However...if your promise to Billy falls through, we're back to square one, and none of you will see a dime. And Billy's promise will break, too."

"Meaning?"

"You figure that out," I snapped defiantly.

Billy smiled, full of pride despite himself.

"But if you hold up your end of the bargain, I will heel and help reinforce the confidence these people have in you. My father would have to chase down Susan McSween in order to have her sign over my guardianship, and I doubt he'd work things out with her before my eighteenth birthday. I even doubt the widow McSween is any longer concerned with the issue of my position. Handing myself over will be the only way for him to get me back. If you can secure a firm agreement based upon my going home as well as the pardon you promised to Billy, then we'll not make a fool of you."

Humoring me, he replied, "I promise to do what I can—"

"—Who are you horseshitting, Lew? And you don't want to be in this town any more than we do. You should want to reap a stately sum for your trouble. Don't say you'll do what you can, say you'll do it."

Wallace looked to Billy. "Mr. Bonney, have you changed your mind based on anything that's been discussed?"

"No sir, I believe this must be my only chance."

I cannot say, to any degree, that the meeting with Governor Lew Wallace had done anything to stabilize my confidence.

With Tom in his own room and Jimmy about town, I visited alone with Billy. He sat in a chair riffling his playing cards.

I told him again, "You're doing Jesse dirt."

"Oh," he laughed. "that old gem. There go them chattering circles of yours again. What the hell is it you care so much for, anyway? Ain't we done with this argument, yet?"

"You made him a promise."

"*Oh?*"

I had been facing the wall, but turned to find him looking at me, his eyebrows raised with curiosity.

"There is no honor among thieves, is that it?" I asked.

He gave me a peculiar look. "You're upset that I traited on your boyfriend? Is that it?"

I put hand to my head at that, *traited*? Such southwestern drawling and corn-fed dialect.

As I considered his derision, my thoughts shifted, focusing on his sarcastic question about Jesse. "You don't fool me," I told him.

"Oh, no?"

Curiosity and mischief converged across his face.

"No. Not at all. That waggish tone of yours can't hide the fact that you are a jealous man. You only play at being the cavalier rogue, Billy Bonney."

To me, it seemed true enough that he had made it more than obvious that Jimmy's, and now Jesse's, attentions had tweaked him.

He waved me off. "If you say so..."

"All right then, cut it out and answer my question."

He relented and grew serious. "No, there ain't no honor among thieves, Lu. Didn't Jesse give me up after we took them horses? And what should I care, if all I'm considering is making things right? I'm thinking about me—I only care about me."

"You're always thinking of you."

He gave a half-smile and studied me.

"You don't really care about my breaking that pact with Jesse and Dolan, do you?"

I turned back to the wall and quietly said, "No."

When he said nothing else, I turned back to him and, looking at the floor said, "I don't like the position you've put yourself in. I don't care about anyone else or what you promised them. Except, breaking that pact...you've given yourself up on both sides. It worries me."

Billy jauntily kicked at the chair that sat adjacent to him and held it slightly aloft with the toe of his boot, cocking his head and giving me a sly smile. "There it is," he said.

"There *what* is?"

He let the chair clatter down unceremoniously and hooked his foot on its rung, shook his head, and shuffled his cards again, smug.

"And you think I'm a jealous man," he laughed. "Who've I got to be jealous about? You admit you don't care about nobody else."

His comment forced a smile out of me. He really was an arrogant piece of work, but in such a way that it was gregarious.

"So is it true you only care about yourself?" I wondered impishly.

With his head down he raised his eyes and looked at me knowingly, his blues brilliantly vivid as they reflected the rays of sun that broke in through smudged window panes. He contemplated me, nonchalantly playing with his deck of cards and shuffling them one-handed, expertly moving one half of the deck atop the other again and again, taking his time in answering me.

I continued to smile at this little game of his as he lifted his head and said, "You know you and I are the same. Caring about myself, well it should go without saying that I care about you, too."

I looked at him with such devotion, but I still could not help but say, "Wallace is gonna pick your bones dry."

Ignoring the comment he asked, "Why don't you stay here with me, Bonita? Spend the night with me."

Pretending to be shocked I declared, "Here? I couldn't possibly. How could I?"

"I ain't no real prisoner. Stay with me, I want you here lying right next to me. I miss having you by my side at night."

"Such indiscretion," I joked. "How you could even suggest it, I don't know, and when one of my contemporaries, a dignitary no less, is about. He'll send back a full report!"

"Oh, to hell with all that," he said with a sly air. "It's you and me, darlin'. Nobody else—it's always just you and me. Besides, you know it won't make no difference to them, so long as they got me where they want. You know as well as I there's no chance in hell they'll allow your character to be tarnished such as that. You're in the dirt deep enough as it is already, and I don't see nobody from your hoity-toity little clan begging you off. You're the best kept secret in New Mexico, sweetheart."

I smiled at that. And he was right, after all. As long as my father had use for me yet he would use his money to bury my indiscretions. Already I had been made the victim back home, caught up in a war and unable to make it back east. It was a pity for me, and they all prayed for my safe return.

I supposed I would stay, if I left his room as early as he did mine all that time ago, who could know? And certainly, the reluctant Sheriff Kimbrell wouldn't give us a hard time. He might even find himself more than a little abashed. He was an easy going man who had taken to the Kid.

The people of the town sung for Billy. They would gather below his window and serenade him. He was theirs—their champion, their advocate. But unfortunately, it was not their favor that mattered.

Minxie rode into Lincoln just before the hearings against the Dolan faction commenced on the 14th of April, and Governor Lew Wallace had been gone by then, leaving Billy entirely vulnerable. Billy and Tom gave a near identical testimony that allowed the prosecution to render nearly two hundred indictments against the Dolan side. Billy Campbell was indicted for the murder of Chapman, with Jesse Evans made as an accessory, and Dolan himself was indicted for the death of Chapman, as well as the deaths of John and Alex, in addition to his faction being held responsible for the death of McNab and the others.

Colonel Dudley was charged for the burning of Alex McSween's home. Billy had, as of yet, to stand for his own trial (set for July) for the deaths of Sheriff Brady and Buckshot Roberts. I snorted disdainfully over this. Whoever was responsible for Brady's death was anybody's guess, and as for Roberts', I could categorically attest to the fact that Billy had not a single thing to do with that. But Billy was made to believe that his trial would be a mere formality as part of his false imprisonment while I remained distrustful.

Despite the inconclusive evidence against Billy in the deaths of Brady and Roberts, D.A. Rynerson still had every intention of punishing him and having his neck broke whether he was guilty or not, while the Santa Fe Ring partisans, who were by far and wide a renowned guilty, murderous lot, some of their most vicious and unforgiving massacres having been verified for all to see on July 19th of last year, were granted forgiveness under Wallace's amnesty proclamation, a luxury Billy would never be awarded despite being significantly less culpable than those other murdering sonsabitches who had qualified for it.

Not surprisingly, but quite infuriatingly, Dudley, Peppin, and naturally, Dolan, had their charges dropped altogether, escaping the gallows thanks to the Santa Fe Ring friendly courts.

Billy: They'd have him hang until he was too far gone and decayed not to stay put.

Governor Lew Wallace's alleged influence did not hold weight with Rynerson (not that I ever believed it would), and who could know if the Governor had truly concerned himself with Rynerson's posture on Billy as he'd promised? It was my personal belief that he never had any intention of doing so, but I had failed Billy, too. I could not prove myself an adequate bargaining chip as I had desperately hoped. Twice now I felt as though I had let him down.

Trying, arresting, and ultimately attempting to hang Billy was purely political opportunism, and the dazzling, farcical spectacle of setting to rights the troubles caused by the Kid and the other ne'er-do-wells was merely for the benefit of the citizens and only a quintessential necessity for a prideful little fraud like Wallace. As far as the unwitting citizens of Lincoln knew, Wallace had proven to be just and righteous, promising to do what they had demanded of him. And what a boastful little prat I'll just bet he was after fooling them all into believing he was an honorable man.

But if the Ring had intended to discredit Billy's appeal with the people who fiercely adored him by attempting to bring down their champion, making him out to be just another lowly imprisoned, common, contemptible thief and murderer by denying him his promised pardon, then they had overplayed their hand—their move was too bold and imprudent, for Billy's bravery in testifying against the all-powerful Ring only created an intense enkindling to his already unwavering popularity and allowed him to gain even more momentum which garnered him an even greater loyal following. But this, in turn, only managed to cause his impairment with the law to become all the more fatally destructive. He was already at a great disadvantage with Rynerson, a Santa Fe Ring man. Now New Mexico loved him, and Rynerson all the more wanted to crush him explicitly.

Billy continued to hold out hope, though, still believing that Wallace would come through for him as promised before his trial in July. But, just as I had foretold, Wallace was finished with the Kid, and dispatched him from his mind once he had gotten from him what he wanted. Justice, for Wallace, was done. His omnipotence, however illusory, was proven to the people of Lincoln.

I continued to visit with Billy every day in his contrived prison cell, and every day he grew more nervous. *Good,* I thought, *let his fright catch up to mine so we can finally agree on things.*

As the days passed with no word from the Governor, Billy became increasingly troubled, but I remained patient and quiet. I would not confirm his anxiety with my own, nor would I remind him that I had told him so. Now was the time for me to exhibit strength for his benefit.

But I was proud of him, yet. He had not only accomplished what he had intended from the outset, but he had proven that he was not a devil, the bad person he had once tried to convince me of to push me away, though I had always known he was full of it. He had courageously risked his life to stare down the Santa Fe Ring and had, in principle, brought Dolan down—it was not his fault that Dolan had a fail-safe in the D.A., and would not suffer the consequences of his deserved comeuppance. Billy, The Son of New Mexico, was honorable, but was yet again abandoned and would need to find a new and creative way to survive. He kept his faith in Wallace much longer than he should have, but I applauded Billy for holding out hope against hope despite knowing that even the smallest shred of it had eluded him since before I had ever known him. I hadn't known anyone before who hadn't grasped the sense of defeat when it seemed they were beat. But, I guess when one fights for one's life so valiantly, a faint ray of light will break through the dreariness of futility and continue to instill faith. Disappointment never seemed to dampen Billy's spirit for long, and I admit, I found a modicum of comfort in this. So long as he could remain unremitting, I could breathe easily enough despite the walls closing in.

Watching him, I was reminded of Sisyphus, the mythical king of Ephyra who was punished for his constant deceitfulness by having to roll a boulder uphill time after time only to watch it roll back down again. That boulder would never get up that hill so long as Billy stuck around New Mexico. He was a condemned man, and I couldn't help but place the irony of the reason for Sisyphus' punishment squarely on the shoulders of Billy, either, even if it was unfair.

Back in my room at the Wortley I paced and paced, arms folded behind my back, worries upon worries furrowing my brow. I thought of writing to my father, of begging him to use whatever influence he could to get through to Rynerson, be it money or position, but based on my father's current stance and past communications of help I had made to no avail, I thought better of this action. What if he were to use his influence against Billy? After my previous pleas for my father's help with disappointing results I had no trust in him.

I never loved Billy more than when I feared for him terribly. It was a cruel sort of torment. I took him for granted far too often when harm was only a gentle concern. Complacency was a true vice and detriment.

The five of us: Billy, Tom, Jimmy, Minxie, and myself, often sat together in one "cell" or another playing cards or talking. Nearly two months had passed since Billy and Tom had willingly made themselves rats in a trap and the two were making their plans to get out. During the time it took Billy to admit he had fooled himself, I turned to one of my most loathed pastimes: needlepoint. Inanely, I poked canvas with a needle and thread in an attempt to forget this awful, stupid mess. Focusing on the tediousness irritated me but it was actually a relief to have something else with which to tax my nerves.

Ultimately, Billy's testimony was dismissed as the testament of a liar. He was a "criminal of the worst sort". None of his truths would be considered, just as my own veracity had been discounted when I had given my own testimony towards Finny.

Part II
The Outlaw

Between this news and the elusiveness of Wallace, Billy finally saw the forest despite the trees and wagered that he'd not stick around this town any longer in recognizing that his enemies received such favorable verdicts while they planned to have him kneel on the chopping block.

When it conclusively became apparent to Billy that he was lost on Wallace and that he would swing for certain if he stayed, he made up his mind to strike out. Wallace was another in a long line of men of position who had failed him, further disinclining him towards trusting any form of authority. The law and politicians alike may have considered him a criminal of the worst sort but, so too did he consider them as such, as there was no such thing as an honest politician or lawman in Lincoln. They were *all* crooks, and therefore, as far as he was concerned, he was on level playing ground.

It was June before Billy finally tired of playing the stooge, being holed up in Lincoln under the misguided trust of Governor Lew Wallace for three months with nothing to show for it but lost time.

We left for Fort Sumner and I took care when I told Billy I was proud of him for trying as he did. I feared that saying this might seem disparaging or condescending in some way, afraid the word "trying" might hold subliminal as a means of saying "I told you so," as if I might mean to remind him that I said he would fail, a way of expressing that he'd only be able to *try* but never *succeed*.

I was afraid my compliment would cause my old warnings to resonate, unbearably humbling him as it was all too apparent now that I had been right from the beginning. A man can tend to read a thousand negative aspects in what a woman says when he's feeling low, and it's critical that a man's pride remain intact, especially when he's feeling defeated, but I wanted to be sure he understood that I supported his decision and his desire to be found out as a good man. And it must be understood that I would never—not now, not ever—use this horrific incident to make the point to him that I knew better than he. Though his decision to chance things was slim, it was, after all, still a chance, and a bold and courageous one at that. And probably the best opportunity for him to prove himself honorable, and I understood the importance of that. I knew he was frightened for his life, yet he went through with it. He put his faith in a law he did not trust with as much hope as he could muster and that stood for something. His fine character was secured under God and those who understood the cause. And better still it was he the "villain," the *criminal*, who had kept his side of the bargain, while the refined, cultured gentry and noble law issued betrayal and deceit, two of the utmost wicked iniquities a man could possess. Once again, the irony was not lost on any of us. They, too, were thieves and murderers, hiding behind a fraudulent, gauzy veneer of integrity.

Stopping off to camp along the Rio Pecos on our way to Sumner, Billy and I sat close together along the water bank.

"You are a good man by misadventure," I told him.

He smiled solemnly at me. Then he began to laugh at the truthfulness in my idea of him.

"Thank you, Lu."

"What for, Bill?"

"For not saying 'I told you so.'"

I gave him an honest smile and he returned it. I then told him, "I know you agreed all along with me, but you did what you had to do and hoped for the best. You took a very high road, and I'm very proud of you for wanting to bring justice to the murder of that poor man and the others at the risk of your own life. And you did just that, regardless of the outcome. God sees that, and the people know the truth now, too. Dolan and Dudley may get to walk away, but they do not walk clean, and it's not lost on the good citizens that they are ghastly creatures and not the respected figures they think themselves to be. They'll have to live with that. You are by far a better man than any of them, and you will be known for that."

Again, we smiled at one another, and he took in a breath as if to say something, his eyes curious about me.

"What is it?" I asked him.

He stared a few seconds more and squinted, like he was trying to figure something out, then asked, "Was you really gonna give yourself up for me? If it meant I'd go free?"

I smiled widely, conveying that I did in fact mean to give myself up if it would spare him. He put his arm around me and pulled me to him, kissing me on the mouth before nuzzling his nose by my ear and resting his head atop mine. He then placed his other arm around me, enfolding me as tightly as he could.

"I'm glad for that, at least—that you didn't have to go."

I beamed at his avowal, though he couldn't see me, and then he said, "If it weren't for your generous perspective of me, I wonder how low I could think of myself."

"Well," I teased, "you should take time to mediate on the vagaries of life. You might find your answer."

He gave me a needling look. "Little girl, sometimes I don't follow the words you speak to me, but when I do catch on, I like what you say."

He smiled at me and flicked my nose with his finger affectionately.

11

June 1879

We sat around the fire and reflected on the past couple of months.

The letdowns, the unfulfilled assurances, and the lies had ultimately become a burden Billy no longer wished to carry. The promises made to him had always been hollow, and he would never hang is hat on the word of others again. John promised him that he would someday have a ranch of his own, and he was promised compensation by Chisum and McSween. When meeting with Dolan and Evans, they had promised him a release from the fringes of the late Lincoln County War, but they only managed to turn matters into a perpetuation of that conflict, placing Billy even deeper into the mire of tribulation with the murder of Chapman. And the most extraordinary breach of them all was the lie of the pardon, promised from Wallace. Empty agreements, all. Billy had always subsisted on his instincts of self-preservation, but he had gone against those instincts because of faith, ignoring his own rules of survival on the basis, of all things, trust. Trust in a life such as this, he would explain, got you nowhere. You could trust no one but yourself. Trust, if misplaced, could get you killed, he warned.

When we had arrived in Sumner, I told Billy that I did not want to stay at the Maxwell's any longer. When he asked why, I explained that I did not care for Paulita's passive-aggressive offenses which she attempted to hide through her native tongue. I explained that I also did not care for her brother Pete so much. Asking me why I shouldn't care for him, I told Billy that I sensed something about him—I felt him untrustworthy. It was plain that he did not think much of Billy spending time with his young sister, and I warned him that he ought to take this into consideration. Impassive, Billy remarked that if I felt this way, then the best thing for me to do was to stay as close to them as possible.

Humoring me, he said, "Guarde a enemigos cerca." *Keep your enemies close.*

I knew he believed I was only imagining my suspicions, but I ignored his obtuseness and insisted that I understood the measure of watching closely, but all the same I was simply not up to the task of tolerating the Maxwell's. I told him that perhaps *he* ought to keep Pete close, especially if he were planning to pay any attentions to Paulita.

He accepted my feelings of not wanting to stay in the Maxwell home any longer and told me he would secure the single room that was attached to the bunkhouse that had served as the old soldiers' barracks.

"Will you stay there with me, then?" I asked.

"*Sí, contigo*. I'll stay with you, of course."

What I could accept in coexisting with Paulita in Billy's life was this: we both understood the importance of our roles, she the dear friend whom he had innocently loved and shared confidences with, and I the object of his devoted, fierce adoration—one who knew not only his deepest secrets, but who also shared in his plight. Our communal value to him was indispensable. Neither of us would attempt to disarm his feelings for the other.

That said, I had no doubt that should I discuss my displeasure of Paulita's presence he might relent. He might lessen his interaction with the girl. But we were his family, and neither of us wanted to take away the comfort he found in the both of us, even if it meant sharing him with one another. We would spare him the grief. And we both knew and believed that the other sincerely loved and cared for him profoundly, regardless of how we felt about each other.

Because of our mutual respect regarding our significance in Billy's life and our agreed upon places in it, we banded together when another girl of triviality, Celsa Jaramillo, had managed to ingratiate herself into his interest.

Celsa had traveled from Mérida, Mexico with her family, living in Texas for a time before coming to Sumner not more than a few months prior. Paulita and I declared that we would make her our focal point and use our wiles to deliver her from our pains. We had no time to waste when it came to spending time with Billy, and so therefore we could not allow some frivolous Bessie to enter the picture and cause us any further time deficit as it was clear that Celsa Jaramillo was of no real consequence to him anyway, just one of those girls for him to dally and pass the time with, and so we felt confident in our decision to remove her from the playing field.

We came to the definitive conclusion that Celsa must go. Her proud, nasty little attitude toward us (I more so than Paulita) in gaining Billy's attentions expedited this decision. I was used to this as this was always the case. Girls expressly attacked me both vocally and with scathing expressions, always fancying themselves competitors of mine who surmounted me in Billy's devotion. The girls of course clashed with one another as well, but as they regarded me their only real adversary, my occupying an inordinate portion of Billy's heart, therefore making no room for any other, they caused me to suffer their endless streams of jealousy and bitterness, imagining that they could defeat me as a rival in his eyes. The naiveté of these girls never ceased to amaze me as they so very clearly expected to achieve the sort of ardent feelings Billy reserved for me though they had not managed to put in the effort I had and lacked the important history I had shared with him, both the horrific and celebratory moments alike. There was no detail, divine or immoral, that he could not speak of to me rather than let it fester in silence. I had seen that beautiful soul of his turn mean and nasty and back again with a devil-may-care simplicity. It was guaranteed, no matter the plane of torment, that I would understand him without explanation or worry of offense.

And so Paulita and I plotted out our strategy against the bitch Jaramillo, but being of different but prideful dispositions, both of which Billy was well acquainted with, we knew we must be careful in how we approached the situation. Paulita must avoid or curb any display of jealousy or wounded feelings, and I any of my typical, spirited outbursts of annoyance at the girl's presence. If we pushed the ballot he might get wise, perhaps even livid, then lecture us before shrugging off our efforts as petty. But to hell with it. That girl had it coming.

Having to execute discretion, we would play harmlessly enough. We would draw him away from her casually in an offhand manner and engage in subtleties that would in no way tip-off any suspicion on Billy's behalf of our usual strengths of opinion. We would make it easy, effortless, but all the same a success. Paulita and I would simply make it a point to interrupt them and loiter about if we found them together, and I would send often for him, having one of the boys fetch him to me and tell him that I was in the mood for his company. It was beautiful in its simplicity. By whatever means necessary, I made it a point to keep him by my side, an endeavor which he never denied me. Celsa never stood a chance. Nor, for that matter, did Billy, being ignorant to the whole charade.

I might have let it pass and let her have the small fraction of his company that she occupied if she were not so horrible. But the worst infraction of all were the fabricated rumors that she'd divulge about me, spreading her malicious propaganda to anyone who would listen, spilling such fictions as to Billy's true feelings for me, that the well-known accounts of his supposed great adoration for me were in fact false and created as a means to romanticize him. She attempted to further my dishonor by telling the villagers of the little Mexican settlement that he claimed I was a whore, and that he would use me and pass me off to the others for the trouble of being stuck with me, especially when we found ourselves out in the middle of the desert for a period of time and the boys needed entertainment. They would deal me out to make money in the little towns we sought refuge in or to buy silence concerning our whereabouts. She would say that he had confided in her intimate facts, such as how he wished I would leave him be and find another's bed when he was finished with me, or that I would finally take off for home. But, she'd say, he couldn't truly complain, as I was always by his side and, therefore, was always readily available for a tumble and to satisfy his needs. And so, she'd say, he conceded I had some use.

My cheeks grew hot as embers at these accusations, embarrassed as I knew full well that most of the townsfolk had heard these slanders against my character, but Billy himself remained unaware and oblivious, nobody wanting to incite his anger by telling him of such vile accusations. They would come to me and keep me informed on the matter, nobody more so than Paulita, and despite our trifling little rivalry over Billy I knew she took no pleasure in relaying these insults to me. Whatever little snipes and quips that lay between Paulita and I did just that, remained between the two of us with only Billy to roll his eyes at our absurdity. She knew any smear on my name by Celsa was an outright lie and so it would bring her no hope—she would not find any comfort or inclination in it, and to that end and her great credit, what would be the point of gloating over such information that had no basis whatsoever? The point of Celsa's psychological warfare was lost on her. She found the whole sorry, twisted and pathetic little scheme as base as I did, and was reviled by it just the same.

"Would you want me to tell him?" she would ask.

If anyone other than I could gently share with Billy such awful news and keep him calm, it was Paulita.

"No, please. Don't tell him anything. It'll only make him hurt and angry. Nothing she says is true and nobody believes her—I can't see the point in bringing him any unnecessary grief. He thinks I'm vulnerable, and he would feel guilt at the thought that I might be affected by this."

As I had said, those who knew me well, which consisted of nearly everyone in the entire little fort, knew the claims that Celsa professed were untrue, but again, to tell Billy, nobody wanted to be the one to get involved by being the messenger of such disgraceful defamation of his *amor verdadero*.

Josiah and his wife lived at the old fort and had been touched by the rumors but did not know the severity of them. I dare to say that if that had been the case, Josiah "Doc" Scurlock would have come to my defense and allowed nothing in his way of it. At the hearing of my being a subsidiary "whore" to himself and the others he would have been inflamed something awful, and he would have dealt with things then and there and hear of no urging to the contrary by me or anyone else.

Jimmy and Tom threatened several times that they would put an end to it, Jimmy asserting that he would knock her teeth down her throat if she didn't quit, but I made them promise to leave it alone. What would be the use in acknowledging her petty little game? Everybody knew these contrived falsehoods were made by a silly, jealous girl, and that my honor was indeed intact. Still, the whole sordid event proved very difficult for me to accept—jealous, silly girl or not. I had no sympathy for her, understanding she foolishly loved a man whose heart categorically belonged to another with no way for her to change and capture it, so she would lash out with cruel intentions. The attempt at marring the sacred bond between Billy and I sat very uneasily with me as one could imagine. And truth be told, I didn't want anyone to reveal these revolting state of events to him, to have him know and be upset over such an unfortunate topic. I could and *would* handle it.

After all, she meant nothing but squandered time, and she was especially gratuitous in imparting her proud ego toward me, making it a point to try and tempt my ire and pique my envy by working to fool me into believing that he'd chosen her over me. I'd see them walking together. He'd smile at me greatly and she would make a terrific production of looking down her nose at me to demonstrate her imagined prominence over me. I knew the truth of my value to Billy as it compared to hers, and perhaps I should have parlayed that into being the better person, but then an even greater offense was made at my expense when she deliberately brushed against me causing me to bump into a cart as we passed one another on the street. Naturally, as one might expect of me, I took umbrage. Until then I had been taxing myself over how to go about dealing with her and making her pay for her affronts without causing a magnificent stir, but her physical mistreatment of me forced me to make a mistake in the plan to edge her out quietly. Celsa had, for all intents and purposes, upped the ante of the game.

Once careful not to alert the girl to my displeasure of her lest she complain to Billy and place me in the awkward position of having to sit while he sermonized me on appropriate behavior toward the locals, I had blundered grandly when again I had found the two together and, after a bout of rainy weather, tripped her into a rather large, muddy puddle. I had intended to pull the coup off carefully by nonchalantly, if diligently, sticking my foot out as they walked along—the convenience of that puddle presenting itself before them at the right moment was too appealing to pass up—but I had become positively ecstatic at the thought of watching her falter so spectacularly and grew ambitious in my excitement. Giddy with a laugh, I thrust out my booted foot and gave my leg an extra jolt forward to ensure her calamity. Down she went into the muck and I laughed blissfully. She began to cry hysterically as I cackled, and I laughed even harder at this. Billy gave me such a look of fury that my breath caught in my throat, interrupting my amusement. Helping her up, he continued to stare me down while he comforted and soothed her. The dumb girl didn't even have the presence of mind to become angry with me after she had showed her distaste for me, causing me nothing but aggravation all along. *When it comes down to it, you haven't the nerve,* I thought. Or perhaps it was only a trick meant to make me out the villain. Regardless, the disdain I felt at her weakness freed my breath and I petulantly clucked my tongue at her stupidity, forgetting all about Billy's anger. What could he do? Cut me loose? He wouldn't dare. My knowledge of this put him at a tremendous disadvantage when it came to the unpredictability of my potential to embarrass him.

"What can you expect when you flaunt your little romances so casually?"

"I think I can expect better conduct. Where've all your grand little manners gone? My God! We shouldn't let you be so unhappy unless we all wanna suffer along."

With a tut I replied, "I've always had a meanness in me, and for that I am certainly no patrician, so don't pretend it's so. If not for her mistreatment of me, then I would not have done something so audacious. If a man insulted you the way she's insulted me, you would outright murder him."

"What's San Patricio got to do with this?"

I looked at him cockeyed. "Who said anything about San Patricio?"

Now he looked at me funny. "Well, I'll certainly say a Patrician'd act a sight better than you have."

"I said 'patrician'! Not as in San Patricio, as in aristocrat!"

"Who the hell can understand half of what you say? I sure as hell don't."

"I could say the same to you with all that Spanish bullshit, compadre! I'm speaking plain English at you, boy! Get a goddamned dictionary!"

I had not, as of yet, told him the truth of the abysmal nature of the dispute that ultimately sent Celsa flying into that puddle. I wondered if I should even bother.

He waved off our digression and continued his lecture.

"Mistreated you how, anyway? All in your head is all. What's it she's done?"

I ignored the question and continued my lecture.

"As long as you conduct yourself so improperly then you might as well expect me to conduct myself the same. My patience is wearing thin with these girls and their brazen pride at being your companion while they think me a fool. Maybe I should take my anger out on you if you so fervently disapprove of my actions since you're the cause."

"Hell hath no fury..."

I thrust my fist at him. "You have no idea!"

"Sometimes I honestly don't know how to stand you. You act out like a god-damned vicious little cat. And that high and mighty attitude. My God!" he scorned.

We stood in the singular bunk room glaring at one another, and I tried to reason with him, albeit irritably.

"Paulita is one thing, but with that other one it makes *three* of us in such a small community, and the time I spend with you is precious enough as it is, you know I feel this way. And of course there is also the matter that I don't want to share you with her—or *anyone* for that matter."

"Christ, *of course*! That jealous temper of yours! The things you're capable of when you don't get your way! How's it a girl like you could have so many years of proper breeding and have it all go to waste like you was born in a barn? If I believed you were capable of an apology I'd make you give it."

Make me give it?

It seemed that Celsa Jaramillo would have the last laugh. Billy hurt me further by not putting the pieces together, knowing me as well as he should have.

"You're to come to me if there's a problem. How many times should I tell you?"

A problem? This was, by far, more than such a thing by leaps and bounds. I wished wholeheartedly that I could just tell him how awful things had been—just how mean-spirited and relentlessly cruel Celsa Jaramillo was, how terribly she had tortured me. But I refused. My pride wouldn't let me. No self-respecting man would let himself believe he owed an answer to anyone, and so therefore neither would I. It was my problem and I handled it. I only wished Billy weren't standing before me now giving me such a hard time and making it worse. I never did like disappointing him, and though I was full in the right, I felt guilt. Not because of what I had done to Celsa, but in how Billy thought of me in this instant. A rumbling of intense emotion nearly felled me and I struggled to hold back tears that grew hot behind my eyes and threatened me at his reproach. It never ceased to amaze me how, since the day I met him, someone of his orphaned, baseborn rank could not only make someone of my celebrated station feel so terribly small, but because of how close we were, could not know the magnitude of the slight I had suffered at Celsa's hands when it was so well documented. The entire little community was aware and yet he knew nothing. And how could he not suspect something was terribly amiss by my callous retribution? Certainly, I did not treat every girl he paid attention to in this way. That alone meant he could have guessed that I had been provoked, but instead was too angry to see it and could only be bothered to yell at me.

Despite my best efforts, I could feel the hurt beginning to register upon my face as my resolution ebbed, and his expression went somewhat slack at this. He never could bear the sight of me upset. He took in a deep breath and expelled it slowly. The airing of his grievances had allowed his body to relax a few degrees and he squinted at me, his mind working out how he ought to act now that he had begun to calm, understanding full well that I was capable of acting out in such a profane manner when offended, and he placed part of the blame on himself knowing that his romantic behavior gave the other girls a false sense of entitlement with which to deride me. He began to assume that perhaps Celsa had indeed struck out at me in some way but never guessed at the brutality, so he was absolutely unwavering in his feelings regarding how poorly I had conducted myself with her. Still, he smiled at me and gave a slight, amicable laugh. At this, the danger of my tears subsided.

"Okay, sweetheart, you win. If you don't never want me to see her again, that's what I'll do. That's what you want, isn't it?"

I nodded briskly. "Yes. I told you it's what I want, Bill. Have Paulita by your side, be my guest. But don't allow anyone else to come between us."

His temper now cooled, he put an arm around my shoulders and pulled me to him, kissing me heartily upon the cheek and smiling dashingly.

"Look, niña pequeña...all you had to do was tell me. If you have a problem it's my problem, too. You only need to let me know so's I can fix it."

He then looked into my face lovingly and said, "Comprender, niña?"

I nodded, tears nearly welling in my eyes again as he exhibited the usual sweetness he saved for me.

"But good God, please behave yourself from now on and quit acting out mad as a hornet. That poor girl didn't deserve such a thing."

Naturally, he said this with a straight face, being unable to appreciate just how truly deserving she was. Of all the horrible things we had witnessed this past year and a half, what I had done to Celsa was trivial if spiteful. I was tempted, wanting to blab to him like a child needing an adult to take care of its troubles, to lay before him every humiliating detail of the entire, ridiculing account and anatomize it, even if only to cruelly witness his regret in blaming me. But immediately, I felt ashamed by the thought of hurting him deliberately, and now that he was looking at me again with such affection I wanted to let it be, and so I said nothing, promising him I'd be a proper lady from this day forward. Afterward, I went to Paulita and we had a cathartic, sisterly laugh over the cruel little incident I had caused.

Two days later I had received my redemption. After witnessing how I had acted out on the street, and having no loyalty to the girl, there was a collective set of finger-pointing by Fort Sumner patrons who clucked their tongues at and began to shun Celsa. One by one they came clean to Billy with the truth, certain he must have been made aware after my actions. When he had found out how appallingly his niña dulce had been abused he was horrorstruck. Hearing the lies of Celsa spill out, he put his hands to his ears and exclaimed *No. No más. No more.* He was sick with rage and refused to confront Celsa for fear he'd kill her.

Celsa, knowing everyone had turned on her and that Billy wished her dead, broke down and cried, spending two days in the little church outside the fort on her knees begging Christ and the Father, *por favor*, clutching her rosary to her chest so tight the beads had imprinted themselves into the palms of her hands, sticking there when she tried to release them.

It was not Billy's rejection that caused Celsa such a miserable, overdramatic descent, but the shame placed upon her by the whole of the town. No one would speak to her. I only sat back and took it all in. I was not smug at her misfortune, though it was well warranted. I was relieved. I felt I had been thrown from a whirlwind, tousled and bullied.

It took Billy two days to come find me, mortified by the things said of me and feeling wretched over his mistreatment of me, which had added insult to injury.

Under different circumstances he'd have come straight away, but now he could not face me, and I felt miserable that the boy who loved me so much was hiding from me because of his dreadful self-loathing brought on by some filthy mab.

Jimmy was with me during the two days Billy's confusion mounted, and it was because of him that I knew of Billy's misery. I wondered aloud why Billy stayed away, confessing I did not understand.

"He's done worse," I said. "I would think throwing me into that trough was bad enough."

Jimmy laughed. "Yeah, but what else was there to do? If you was gonna mess around with the midnight oil, the best he could do was scare it the hell out of you."

I nodded. "True. But his remorse was far less than it is now. What's he done? Taken her side when he only knew that I'd attacked her? I hadn't told him the truth—there had been a misunderstanding and I didn't correct him. He's only guilty of leaping without looking." I waited a second before adding, "I honestly couldn't have expected he'd feel so terrible."

Jimmy gave me a funny look.

"What?" I asked.

He seemed unsure and took stock of me before explaining. Billy, he told me, was racked with guilt because he was bedding the girl while she tried to ruin me. Yes, he was upset that he had taken a misstep and failed me, but he was horribly disturbed that he enjoyed screwing the evil bitch even as she made me suffer.

When Billy came to the bunk I had been occupying alone since he'd disappeared, he knocked on the door quietly instead of his usual allowed, natural entrance. He opened the door slightly and peeked around it until he found me. Pushing the door wider and then shutting it behind him, he only stood staring at me before quickly removing his hat in atonement. His eyes refused to meet mine, and he stood there looking pained. I thought hard on what I could say, finding it strange that comforting him in this came with difficulty. He had never felt so displaced with me before, and this unfamiliar condition caused me some doubt in how I should approach him. When I thought to speak I could only think to tell him to forget all of it, but I knew this would be impossible for him and would resolve nothing. To suggest he let it go would be to suggest that he forget how irresponsible he had been with my welfare and trust. He would rather suffer than have my feelings mean nothing to him.

"How can you expect me to protect you if you won't tell me anything?"

I hadn't expected him to speak, and he said this so quietly that my unpreparedness to hear him out forced me to stay silent while I assured myself that I'd heard every word he said. It wasn't an accusation or complaint—the question was entirely unassuming. I was dishonest by omission and he had faltered. His guilt at this was overwhelming.

I smiled at him and said, "Perhaps I don't need your protection."

He looked on before smiling in turn, saying, "Sure, you can take care of yourself all right..."

I went to him and, standing on the tips of my toes, putting my arms around him, said, "Nothing is out of joint between us. I should have confided in you as I always do. If I had done that, you would have made things right."

He didn't respond, not with words. He only held me tightly and buried his face into my neck. That was all that was necessary to mend the rupture he imagined.

With Celsa shamed and shed of, the boys sat with one another playing a friendly game of poker in Beaver's Saloon. Never bothering to learn the game, I was told that it was unwise and a detriment not to acquire the skills as it could bring me a decent income should I need it. It could, they'd say, make all the difference between living comfortably or starving, having to lie around on my back to remedy the latter. I knew it was foolish, but these boys had always been my benefactors, and wasn't I used to always being cared for? And anyway, none of them knew of the money I had secretly stashed away. I had learned a little by playing with them to pass the time, but I was not keen enough to play for high-stakes as they often did.

I stood watching them bluff each other and have a grand old time as they nearly forgot I was there altogether. Becoming bored, I got myself up to no good. Mischief grabbed a hold of me as it was sometimes inclined to do and, situated on thinking about the irritating things Billy had done to make fun at my expense, especially that horrible Apache joke he made on me last year in the middle of the desert during the war, I decided I would pay him back with my wickedness.

I stood near him as I often did when he played, using his lack of concern for me against him. I planted myself behind him as he sat directly opposite Jimmy and sleekly got Jimmy's attention by making an innocently enough racket with my spurs. When Jimmy glimpsed at me, I quickly shifted my eyes to Billy's cards and back again, flicking my nose with my forefinger to signal that Billy was bluffing. Jimmy put his eyes back down to his own cards with hardly a change of expression. His attention toward me should have gone unnoticed altogether if not for the fact that Billy never missed much. And so, though the communication between Jimmy and I was slight and brief, Billy nonetheless caught a notion of misgiving and locked his cards, vesting them. He turned to look up at me and squinted distrustfully. I looked down at him and, meeting his gaze, raised my eyebrows, giving him an air of innocent curiosity. Still uncertain, he turned back to his cards and again fanned them out slightly. The calls and checks made their rounds and came back to Jimmy, who only just skimmed his eyes over the top of his cards at me to find a marginal shake of my head. Jimmy raised and the rest of the boys, catching on, snickered. Billy's head whipped around and up at me.

Turning and running as fast as I could, I heard his chair noisily scrape the floor and his boots pound the wood of the floorboards behind me, the sound of his spurs punctuating each step he took in his intent to capture me.

Nimbly, despite my panic, I weaved between people and tables and cleared the exit onto the street. Though I ran as fast as I could manage I knew it was pointless, that the game was up since I'd still never outrun him, for his agility was by far defter than my own—the son of a bitch was fast!

But fortune was with me. It had rained earlier and, in a stroke of good luck, he slipped on a wet patch of mud and fell. I heard him shout profanities and I slowed so I could turn and see what the matter was. Seeing him muddied and flummoxed on the ground was more than I could bear.

Out of breath from running for my life, I made no sound as I shuddered from laughter, and I thought I might suffocate until finally I took in a sharp burst of air, making a high-pitched squeal as I stood there giggling hilariously. He stood up and, seeming to forget me a moment, instinctively wiped at his ruined clothes, succeeding only in making his filthy state worse. He looked at me as I made such fun of him in the middle of the street, no longer concerned with giving him the slip. I knew I was caught, but would give myself up happily for the sight I was seeing.

He collected himself and walked toward me, putting his arm around me affectionately, good-humoredly mumbling to himself about my being such a goddamned little devil. He kept his arm around my shoulders as we walked back in to the saloon. He had lost his hat on his way out and stooped to pick it up before walking back to the table and to the awestricken faces of the others who began to laugh in earnest, one by one, at his appearance. Slipping his arm from me he gently grabbed me by the back of the collar, casually pushing me toward the bar and ordering me to stay where he could watch me. Still laughing, I obliged him.

We moved on to Las Vegas, Billy and I, with the others deciding to move along soon afterward. Though we knew it would be a dangerous ride, just the two of us being on our own, Billy knew how to keep off the beaten path as it were, and how to take the safest routes for purposes of concealment which wasn't necessarily a guarantee but, being used to taking these paths, Billy felt certain. Regardless, the both of us got the itch in us to go about an adventure without company.

We stayed at Puerto de Luna a couple of days before continuing along the Pecos toward Anton Chico and staying put there for a few more days. With the exception of seeing another sporadic grouping of what looked to be Apaches from across a canyon, the trip was, thus far, largely uneventful.

We were about a day's ride out from Vegas when Billy chose to put us up in a familiar, secreted cave he had found out about during one of his many tours through the territory before we'd met. As far as he knew the cave was concealed carefully enough so that he thought not many could know of the little cavern—if any knew of it at all. He told me that he had come to this conclusion based on the fact that whenever he had a use for it for the purpose of refuge it seemed to remain unexploited by others and was always as neatly intact as nature would have it, though, he explained, it had been a while since he had visited the earthen cavity. This would be our first campout along our way to Las Vegas as we had stayed at the Gerhardt Ranch on our first day out prior to staying in Puerto de Luna and Anton before arriving here.

It was close to the rainy season, and so staying put inside of the cavern was a necessary condition for us should we find ourselves caught in a storm. The day had burned slow and was heated under a clouded, covered sky. Billy claimed that a storm was a real possibility, basing this, he said, on the friction he felt in the air.

There was a natural enclosure positioned just below the cave which was sur-rounded by sturdy mountain rock outcroppings and boulders with a natural overhang where we could shelter the horses. This would provide them decent enough protection from any rain or should a flash flood manifest without warning—flash floods were always a source of concern out here. They were an easy and near unavoidable death if one were caught and exposed by a merciless desert downpour. Certainly, dangers abounded everywhere out west.

The cave itself was set up high within the mountain, as was the cave in the hills of Patricio (where we had hidden out just before the 5-days-Battle in Lincoln), and it, too, had a precarious ridge one must climb to reach the earthen portico that spread wide before its mouth—the same swatch of land that created the overhang for the horses below. The cave was set back and nestled into the mountainside, and this particular cave boasted something of a fictile shaft made of rock inside that ran up through the mountain like a regular chimney which allowed for a fire to be lit beneath it, the shaft a flue that would suck the smoke right up and out, accommodating the terrene lodging in a way that made it cozy.

We secured the horses and began our ascent of the hazardous, narrow ridge that hitched along the mountain up toward the cave's portico, our backs sliding against the wall of dirt behind us, loosing earth and scree that fell and bounced on its way down. With his right hand he took my left, guiding me along the dangerous edge as he negotiated it. With his left hand he held his gun aloft.

He dragged me as we climbed, causing us to sidle faster than I had expected along the slim berth of ground. He seemed anxious, wanting to reach our destination and get settled, his gun poised and at the ready, ears tuned to any sound that might come from up above. He was primed for misadventure.

He stopped for a moment, listening. An emerging ray of sunlight glinted upon something on the ground and caught my eye. I lent myself toward it with my free hand, attempting to grasp the object that had seized my attention. Knees and body bent, I reached out. The hand that Billy held kept my left arm anchored upward as I angled myself toward the item, making my movement awkward. As he began to move again and pull me along he nearly caused me to lose my balance, but I had managed to grab the shimmering object and correct myself nonetheless. It was a pretty locket, covered by a fine sheath of dust. I wiped at it with my thumb as he continued to pull me along.

We were cresting the ridge and approaching the level ground that surrounded the cave—a gaping maw set back by an atrium of dirt and rock. Suddenly, the wind kicked up and Billy turned his nose away, disgusted.

"*Oh Jesus...*" he sighed.

I opened my mouth to ask what was wrong, but before I could speak I knew. A foul stench enveloped us both, causing us to hunker down into one another against the mountainside and cover our faces in desperation.

"God. What *is* that?" I yowled.

He only managed to say something incoherently and moan dreadfully into his hand.

He rose and turned back, preparing himself to look upon the place in which we sought. Letting go of my hand he turned to me and told me to stay put. Still crouching, I placed my hands down to steady myself along the ridge while he left me there alone. I saw him disappear around the bend at the top and then heard the firm flapping of wings before seeing black carrion birds scatter off into the air. And then...nothing. I waited as patiently as I could, but when his absence proved longer than I would have thought, the silence caused me to grow uneasy. Still attempting to protect my nose against the rotting stink with my hand, I called to him through my fingers. When he didn't answer, I decided to make my way up the remaining stretch of path. Rounding the same bend Billy had disappeared around moments before, I saw him. His hand was over his face, eyes horrifyingly wide at the scene before him.

Two bodies lay by the mouth of the cave. I shrieked in shock, causing him to turn and see me standing there. Reacting quickly, he began pushing me back toward the ridge, firmly instructing me to climb back down. After my initial confusion, I was finally able dig my foot in and slow him from pushing. He fought against my stubbornness, yelling for me to move, but I was able to calm him when he became aware that I was deliberately struggling to make him stop.

"What are you doing? *Go*!"

"Billy, we can't!"

"Like hell! Go! *Move*!"

"Billy...the *rain*!"

Just then a growl of thunder punctuated my point as it sounded in the near distance.

He seemed to think on this a moment, then shook it off. "We'll take our chances. Did you see what I just saw?" he barked.

"We have to stay here. You know we have to stay here, unless there's another place like this we can go—"

His look turned derisive, sarcastically asking me, "Do you think this is like some damned hotel? That we can just *request* a different room?"

Frazzled, I hollered back, "Well, I'm sure I don't know!" I was feeling provoked and uneasy.

We grew quiet together in our shock, and exasperated, I placed my hands to my head, pushing my hat back. So we stood together silently, lost in our own thoughts, Billy considering our situation.

"What the hell are we supposed to do?" he asked out loud, almost as if to himself.

"Move the bodies," I casually responded. Resolute.

His expression toward me could only be defined as repugnant. For the moment he seemed clearly put off and sickened by my suggestion, and then he looked at me as if I were short on sense.

"You must be out of your cotton-pickin', east-side mind! I ain't moving those damned bodies. I ain't *touching* the goddamned things—"

"—I'll help you—"

"—Like hell—no way! If there's one person between us two who definitely ain't going near them things it's you, and I ain't going, neither."

He began to push me along again but I held fast to my position.

"We have to do this, Billy."

I looked up at him, into his unblinking, wide blue eyes. He registered this truth. Twilight was peeking over the desert, and with the prospect of a storm and the sky growing steadily darker, another rumble of thunder closer off in the distance turned the simple possibility of a storm into a devastating reality. He began to nod to himself as if he were mentally gearing up for what he knew needed to be done—teeth working at his lips as his mind worked at the unpleasant task that lay ahead.

"Okay," he said. "Okay."

He started back toward the gruesome scene, and as I began to follow, he turned to face me and placed his hand against my shoulder.

"Stay there," he commanded.

I stopped and let him walk on. I leaned against the mountainside, already feeling exhausted as I thought over the matter and the unpleasant undertaking that lie ahead when I heard him gagging. I moved toward him and peered around to see him sicking up as he knelt close to the body that lay the farthest from the ridge. When his stomach had expended its contents he stood and came back toward me.

"I can't. We have to go. *Now!*"

"I'll help you. We have to do this."

"Aw, hell no, Lucy. Get going!"

I maneuvered around him and stood directly between both corpses, surveying the macabre tableau.

Both carcasses lay with their guns drawn, the body that Billy had first planned to move lay half in, half out of the cave. The half of him that lay exposed was horribly rotted, the gray-green flesh of the head had disintegrated in places, exposing the skull and desiccated tissue. The face confronted me, its marbled, black and puffy green colored flesh blistered, tongue eaten at, with what was left of it protruding through teeth unsheathed by withered, picked-upon lips, eyes gone. I waved away at the flies that had swarmed, realizing for the first time the churning black veil that shrouded the moldering flesh which should have been impossible to miss, the buzzing incessant and quite loud.

I felt my own stomach spasm at this. I hurried away from the bodies and wretched.

Satisfied, Billy yelled over to me, "Not so tough now, are ya?"

When my own body had quit shuddering, I looked back at the morose sight. Billy stood there, a strange look in his eyes as they flitted back and forth between the two dead men, coat sleeve covering his nose and mouth in an attempt to keep the malodor from entering his nostrils. I knew this had to be done. We could go nowhere else. Thunder lightly sounded again from the east, seemingly just beyond a small mountainous range. I studied the situation some more.

Looking at the angle of the bodies I wondered aloud, "Was it a fight? Did they kill each other?"

"Hell should I know? Looks like."

"Okay, let's just get this over with."

He walked with me back toward the body we had both become unpleasantly familiar with.

"Grab him on that side by the jacket," he said. "We'll pull him and slide him over the side."

I nodded and moved to do what he told me to, then stopped.

"Do you think he has any money or valuables on him?" I asked.

"Jesus Christ. I don't know. Can we just get this done with?"

Ignoring him, I scampered around and to the other side of the dead man. I was revolted, seeing a new horror of insects as they scurried and writhed over and around the corpse.

Cautiously, I gingerly placed my forefinger and thumb on the edge of the dead man's lapel and slowly peeled back his jacket to look for an inside pocket, eventually flipping the panel over quickly. When I found it, I very warily placed my hand inside. Billy made sounds of aversion and vocally objected at this, but I pulled out a billfold.

I looked up at him with a wide smile and nodded my head, pleased with myself. He frowned. I opened the billfold and found some dollar bills inside.

"Count it later," Billy demanded.

I counted it right then. Nearly fifty dollars! That would do. I dropped the billfold and observed the body, still waving off the flies that consumed me as well, as if I could make them go away. The corpse's legs lay one over the other and looked to be somewhat intact, but one could not truly tell as the carcass was fully dressed, and so his pants concealed his lower half. The flesh around his exposed hand had grown taught and leathery. The other hand was missing entirely. Thunder sounded again.

"Lucy..."

I glanced quickly up at Billy and, ignoring him a moment longer, checked the torso and found a clean, gold pocket watch which I hurriedly snapped away from the body for fear of the things creeping about, and then finally, returned to helping Billy. We dragged the body together to the edge of the bluff by the shoulder of its jacket and collar and, despite my dragging a festering dead body, of which I should have found very odd, all I managed to think to myself was how light it was. We slid him over the side and he fell a ways down to the ground but still made an audible thump.

We looked at each other and then at the second body. This one was laid out fully in the elements. His right, near skeletal hand lay clutched by his chest, his naturally decimated left hand lay alongside him as he lie prone, his gun resting on the ground as if it had been dropped there after its owner had been drilled by a bullet. There was a rucksack nearby him. Billy saw me spy this and placed a hand on my shoulder.

"After we're through," he said.

I nodded, knowing he wanted to get this over with, but still, I was not swayed from considering the body, looking for anything of worth and seeing nothing. I thought to check his clothing, but this one was by far worse off than the other. The skin of the face was gone completely, the chest appeared sunken in and the rotting shirt had a thick looking, slick stain, the gut hollowed out. *Liquefied*, I thought. I noticed a sticky-like substance pooled around him, biological run-off. The iron nerve I had initially summoned and maintained fairly failed me at this particular sight and I ran off again, dry heaving, wracked by the discomfort it caused my body.

When finally we had fulfilled our unpleasant deed and pulled this dead man over the ledge, we smiled oddly at one another.

Disturbed and with a strange smirk, he said, *"Ghoul."*

He walked off to fetch our things from the horses while I hung back and examined the substantiation of what was here—what remained despite the removal of the grotesqueries. There were brownish, sticky and dry looking stains left behind by both bodies, thinly coated by a layer of grime, but the concentration of the smell had seemed to dissipate. I supposed this might be due to the fact that we had removed its source from the immediate places, but likely it was also because I had grown accustomed.

When we had calmed down after being forced to witness and deal with such an awful scene, ease took over and managed our wits. We had entered the cave and Billy lit a fire, both of us sitting by it. Billy complained, swearing he could still smell the offensive stink and I could do nothing but believe him as I felt the nasty odor clung to us, permeating our clothing and nostrils for good. However, I pointed out, it was nowhere near as bad as before. He agreed to this.

Inside, as the thunder rumbled closer, we had found a saddlebag which Billy wanted no part of. I picked it up and brought it by me along with the rucksack. Studying the quarry I had, I heard him say to me, "You'll give up wealth, you say, but look at you...stealing money off a dead man."

I looked up at him and saw that he smiled as he looked me over, feigning a study of me. I smiled back and then dropped my eyes before putting my head back down. *The clever little Prat.* He had me there. But what he could not imagine was the sort of wealth I was in fact prepared to give up just to sit here with him in squalor and putrefied stink and think nothing of it for a mere fifty dollars and a pocket watch. That small amount would do us well out here, and I could turn the watch as trade or pawn it. Give up all that money waiting for me in New York, yes, but I'm not a complete, damned fool.

We sat quietly as I went through the contents of the rucksack until I had pulled a photo from the bag.

"Look here," I said. "It's a photo."

Billy took the photo and considered it. "Well I'll be! It *is* a photo!"

I smirked at his teasing me when he said, "It's a family. Where'd you find this?"

"In the rucksack."

He turned it over in his hands and read the name on the back of the photo: MacCallum.

"The rucksack was near the second man we tossed," I reminded him. "Do you suppose it must be his family?"

He gave a slight nod and made an offhanded, disinterested sound.

I took the photo back and looked it over myself, observing a dark haired man and blond woman whom I guessed was his wife, with two small towheaded girls and a small boy. I placed it back inside the pack. There was nothing of true value inside, just a few personal items such as socks and a toothbrush with brushing powder—things that were worthless to me. I did, however, find another photo of a woman. It was not the same woman from the photograph.

By the fire Billy sat reading a well-used short story he had picked up for himself in Anton: The Murders in the Rue Morgue by Poe.

"Rue Morgue..." he wondered. "What's those words?"

"French."

"You speak French."

"Yeah. So?"

"So what's those words mean?"

"In the literal sense, they mean "Morgue Street." A morgue is a mortuary, and "rue" means—"

Billy looked pensive. "What's that?"

"What's what?"

"A mortuary."

"A mortuary?"

He nodded. "You get all hard a'hearin' all of a sudden?"

"It's a building that houses the dead after a person passes—"

"What the hell for?"

"Often for preservation of the body so the family could have a wake before burial."

"Oh. So, it's like an undertaker's?"

"Yes. But out this way, don't they generally bury a body quickly? There can't be much of a process for preservation in most of these parts."

"So this story, it takes place in a morgue?"

"No. I think that word might be more of a commentary on the dark telling of the story. They need to solve these horrible murders on this street where—"

"Okay now, don't give it away."

I laughed silently to myself at this and we both went back to minding our own business.

Lightning had now become prominent, accompanying the thunder and pene-trating the cave, illuminating it dimly for a few seconds at a time.

I toyed with a gold chain at my neck that Billy had given me for my eighteenth birthday: a gold horseshoe pendant, affixed directly to the chain on either side, the shoe pinning a gap between the tiny links. He had also given me a little wooden box of chamomile tea, of which he had been told was popular among my kind and had a calming effect. I nearly criticized this particular gift, perceiving him insolent in his intentions by giving such a thing to me as if to say I was a bother who needed sedation—I wouldn't put it past Billy to play such a joke and be as mischievous as that. But in giving me the gift, I could see his proud innocence as he meant the gift as a sincere, heartfelt gesture, and that I was being unreasonable.

As I played with my necklace, I examined the locket I had found and noted a pair of engraved initials upon the back: S.L. & C.M. Opening it, I discovered a small picture of the same woman whose singular photo I had found in the pack occupying one half. The other half boasted a photo of a man whom I concluded must be that of Mr. MacCallum. It was a ringer of the gentleman in the family photo, and I was certain because of the initials on the back: C.M. I told of my find to Billy.

"Seems that man had himself a mistress," I said.

Without looking away from his story he said distractedly, "Seems so. That's quite some detective work, Lu. You should think about quitting all of this and going into the detective business. Maybe become a dagum Pinkerton or something."

I smacked him harmlessly on the arm, teasing him.

I gently put the locket down on the dirt floor of the cave and opened the saddle bag. I rummaged around, hoping to find something useful. I found some cartridges for a forty-five, another small roll of currency amounting to fourteen dollars, a book of poems, a journal of blank pages, the cover gilded with the initials J.S., which suggested the bag belonged to the other dead man, and finally the same photo of the woman I found in MacCallum's rucksack and locket. I looked on the back and read the name: Sara Lang.

My eyes grew wide with disbelief and excitement.

"That other man has the same photo of that woman in his bag, too."

"So?"

"So...You think they got into a scrape over her?"

He peered up at me from his story with a look that implied I was being queer, then, returning to his book he said, "Might could be. What difference does it make now?" He looked back up at me a moment. "In fact, I fail to see how it should make any difference at all."

"Well, I think those two men would disagree with you."

"Looks like..." he mumbled, not really paying much attention anymore.

"Do you think they figured this and that's why they killed one another?"

Clearly losing his patience he sighed and said, "I don't know. Maybe..."

I became enthusiastic by the riddle I believed I was piecing together. "Maybe they argued about it."

"Could be. I don't know many women who haven't been known to cause trouble such as that between men."

"Pardon? But *you're* one to talk so fancy about women causing trouble in romantic relations. You've caused plenty of that yourself, and on me, no less."

He looked at me and frowned.

"Why do you care so much about this?" he asked, honest in his curiosity.

"I don't know," I shrugged. "There's nothing else to do."

"Yeah, I hear that," he said, flipping over a page.

The thunder growled again, louder, succeeding a flash of lightening. I looked toward the mouth of the cave and found an almost complete and utter darkness there. Then, turning back to Billy I went on.

"That MacCallum man...he seemed to be nice looking. Do you suppose we should find his family and tell them about what happened? That's he's passed now?"

Billy looked up at me again, rolled his eyes and sighed, frustrated. "Good Lord, Lu. Leave it go."

"But there are children. Shouldn't they know what happened to their father? Perhaps his wife will be destitute."

"He was screwing around with some whore. If he didn't care about his family, why should we?"

"Maybe she was *not* a whore. Maybe she was his sister. And he found out that the other man was courting her without permission and it upset him..."

"You read way too much, Lucy. Life isn't so romantic as all that."

"Fine. Then what?"

"You asking me?"

"Who else? What do you think?"

"You ain't gonna shut up about this until I have something to offer, are ya?"

"Could be," I insisted.

I smiled arrogantly at him and he sighed.

"You want to know what *I* think? I think that one man was seeing that girl behind his wife's back. A man don't put a woman's picture besides his own in a locket unless there's something between 'em. And she was probably his friend's girl, and then his friend found out, and now here we are."

I thought about this scenario and decided that it made sense.

"Hmm, Bill. That's a good notion of it all. Okay, I think you may have something there."

"Great. Can we forget about it now, then?"

A great clap of thunder bore into the cave just then, startling us both and echoing around the walls of the chamber. Lightening cut the darkness, and for a few seconds I could see out as though it were late afternoon under a green-tinted sun.

"Won't the rain put out that fire?" I asked.

He nodded, "Most likely it'll come down the pipe and do just that...maybe."

I decided to take the photo of the family back out of the pack and look it over again.

"Maybe when we get to Vegas we can find out about this MacCallum person."

"How's that? What makes you think you'll find out anything?"

"Maybe they were headed in that direction, same as us. Perhaps his family is there."

"Doubt it, for the sort of town Vegas is..."

"Well, I suppose. But just the same."

"Lucy, forget about it. That woman is probably a California widow and figures her husband ain't coming back anyhow."

The rain began to poor intensely and so very suddenly. It was as though it had been dumped in earnest upon us—nature did not ease us into it. It fell so loudly that, when coupled with the sound of the accompanying thunder, it gave the illusion that the world was deafening as the sounds reverberated off the walls of the cave.

"Perhaps the rain will wash away the filth that remains from those two corpses and take the rest of the rotten stink with it," I proposed, feeling I had to shout a bit above the din.

"One could only hope."

It rained hard and true for a length of about ten minutes, and just as Billy had surmised, fat drops came down the shaft causing the fire to hiss and wink, but the rain did not drive it out completely. The flames left burning after the deluge passed by had eventually dried the places where the precipitous rainfall had distinguished the flames, allowing the little pyre to flourish again.

"What shall we do when we get to Vegas?" I asked.

"Don't know. I figure we'll make a little money gambling. I've been thinking about making a little stop to our old friend Chisum's after we're through there."

"Why Chisum's?"

"Well now, he owes me more than a little bit of money for my services during the war, for protecting his stock."

"You think he'll pay up?"

"We'll soon find out, won't we?"

"Maybe we ought to go with the others when we stop by there to see him. I would think that ought to be the plan. Perhaps he'll pay up if there's a crowd of us."

Billy laughed, amused as usual by my practical innocence regarding frontier, outlaw living. "You might think right, I reckon."

He sat there then, saying nothing more. I tilted my head and looked at him, wondering why he didn't go on.

"Bill?"

"Yeah, Bonita?"

"What ought we do about Chisum if he doesn't pay up?"

Without lifting his head from the book he raised his eyes at me, meaning clear in them. After looking at me like that for a few seconds he brought his head full up. "We're going to head into Vegas, make some money there to get by. After that, if Chisum doesn't supplement those earnings, I have a sneaking suspicion he's gonna find a few cows missing."

I knew what he meant, but still, like an imbecile I asked, "Find a few cows missing?"

He smirked at me and laughed. Humoring me he replied, "Well, darlin', cows have a notorious tendency of getting themselves lost. And I have a tremendous tendency of getting them found. And something tells me that tight wadded sonofabitch ain't gonna pay what he owes."

I looked at him and nodded my head, a bit unsurely, however. I still hadn't wrapped my head around this wayward way of thinking as of yet.

"What will we do with the cows?"

Billy smiled like the cat that ate the canary. "We'll sell them off in Seven Rivers. I reckon them folks would be more than pleased at the chance to take a large head of John Chisum's cattle. Hell, they won't even mind how we come to have them to sell. And considering how John Chisum's cattle are hard to disguise, they'll know they're the real deal and I'm sure they'll take great pleasure in buying them up, and I'll just bet they'll give us a right kind price, too."

"And then what?"

"Sumner. The farther we go, the harder chance he'll have of pinning us down. And we got a lot of friends out in Sumner. It's our best bet. If I had to figure, Chisum will suspect we went off to Patricio, giving us a hell of a lot more distance and time to be on our way. After what happened between us and the Seven Rivers posse, I doubt it'll occur to him that we'd dump his cattle off there."

I thought on this as a quiet moment passed between us before I heard him shout, "An orangutan! You gotta be kiddin' me!"

I laughed, amused, as he tossed down the pages.

"Ridiculous!" he muttered.

12

July, 1879

We'd been in Vegas since mid-June and Billy had opened up an illegal faro gaming table, occasionally operating it himself before turning it over to Tom, the both of them overseeing the funds and the day-to-day activity, making us a decent turn of profit.

I had a great deal of fun in Vegas. I went to the theaters and watched the dancing girls as they hid behind the ostrich fans that promised to expose what God-given assets they had, but never making good on those promises. They masterfully teased the men in the crowd and it seemed to me that the teasing was a bigger source of entertainment for the men than actually seeing the goods they were teased over. This fact would amuse me to no end.

If I couldn't be found around town the boys always knew they could locate me in one of these theaters, standing off somewhere in the dark, mimicking the shimmying girls on stage.

Men desired these women, and I found it entertaining to pretend as though I were like them, sharing in their talents as if they were my own because my talents, though far more highly regarded and valued, were also far more boring by comparison. I once kidded Billy by asking if I ought to ply my trade as these girls do so that I could pull my weight, bringing in my own source of money. At first he scoffed at this idea, nearly laughing so hard he might have busted a lung which, I admit, managed to hurt my feelings. Before I could express my resentment over his making fun of me, he had quickly curbed his good humor, growing serious and looking at me gravely, making damn sure that I understood I was never to dare attempt such a thing, schooling me on how he'd see to it that I was good and sorry if I did. Though it was only a joke I had made, I took this admonishment of his in earnest, remembering all too vividly the punishment I took from him the day I had been caught in that opium den.

One night in particular, however, after one of the performances, I made my way to the back of the stage and knocked on the door of the dressing apartment occupied by the acting girls. When I was invited in I sat by and watched wide-eyed as they removed their face paint and rouge and got dressed up to meet a suitor who would pay for their company.

"Are you whores then, also?" I wondered openly.

One of the girls I had watched on stage turned to look at me full on, her eyes blisters. The others paid me no mind, as if they were unfazed and used to such accusations.

The girl who had stared violently at me asked, "What's that you say to me, sugar?"

"I meant no disrespect, ma'am, but I don't understand. It seems to me that perhaps you go onto that stage and perform half naked for these men, and then afterwards you agree to keep their company if they'll pay."

Surprising me, she laughed at my ignorance, a reaction I'm embarrassed to admit I'd become accustomed to, having been constantly and consistently laughed at by the men for the knowledge I lacked in frontier, western living. I was forever about a mistake or fumbling over myself gracelessly, and the boys could not get enough of this.

"Darlin', no...it ain't like that. I'm an actress—an artist. Sometimes these men want companionship for the evening because they're real lonely, but that's where my company ends, you understand?"

I nodded my head briskly, eager to let her know that I comprehended her business and that I held no hard feelings.

"So I get paid to perform for them up there, and then I get to have a night on the town on their dime. My meals are covered, and sometimes they buy me such lovely trinkets such as ear baubles or hair combs, which I can always pawn off if I need the cash. Hell, I even have one gentleman who comes into town from time to time and pays my rent to ensure I'll still be here for him whenever he comes back around. So you see, I'm well taken care of—there's no hand to mouth living for me."

My eyes grew wider at this. I couldn't believe it! They were outsmarting the men—beating them at their own game! These women seemed to live a life of debauchery, but it was all illusion. And the men paid up for this! Having made it a joke or not, how could Billy frown upon my offering to live such a life when already I lived a life of depravity that was inarguably legitimate? Surely illusion was better. And I hadn't even the comfort of my life being anywhere near as glamorous as this. I wondered what one would need to do to have this sort of lifestyle.

"If I'm honest, you only need immodesty and a certain lack for shame, but it wouldn't hurt to have some sort of talent. You have any talent, sugar?"

I nodded my head enthusiastically.

"Well, then. What is it you can do?"

"Well ma'am, I play the piano, and I can sing—real pretty. I have an unparalleled education in most social-pleasing skills. I had a modest training in ballet as a girl so I have a real graceful movement."

She smiled at me and then looked me up and down with her eyes.

"Educated, huh? I would assume then you're from the east, but if you'll pardon my saying so, you don't talk so much like an easterner."

I frowned a minute, attempting to catch her meaning. When I understood I said, "Oh, you mean how my speaking manner is sometimes languorous? That sort'a means "lazy". Well, I can assure you *that's* more to do with my associates and environment than any lack of education. You pick things up when you're surrounded as I am."

She nodded in understanding.

"Well, you certainly have a prettiness about you. And you do have a darling little figure. A little on the thin side, and such an inadequate bosom." She frowned at this observation and so did I as I looked down at my chest with disappointment.

"But if you can do all those other things you say, and do them as well as you say you can, well, you'd do all right then. Singing like a bird with as much grace never hurt anybody."

I smiled at the thought. Me, a theatre girl! I couldn't have imagined it. How would my father like that? *Ha*! Won't he wish he'd have helped me when I'd asked for it!

Watching those girls up there on the stage seducing men was about as exciting as it got for me. I saw now that there was a whole other side of freedom out there that I was deprived of. A whole other side of independence that did not hinge on waiting for men to give me an allowance or absconding from the law and hoping tomorrow wouldn't find you caught or strung up, and hang Billy if he didn't like it.

"My name is Elucia. My friends call me Lucy, for short."

"I'm Theda. Just Theda, dear."

She reached her hand out and I took it, shaking it.

I spied a set of ostrich fans and Theda caught me at this.

"Would you like to try them out?" she asked.

I nodded, delighted by her offer. She handed it to me and I stood, attempting to mimic what I had often witnessed on stage and having great trouble at practicing keeping the most intimate parts of my body covered as I moved this way and that. Theda laughed heartily and grabbed another fan.

"Here sweetheart...this is why we use two pair."

I took the other and, though it was easier to play at covering myself up I still had a hard time keeping the plumes in place without flat-out dropping them, or causing them to move and fold shut. We both laughed at my difficulty when a knock came at the door. Fully dressed, Theda offered for whoever was on the other side to enter. To my horror it was Billy.

He took his hat off and gave Theda a smile which faded when he looked at me playing like a burlesque courtesan. In an attempt to liven the mood and save myself from any misfortune, I quipped, "Hey, look at me, Bill!"

I put the fans up around me and performed for him a mockingly ridiculous rendition of a shimmy while simultaneously giving him a great show of facetiously batting my eyelashes. At first he strained, trying not to betray his amusement, but ultimately he could not hide that he was in fact entertained and laughed at my displayed absurdity.

"All right, girl...put those down now. We're all going for some supper." He reached for me and put his hand on my shoulder, squeezing a bit too hard and causing me to cringe. Clearly, despite his momentarily surrendering to fun, he wanted it known I had rattled him nonetheless.

He turned to Theda.

"Thanks for putting up with my girl here."

"It was no problem at all. She's a real pleasure to speak with."

She looked at me and smiled and I gave her a wide, toothy smile back.

When we stepped outside Billy soberly asked me why I decided to play around like that. I told him there was no harm in it—that I was only diverting myself.

"Well, see to it that you don't divert yourself right into an occupation."

I nodded obediently but glibly replied, "Whatever you say. How'd you even know where to find me anyway?"

Squinting, he shifted his eyes to me and smirked peevishly.

"I guessed."

Billy and I had dinner at the Adobe Hotel in which the two of us presently had hired a room. I looked forward to having him all to myself as we dined, but as we sat there a man Billy recognized walked in. Because I had my back to the entrance I did not see him, and so when Billy waved him over I turned myself around as far as I could so as to take a look at who he had signaled. He was a stranger to me, tall, six feet or so if I had to guess, and bearded. He walked toward us with a relaxed gait and a lanky pace. He smiled at Billy and I noted that an upper tooth on the left of his mouth shined silver in the light. When he reached our table, he coolly slid an empty chair back and sat himself down with such an air of confidence that it struck me powerfully. He might as well as owned the joint by the way he sauntered through it.

Billy, looking awfully pleased with himself said, "Bonita, I want you to meet my friend here, Mr. Thomas Howard."

I only stared at the man, studying his face. There was something grippingly treacherous about him.

"Cat got that tongue a'yours, Lucy?" Billy's tone was innocuous, though I registered its hidden irritation, knowing he wanted to convey the point that evidently he considered this man of some importance, and me rude.

I broke my contemplation and looked at Billy, dumbfounded.

"Huh?"

Billy nodded his head towards Mr. Howard who sat across from him and to my left.

"Say hello to my friend, Lucy."

"My apologies, sir. Hello."

"Sometimes her mind wanders," Billy said dismissively, making excuses for me.

I gave Billy a look of petulance, which only made him chuckle whimsically over my displeasure of his attitude. There was certainly nothing new there. He seldom bothered to concern himself with my suffering of him over such matters.

Mr. Howard spoke, "Pleasure to meet you, Miss..."

"Howard," I replied.

Mr. Howard smiled at that, our names being one and the same. He respectfully bowed his head toward me before removing his hat and extending his arm in greeting. I accepted and he pressed my hand.

"Don't kid me and tell me you're *the* "Lucky Lu" Howard I'd been hearing about."

"The one and the same," Billy interjected with pride on my behalf.

Mr. Thomas Howard seemed impressed, but still left me feeling ill at ease. He lit a cigar and turned his attention to Billy.

As the two conversed they talked of deceitful dealings, having themselves a few laughs over this shared trade of theirs. Billy may not have been the most honest man in the territory, and certainly not in the U.S., but I knew that Billy Bonney did what he did in the interest of combating despots and a way to make a meager, if dishonest, living. This man, Mr. Howard, made the short hairs on the back of my neck stand on end. There was something about him, his posture, his countenance, his ease of physical presence. There was something menacing in his entire being. In listening to their conversation I concluded that Thomas Howard's duplicity wasn't excusable in any light.

Looking at Billy, it was Mr. Howard who now cocked his head in my direction as he took a pull from his cigar.

"This one trustworthy?" he wondered.

"Ain't it a little late for you to wonder about that after all the gum-flapping you've been doing?"

Billy was mortified and shot me an angry look, but Mr. Howard only laughed, saying to Billy, "This one's got guts."

"Yessir," Billy nervously laughed.

Ignoring my belligerent statement, Mr. Howard puffed again on his cigar and surmised I must be trustworthy if the Kid allowed me to hang around him with a mouth like mine.

My transgressions seemingly forgiven for the time being, Billy beamed with pride when he looked at me. "The only person in this whole goddamned world I'd trust with my life and lay it down for."

Mr. Howard glanced at me and raised his eyebrows with an impressed appreciation of Billy's admission, his eyes regarding my own.

Billy went on, "I keep no secrets from Lucy. She's the other half of me."

Billy looked at me with intense, unfettered affection upon saying this, his intonation reflective as though he had unintentionally spoken a private, evocative thought. I looked at him and smiled tenderly, a brief moment of familiarity as though just us two were present in the room.

"Do you know who I am, little girl?" asked Mr. Howard.

I reluctantly pulled my eyes away from Billy to respond honestly.

"Can't rightly say that I do, sir."

The two of them laughed nonchalantly over their private little joke at the expense of my ignorance and continued to stare at me. I didn't like it one bit, the way Mr. Howard observed me—it was obtrusive. His eyes were scrutinous, as if he were sizing me up, deciding for himself whether or not I truly was trustworthy, Billy's word or not. I didn't care for his officious arrogance in the questioning of my character. Who, I wondered, did he think he was in deciding my worth?

Billy's voice broke through my thought. He lowered his voice and said, "Let me give you a hint, sweetheart. You're currently sitting at the very same table with two of the most feared men in these United States. This here is none other than the infamous Jesse James. How do you like that, niña?"

Just what the hell was I supposed to say to that? I've been begging Billy to challenge the wind in riding the hell out of here, and not only had he refused, but here he was cavorting with the country's most wanted murderer. He didn't need any more trouble than he already had, therefore he certainly didn't need acquaintances such as the likes of one Mr. Jesse James, or Mr. Thomas Howard! And here I was, caught between these feelings and the need to behave adequately for Billy's sake. However, if Billy believed I ought to be impressed, he was severely mistaken.

"Is that right, Mr. Howard?" I asked with indifference. "Am I to be impressed?"

Jesse studied me intensely a moment, deciding to let my spiteful remark pass as if unnoticed.

"Yessir, ma'am. I am he."

I frowned and asked, with obvious contempt and a flagrant disregard for my own conservation, "So then, you rob trains, among other things?"

I kept my spine stiff even as my insides cowered, half expecting Jesse James to lunge at me from across the table for my insolence as my attempt to behave civilly was failing epically. Billy's expression changed from good-natured to hostile as though his countenance had been cracked by a whip. Could he truly have been that staggered by my foul reaction? I would have bet he knew me better than that.

"Keep your voice down, Lu," Billy commanded sternly, his tone compressed.

Ignoring him, I pushed on, "Well, Mr. James?"

"That'd be a fact, darlin'. I sure do."

"You seem so very proud. So then, are you proud to rob the poor farming men and innocent passengers who ride those trains alike, then? Might that be a fact as well?"

Visibly off-put by my audacity, Jesse leaned over to Billy and remarked, "Your girl's got quite an observation on her, ain't she? Not to mention quite a mouth."

It was fleeting, but I caught Billy close his eyes and I knew he was begging God to grant him serenity.

Jesse maintained a forced calmness as Billy stared miserably at me. I knew Billy was irked but how could I help myself? And what could I care with the exceptional opportunity that lay before me? I was presented with the very man who was responsible for the cruelly egocentric corruptions that caused so much strife and fright and misplaced sensationalism that raged wildly across the country—what Governor Crittenden wouldn't have given to be in my place. Here was the man that I had myself once petrifyingly feared as I rode the Union Pacific to New Mexico, and who now, after all I had witnessed, merely only piqued my nerves. In my defense, he had offended me first with his exploits as I dreaded the thought of him on that train, *long* before this day of meeting him face to face.

Jesse James was nothing more than a cowardly, cold-blooded killer who terrorized people and robbed them of what modest possessions they owned, taking deliberately their hard earned, paltry wages, wrenching them directly from their tired, calloused, soiled and work-worn hands. Why, then, should I even pretend to display good manners and feign politeness to such a low-life, even for Billy's sake? And what I wouldn't do for Billy made for a very short list. But I viewed Jesse James as nothing more than a bug to be squashed beneath a well-placed boot heel. Mr. Howard would receive no well-bred, cordial disposition from me.

Sarcastically, I lamented, "Well, I do apologize, Mr. Howard, but it wasn't all that long ago that I made my own trip out here from the east, terrified that I would suffer a hold-up by the likes of you. I cannot abide such a man and I would hope you could afford the disposition to be able to understand my feelings on the matter. The fact that you hide behind the moniker of Mr. Thomas Howard tells me you must, for it's plain that even you wonder who could tolerate Jesse James."

Yes, it was clear he was a coward, having to live his life under an assumed name. He was a truly bad man, yes, a coward indeed.

Jesse nodded slowly to himself, seemingly in thought. "Well, I reckon that I do understand that young lady. I'm truly sorry if I gave you such a fright."

Billy looked at me, extremely incensed—he was upset and made no effort to hide this fact.

"Fright!" I crowed. "Now that I know better, I hardly count the thought of your presence as frightening, considering it tame by comparison to the terror that has been my life for over the past year. I suggest you recalculate that egotistical pride. And isn't it true," I further prodded. "or at least it's what I've heard, that you kill your own men?"

"Lucy!" Billy warned.

I ignored him.

"Such tall stories! Where is it you could have heard such a thing as that, darlin'?" Jesse asked.

"How extraordinarily unbecoming coyness is on you. I've heard tell that you hire men of a certain...rudimentary intelligence, contrived partners in crime who can conveniently take the fall when the law gets too close. All the better for you to make off with your ill-gotten gains. And I've also heard it said that when your paranoia gets the better of you, you lack trust for the very friends a better man than yourself would consider worthy confidants, friends who stick by you, helping you steal from the very people who work hard for what little they have. When your suspicious fancies strike you, you outright murder those friends to ensure that they cannot give you up. I believe it is safe to say that there is not one trace of loyalty in your rotten bones."

Jesus, I finally began to wonder. *What has come over me?* Why is it I could say such things and tempt fate with this seditious murderer? I meant less than nothing to him, but what did it matter? I had gone too far, just as I had with Brady and Finnegan Flynn, but I wouldn't stop. I never could figure out how to keep my harsh opinions to myself when challenged with those whom I loathed, even knowing as I did that the cost could be my life.

Jesse was angered. "Those friends of mine, I can assure you, look to turn me in for the reward."

"Interesting. They must think on you as I do, then. It says so much about you. Billy's friends do no such thing. Perhaps he commands their respect."

He opened his mouth to speak, but I interrupted, "And then there are the innocent lives you take aboard those trains or in the banks you've robbed, good men whose vocation was only to feed their families. You are in the business of making widows and orphans."

Jesse James, aka, Mr. Howard, sat there and smirked at me, his left arm slung over his chest, its hand suspiciously close to the pistol resting within the scabbard that hung by his side. Billy's eyes surveyed this display and he grew cautious, his own hand deftly lingering by his Colt.

"Well, darling, perhaps you are uneducated as to why I do such things—"

"Sir!" I interrupted again. "Uneducated? On the contrary. I'm one of the most educated people you'll meet out here! And I know all about you, Mr. Howard. *All* about you!"

"Do y'now, sweetheart? And just what is it you think you know?"

Sweetheart? Such an unbelievably cool, patronizing nerve he exhibited.

Billy put his head into his hand. I knew him so well and understood he was sitting there tormented, quickly trying to think of ways to get rid of me or praying for this all to be over without a riot, and though I hated to cause him such anguish, only ever wishing him to feel the boundless affection I held for him, I would still have my say.

"Have I not read the tea leaves correctly?" I asked mockingly. "But all right, if that's not good enough, I'll try again. There's the fact that I've read much print on you, and I can tell you if my father had his way—"

"Father? Now I'll just bet he's a Yankee, ain't that so?"

"General, yes."

Jesse snorted, "No wonder you think as you do."

"Well...he's a better man than you, anyway, and I can't rightly say that I'm appreciative of even *him* at present. So you can imagine how low a man such as yourself sinks in my mind."

We stared at one another, Jesse amused, and my disposition stark. I went on.

"And I don't need my father's political stance to determine my own. I'm well aware of the fact that you use your thievery and terrorism as an excuse to right the imaginary wrongs you've suffered during the war, exacting violence against innocents whom you selfishly and unjustly hold responsible for what you consider a destroyed life, your own as well as the lives of those who fought on the side of the confederacy. But you'll have to pardon me, as your wicked, evil deeds exercise zero discrimination in that respect as your victims often include southerners alike. It is nothing more than an excuse you employ to carry out such cruel actions of pure and immoral greed for a dead, insignificant cause."

"I'd beg to differ," Jesse said.

"Oh. But I'm sure you would. Any misdeeds you believe the North played against you are nothing more than misperceived notions. Your ego brought them upon yourself by imagining and then playing them out all in your mind. And but for the life of me I cannot see how you'd be able to disagree with me when the glaring reality is that your crimes know no bias—your crimes seldom have anything to do with those you consider enemies of a defunct confederacy. For you, leveling what you consider the opposing side in this imaginary war of yours is all about the payout the convenient timing of an ill-fated mail train will bring you. And to that end, even if your subjective reasoning were intact and defensible, do you honestly believe that those from whom you pilfer are directly responsible for your illusory abuses, and therefore, have anything at all to do with them? Even if you swear it's true, I call you a liar."

Billy had had enough. He cleared his throat and spoke up. "Mr. Howard, if you'll excuse Lucy, she's a passionate advocate of her own beliefs. I hope you won't take her too seriously," he pleaded.

I rounded a nasty look at Billy. "I'll thank you to not make excuses for *me*, Billy Bonney. And to your own shame, too. *You're* the Kid, under no one's level. You make apologies to no one, especially this guy."

I displayed a deliberate lack of respect by absently jerking my thumb in Jesse James' direction without so much as bothering to look at him, my eyes ablaze at Billy with keen fury.

"You're worth a countless number of the likes of a Mr. Jesse James. He hides behind an act, a false life—you proudly live your life right out in the open, proud of who you are. Don't you dare defer to this man!"

Billy was struck dumb and sat there looking senseless, shocked by my audacity—the audacity I possessed that he knew only too well. I turned back to Jesse who merely looked amused. But underneath that veneer of glee was a mind fraught with hatred.

"Look here, Mr. Howard...you're losing the war twice, now. How long do you think you can keep up this foolish game?"

"Been long enough—"

"—Time's almost up."

"Perhaps if you'd allow me a word in edgewise—"

"—And what? Allow you to try and fool me with more nonsensical excuses that you and others like you haven't conveniently chosen to believe in? What is an obviously prejudiced imaginary slight so that you can justify stealing the money of others? How gross. You believe in it so thoroughly that you couldn't be bothered to tell what reality is and what is a lie. So long as the shoe fits the cause, I suppose.

"And Mr. Howard, the southerners you rob alike? Would you not consider them victims of the war, same as you? Yet you make them pay as well. The justifications of thievery and murder you proclaim as payback for Union mistreatment are nothing more than the sentiments of a bitter, resentful man. Mr. Howard, it is the actions of men such as you, the extremist, southern supporters, who demonstrated that the south was indeed in need of gross reformation. Your illogicality seems to know no bounds. You are the embodiment of contradiction—stealing from this one and that, no matter which side of the delineated breadth they fall on, North and South alike. If the president you hated so much, one of the greatest leaders this country has ever had the privilege to know, had not been shot down by one of your own, the South would have known forgiveness. But that scoundrel Booth set quickly the wheels of reconstruction in motion with his action of anti-heroics. It was proof that the South needed a continual slap upon the wrist. Such behavior is abominable and inexcusable. I'll just bet you hail John Wilkes, but what irony!"

Jesse's look changed. He now seemed a man eager to desperately change my mind by clinging to a remembered hurt. He appeared small and fragile, certainly not the great, heroic man James.

"You cannot know the injustices my family suffered during such a time."

"Well, a Quantrill man deserves hell to pay. What do you say to the injustices suffered by the families of Lawrence?"

Jesse's look was stern as he stared at me.

"And I can *too* imagine such a thing," I avowed. "Do not presume to perceive that I am so dense as to not understand the horrors of war. I sympathize with your people—the South. I sympathize with them because of the punishment the Union bestowed upon them. But it's time to get over the inequities you have taken personally. It is also time for you to quit causing the suffering of innocents to make up for the suffering of your own. Your hateful deeds make you no better than those who have done dishonorable things to you and yours. Therefore, you in particular will get no sympathy from me."

"Goddamned Pinkertons killed my eight year old half-brother after blowing up my home, wounding my mother. It ain't the first time they struck at my family's farm, beating my step-father to within an inch of his life!"

"Not before you killed one of those goddamned Pinkertons first and wounded two others when they came for you and attempted to face you as a man. Clearly, you were a detriment to deal with as such."

"I tried to surrender. They shot and nearly killed me!"

"Too bad it was only nearly."

I was taken aback by my bold declaration, nervous at my daring—spite controlled my tongue. I looked at Billy and saw that he was pale-faced and appeared ill as he stared at me. Clearly, he was too stunned to speak, watching this tête-á-tête with disbelief. I wanted to let him off the hook and behave for him. But I was also aware that the infamous Jesse James was answering to me. He wavered here before my very eyes and I was determined not to lose the upper-hand no matter how horribly I had displeased Billy and that I'd have to answer to him sooner or later. At present I was far too smug, seeing that both of these vicious men were done in by such a little woman.

Jesse James suddenly righted himself. The conduct of this change was subtle, but I saw it nonetheless, as if he had flicked a switch deep within his psyche. He struck a match upon the table and relit his nearly expended cigar so as to bring it back to life when the ember floundered. Then he looked over at Billy, disregarding me. I could see he held sympathy for the poor boy, but I could also see he was feigning courage for Billy's benefit. I had undermined Jesse, making him look a fool and making myself unpopular in doing so.

"You oughtn't to worry, Bill. I often don't pay any mind to the squealings of a woman, but this one is fascinatin'."

He uttered the word in a forcibly mellifluous manner: *fasss-en-ATE-in'*.

I frowned at him. I didn't care for his condescending attitude.

"Let me guess, sweetheart...you're from the North," said Jesse.

"If memory serves, you've already guessed this, not that it isn't obvious. And so? What if I am?"

He leaned forward and dispatched his spent match into the ashtray on the table, saying, "It's not surprising to know. People like you often don't understand or recognize a hero when they see one. I certainly wouldn't expect that a girl should recognize one if he were a rattler that bit her on the rear."

He hit me twice with that sentence, suggesting I was dimwitted and belittling my gender while lauding his own, and I made an unfortunate, high-pitched squeal of disbelief.

"I will have you know that I know *plenty* about that war, Mr. Howard. My father is a decorated general. And I highly doubt, Mr. Howard, that you are considered a true hero anywhere with the exception of in your own mind and among the most ignorant in Missouri. Your own people who do not know any better and who are led to believe that you share your illicit contraband with the poor and to fund the lost cause of the Confederacy. But you and I know that is a lie, don't we? And I must also point out how very mistaken you are about my knowing a hero when I see one. Why, there's one right there." I pointed to Billy who immediately dropped his head into his hands, raising his eyes to look at me with incredulity at seeing me finger him as an example. His eyes warned me to quit dragging him into this.

"You are not fit to sit at his table," I shouted, staring back at Billy as my own eyes besought him to understand that I was calling his bluff. I smirked a little, giddy at playing my sick little game even as he squinted those enchanting blues at me, full with powerless ire.

Before Jesse could respond, Billy's friend Dr. Henry Hoyt walked in to the hotel. Hoyt was eagerly waved over by Billy and asked to join us. Dr. Hoyt happily accepted the invitation and sat down with us, bringing my conversation with the illustrious Jesse James to an end. This was fine by me as I shook with fear and anger, and I was through with speaking to that murdering son of a bitch anyhow. Besides, it was I who got the last word.

I immediately excused myself and went elsewhere in search of entertainment. But before doing so I looked to Jesse James one last time and assured him, "You have nothing to fear from me, sir. I won't let on one stich about you. I may live my life now as a thief, but I am no liar—there is honor among thieves at this table. Furthermore, I'm no hypocrite, and I couldn't care to turn you in anyway. That would mean having to admit that I know you."

I wound up back at the theater, losing myself in the burlesque shows as I often did in order to placate my fascination of this place.

Eventually, Billy came along and found me again, dragged me outside into an alley, and attempted a reprimanding of my poor behavior. He was unsuccessful. I was not, nor would I be, sorry for my misconduct.

"¡Estás loco!" he asked.

"English, please, you Irish Mick!"

Hands on his hips, he pressed his lips tightly together and let out an angry snort.

"Are you fucking crazy? You could have gotten us into a world of hurt back there!"

"Oh? How do you figure?"

"I don't believe I need to remind you of who that were!"

"Yeah, yeah...the infamous murderer Jesse James. I don't believe I need to remind you that I am well aware. And after spending over a year with the formidable Regulators I should be concerned, why?"

Billy seemed at a loss for words now. I had a point, after all.

"You've all taught me to temper my fear by now. And perhaps I oughta again remind you of who *you* are, then, if you're so worried about *that* little devil. You're the notorious Kid. People are fearsome of you, too, but I find you're not so scary after all. Anyhow, it's doubtful that that rat would dare make a move against me with you so near. And then there's the fact that you're surrounded by your own band of men. Mr. Howard would be wise to watch his step out here since he's out of his territory. And the little coward would do little if anything at all, deficient in the courage to face adversity like a man, donning his mask and waiting for unsuspecting backs to be turned. Would he dare blow his cover as the genteel Mr. Howard with so many witnesses? Besides, he doesn't murder women—his one redeeming quality."

"I should never let you out anywhere! Shit, you're embarrassing. I don't know why I bother with you—you oughta be whipped. I can see why Brady was so furious with that big mouth of yours and all. That same, prideful stunt you pulled in there is what put you here in the first place. Haven't you learned a goddamned thing?"

"Apparently, I have not. Anyway, you're operating under the assumption that I don't like being stuck here with you, and you know that ain't the case at all. Maybe I'm just trying to force more of a reason for you stick by me."

He rolled his eyes. "That isn't any way to treat a person—"

"Oh, no? Isn't it? Perhaps I should allow Mr. Howard to lesson me properly in how to treat others, then—treating others horribly, frightening and terrorizing people, robbing them of their worldly goods! And behind a mask no less! At least I provoked him to his face! And you'll have to pardon me, but I'm not all that concerned with giving Mr. James the great big welcome you seem to think he deserves. It causes me a great disappointment in you that you should kneel at his altar when you are who you are, but I'll not kowtow."

Billy opened his mouth to say something, then decided against it as I went on.

"Jesse James robs trains. I should think he could handle my derisive outlook on his pitiful character. I am, after all, only a mere woman. Surely he's aware of the fact that there are bigger fish who are displeased with him and his dastardly little actions. Crittenden, for one. Robin Hood, indeed. *Ha.* By definition the title belongs to you alone."

"Pardon?"

"Don't you know? The people call him Robin Hood: Champion of the poor. Isn't that your calling? A calling you hold true where Jesse James only hides behind the commendation."

Billy waved a hand dismissively. "I ain't no Robin Hood."

"True. But you do care about the people."

"Couldn't you have kept your thoughts to yourself? Telling him what you think of him ain't going to make one lick'a difference."

"Then what I said shouldn't make any difference to you, anyhow, either."

I looked at Billy, my glare full of impatience.

"Oh *dear*..." he lamented sarcastically, impishly placing his hand to his cheek and rolling his eyes in that playfully, melodramatic way he reserved for when he found me curious or insufferable. "Of *course*! When have I *ever* known you not to speak that haughty little mind of yours?" Then he dropped the histrionics and simply said, "You have a big mouth, and you're always getting yourself into trouble with it. I don't know what it is I ought to do with you."

Regardless of my being annoyed with his spiteful behavior, I admit I could do nothing but agree with his opinion of me. After remaining quiet for a moment, he put his hands to his head, sighing resignedly after his being justifiably provoked.

"What is it now?" I asked.

He seemed flustered as he tried for an explanation.

"That attitude of yours—it frustrates me something awful. I've never known a woman to speak so goddamned direct and with such spite, having no thought for courtesy or repercussion. Them high society, eastern airs you put on! For God's sake, Lu. It used to be I would think people like you were bred to be refined, and I almost believed you were when we first met."

Exasperated, he took off his hat and rubbed at his brow in frustration, expelling air from his lungs as though the batch of breath they held was acerbic.

"It drives me crazy but *goddammit*! It gets me all twisted and agitated, and all the same it excites me. Jesus Christ, sometimes I can't stand it—sometimes I even hate it. But I just can't...*deny* you."

I smirked impishly at him. "That's because, Bill, it's a big part of what you love about me. You don't fool me one bit."

He smiled back and conceded, throwing his palms up in surrender. "All right, all right...you got me. I love that fire a'yours. If only you didn't go wandering in to trouble so carefree-like like you always do..."

As we lay in bed I asked him, "So what did you and our favorite mid-western bandito have to say after I left your company?"

Billy lay back on his pillow, his head resting upon his splayed arms, and let out a quiet sigh. "Nothing much, really. He offered me a place with him and his gang, said he could use a man like me and would be glad to have me aboard."

I turned to him and stared hard. He grinned and rolled his eyes, turning his head the other way.

"I don't rob trains."

I softened and lay back down, haughtily declaring, "Damn right you don't!" I then ridiculed Mr. Howard for his nerve. "And after all I'd said to him and still he has the audacity to ask you to be a part of his no good posse of thieving cowards."

Billy laughed. "I don't think he sets much store by what it is my little woman says. Anyway, you won't have to worry so much about him anymore. We're pulling up stakes in a day or two."

"Why's that?"

"We've been here a long enough while. It's time to move on. You know how it works."

Indeed, I knew all too well by now how it all worked. It wasn't prudent for those in our lifestyle to stay in one place for too long, but in a town like Vegas, it was easy for one to get lost among the other societal dregs, buying one's self time.

13

July, 1879

Before leaving Vegas there was a somewhat interesting turn of events in my opinion. Harper Dealy and some of the other Ladies were in town and I hung around with them, soaking up the female companionship while the getting was good as an irritated Billy constantly muttered beneath his breath, "*Those fuckin' girls...*"

While I spoke with them, however, a topic of interest arose and caused me a great amount of wonder which I knew I must take to Billy.

"Have we ever fucked?"

His head whipped around astonishingly fast. He stared at me silently, his expression a strange blend of shock, fright, and confusion. That fatherly air of his was upon him, the one that came about when he would react to some ignorant blunder of mine that caused him awkward pains and forced him to maneuver an explanation or impart a sermon with the intent to learn me something.

He embodied the tension of a tightly wound spring that would start if further provoked and so I stayed silent, letting him stare at me like that. He didn't move as he looked at me, not one bit. I realized I had overstepped some boundary, but unsure of what boundary that was, I felt it best to remain quiet and let him make the next move.

"Pardon me?" he asked, seeming to choke the words out.

I curled my lips inward and bit at them. Clearly I had made him somewhat uncomfortable and I didn't know how to correct myself. *What was it that was wrong in what I said?* Was it the vulgarity of that word? That mean word that meant "*sex*"? I had heard it so often and had even spoken it prior without consequence, so I didn't understand his mood. I supposed I would need to puzzle this out by treading lightly.

"When I'm with those girls they talk about a lot of things, many of them lewd in nature—"

"I'll just bet."

"Well...they asked me if we had ever done such a thing, and I thought to tell them *yes*, we must have. But the accounts I gave of our actions assured them we had not, and so now I'm uncertain. I never felt there was a difference, but they assured me there is."

I had vexed him with this confession. He took in a breath and pressed his lips together in an obvious attempt to keep his temper in check.

"What business is it of theirs for you to even talk about...about what we *do*?"

"I didn't suppose it was any of their business at all, but all the same it was of interest to me. The conversation was intriguing. What's the difference? Have we or have we not?"

As he was all too familiar with my tendency towards accidental transgressions, his irritation relented and he reluctantly excused my faux pas, taking in another deep breath as he prepared to articulate for me an explanation while weathering a storm of discomfort.

He scratched at the back of his head distractedly and made his eyes as big as saucers.

"Lucy..." he began.

I waited.

"Yes, there's a difference, and..."

I stared on at him with anticipation, eagerly awaiting his explanation.

"No we have not."

He spilled those words out as one: *nowehavenot*. It was apparent he wanted this conversation over with quickly. He must have felt confident that his brief reply had answered my question sufficiently, believing I'd have no cause to push the topic further, but I was never one to concern myself with the emotional collateral damage that sometimes manifests in the pursuit of knowledge.

"But *what* is the difference?" I pressed.

Exasperated, he rolled his eyes and blushed, annoyed with being stuck in this situation. I thought to take a different tack.

"What is it we *do*, then?"

"Oh Lucy, can't you *guess*?" he replied, impatient.

He was clearly ill at ease, and his anxiety caused him to raise his voice as he asked this of me. I looked away from him and furrowed my brow as I thought on his harried response. I suppose I could say that I *could* guess, but how could I be sure I was right?

I decided to drop this, but not before I tried for a clue once more.

"Have you done this with other women?"

Galled by my ignorant nerve, he sighed and stood to leave without saying a word.

Seeing Billy so troubled by my inquisition left me more interested than I thought I had been otherwise. What had started out as an innocent curiosity had now taken on a shade of obsession.

I was sitting with Jimmy and playing a lackadaisical game of Knucklebones, neither of us caring much to keep score, when I thought to pose the question to him. Being my second most best friend, choosing to ask Jimmy seemed only logical. Unsatisfied with the answers Billy had given me, I was now armed with a newfound, keen need to know. I could only ask someone else to help me find the absolute answer. I thought nothing at all of asking Billy such a personal question, but despite being close to Jimmy, I didn't share the same easy comfort. It didn't manifest. I knew asking Jimmy would be plainly embarrassing considering the delicacy of the subject matter. Though I had once tried at seducing Jimmy, my attempt had only been halfhearted and trivial, which made the thought of asking such an brazen question all the more unpleasant. And then there was the realization that asking Jimmy would only serve to enlighten his familiarity of my private affairs with Billy. I would have preferred to avoid sharing my curiosity with Jimmy, but my resolve unhinged my rationale and gave me a profound sense of C'est la vie.

"Jimmy?"
In the middle of collecting his bones he acknowledged me.
"I asked Billy what turned out to be an odd question, and he became disturbed."
His mind still on the game, Jimmy sort of grunted and followed up with "Huh?"
"Well..." I began.
I swallowed nervously and felt the color rising in my cheeks, burning them. I had to force my daring, lying like a heavy rock in the pit of my belly, to rise.
With a great amount of hesitancy, I forced my nerve to the surface and let it do what it would.
Forcing the words out while trying not to think of them, I said, "I asked him if what we did was...If what we did was...*fuck*." I cleared my throat. "Why should that get him in such a state?"
Jimmy produced a shocked sound, peculiar in its semblance of a laugh and

cough, before rendering a similar version of the insecure stare that Billy had given me.

Taken aback, he exclaimed, "What?"

"He seemed upset by my question," I explained again. "I realize it was a bit crude, but I've said that word before, and you must know that we've been...*intimate*... in such a way that I should be able to ask these things of him without repercussion, so I can't understand his reticence."

Jimmy laughed somewhat hysterically out of astonishment before going back to the ball and picking up his quarry.

"You really asking me this?" he marveled, stunned. Still, he gave me a rather mischievous smile.

Mortified, I unintentionally shouted back in self-defense, "Well I don't want to!"

Still laughing, he shook his head. "All right, sweetheart, calm down. It's all right. I'll do the best I can to help you out."

He looked at me and smiled sympathetically, but I could still see he was amused.

"Well," he began. "I don't think he cottons to the disrespect behind the meaning."

"Disrespect?"

He stared on at me, wondering how to explain.

"Yeah, disrespect. Like, he doesn't think of you in that way. It's like—that word...it's usually reserved when talking about women of a certain...*immoral* profession, to put it plainly. If you understand my meaning."

"Was it too bold of me to ask, then?"

"Well, maybe. I'd just bet with all the odd things you say, he wasn't expecting *that* to come out of your mouth."

This thought sent him back into fits of laughter.

"Well, what's so wrong with my asking anyway? Our relationship is such that I should be able to ask such a thing without taxing his nerves. He knows how inquisitive I am."

"Yeah, but that's something men do with whores. I don't think he wants to think on you like that."

"But how's it truly much different from what we do when we share a bed? I would've thought it was all the same. There's only one thing to be done when a man and woman bed together."

"Well, there's a *few* things to be done, now that you mention it." He sniggered at his dumb little joke.

"Yeah, I heard all about that other stuff. But mostly it's just the one thing."

I waited for him to say something else. When he didn't, I asked, "So?"

"So *what*?"

"So what's the *trouble*?"

"I told you what's the trouble. That's what whores are for. He thinks on you like...maybe like a man thinks on a wife, and men don't do that with their wives—what they'll do with a whore. That's just the way it is."

"So was that what he was doing with Celsa and the others?"

"Probably."

"But they're not whores."

"Not professionally, but close enough, anyway."

"If they are, then it only stands to reason so am I, and I can't rightly say that I am."

"No, I don't think you are. Those others, they get around. You don't because you're his, and he makes damn sure it stays that way. I think that's his problem with your forwardness on the matter."

"I don't feel you're explaining this to me right."

"Well, I guess it can be complicated." Exasperated, he said, "Look...when a man fucks a girl, he's just using her to get it out of his system. That's all it is. There's nothing else. No love, no sort of commitment. The man is in it for himself. It's just sex, and it's quick—and exhausting. It's really actually quite a lonely experience, truth be told, because there's no caring involved. But it's something a man needs to do."

I thought on this. I've been there to help Billy get "*it*" out of his system before, and sometimes it *could* in fact be exhausting. Sometimes it even felt like work, but I had to admit that it was in fact a pleasant sort of work.

Jimmy explained that when Billy was with me, the "it" Billy was most likely ridding himself of was his desire for me, and he guessed that probably he might just be ridding himself of that same desire for me with others as well, only there was no meaning behind it with them.

"Now I'm almost positive you're not explaining things right to me," I asserted.

"How should you know, anyway?" Jimmy said with an aura of affront. "You're the one doesn't know but is asking."

"Why not just be with me always then if it's me making him so agitated? Why waste his time with others as a distraction?"

I of course knew the answer to this, Billy explaining it to me time and time again. Our relationship was a complex mess. He wanted me, but he refused me so often because of the odds: he did not want to get me into trouble and ruin me. My future, should I choose to end this life and go back to my life in New York, would be irreparable if I were to fall pregnant, so he took his desire for me elsewhere. He took it to women who didn't deserve it. Can it be imagined? *My* just desserts being offered to lesser women to enjoy? It was infuriating. So infuriating that, naturally, as was my way, I continued to ask Billy the same question, phrased differently, in the hopes of receiving a different answer for this, knowing damned well there wasn't no different answer. There was nothing that would be said that could make me feel better about Billy's warped sense of logic. Though, I was being unfair, wasn't I? My frustration sometimes got in my way, I supposed. When my mind was well-grounded, I saw his logic perfectly. He still meant for me, at the very least, to present the illusion that I was untouched and perfect, doing whatever he felt necessary to keep my future intact. His illusion was, should I get out of this hell and go back to the fold in New York, I could parade myself under the guise of innocence and be accepted by my own people with open arms.

The sound of Jimmy's voice broke my reverie and brought me back to our conversation.

"How should I know?" he said. "Except to say that maybe he just wants it over and done with—with them."

"So?"

"So I guess he respects you too much to make it quick and run out the door. When he doesn't want to miss out he'll come to you. That's why whores are so important—they're there to serve a purpose: quick satisfaction." He nodded matter-of-factly to himself, pleased to emphasize this justification.

"How can you call those other girls whores but not me? As far as I know, Billy doesn't lay so much with prostitutes because he has his little legion of townie admirers. They're not unlike me. So at best, this all seems very confusing."

He gave me a smug chuckle and rolled his eyes at my naiveté.

"He's had his share of calico queens, Lucy. He may flirt with a lot of girls in the towns, but it ain't like they *all* fall on their backs for him. He'll go off with the rest of us and find relief in the town brothel." He blushed a bit at this brazen confession to a lady that her compadres sought comfort in the arms of prairie nymphs. "And anyway...those other girls? In the towns? They're not much like you at all."

"So tell then. How so?"

He looked at me while considering his answer, slightly scrunching his face in thought as he did so.

"Do I have permission to speak freely?"

"Naturally."

"Some of them, the ones you'd think were proper? Well, it's true that many *do* fall right on their backs. They cling to him, and when he chooses one, they encourage him to come to their bed."

"That's just because Billy has this way about him. He's charming."

"It's just because they're *whores*. They may not reside in a brothel, and they may seem as if they're respectable, but they're whores just the same. Lucy, do you mean to tell me that you think no girl could resist him?"

"No, of course not. But—"

"Even if a woman finds him irresistible, she still has pride, don't she?"

I saw his point, but myself being someone with a proud disposition who would not have been expected to fall prey so easily to a man's charms, I knew something of this. I made this point to Jimmy who sat up straighter when he explained.

"Billy doesn't talk much about you, not in a personal way, so I don't know much about y'alls private relationship 'cept for what you tell me or the hints I pick up from watching the two of you. I know from your own mouth that you two were close before anything else. And knowing you as I believe I do, I'd guess that that's not exactly what happened between you both, you succumbing easily to him because he fooled your pride. Fact, I believe you checked your pride when it came to him and found he was worth your trust."

This was true.

"Yes, we were great friends, and I loved him. And he told me he loved me and I believed him then as I believe him now."

"I believe he did—I know he does. He respects you in a way he doesn't anyone else. He answers to you, but them he could take or leave. It's remarkably clear that you two have very strong ties and he's certainly never shy to threaten anybody away from you. Do you think he cares if those other girls sport with other men? And they do, Lucy. Face it, Billy the Kid dotes on you, sweetheart. You're different—he loved you first before any intimacy, and I know that's a fact. He didn't simply want sex, he wanted you, and that's not so with anyone else. And I know it that the other girls want what you have. They want Billy the Kid, but they don't have the history to truly have him as you do."

I frowned. "I know it, and I hate it. That loathsome cross of a name makes him that much more attractive to the girls, and in my opinion, I find that...that *prestigious* epithet ridiculous—a blight on his character. I find it foolish and scornfully reject it! But, Jimmy, he was never left wanting in affection from the fairer sex since before all of this."

I considered the truth of what Jimmy had said, about the girls wanting Billy more because of his reputation as an outlaw. But the more Jimmy had talked, the more questions I had. The only person who could give me the straight answers I wanted was Billy.

That night as I lay in bed, I waited up for Billy. As soon as he entered the room I started in on him.

"Billy," I said, "what made you so upset because of the question I'd asked you earlier? Oughtn't *you* be the one to explain to me what it is you do with me when we're alone and at our most intimate?"

He took an anxious breath and put his hands on his hips, staring at the wall with an exasperated look on his face.

"Why's this such an issue with you? I should'a thought you'd be satisfied enough to know that I do nothing if not make love to you."

"I'm told I'm missing out."

"Then you're missing out, then."

"What about you? Are you missing out? With me? Is that why you go to..." My breath caught nervously. "The *others*?"

My question was sincere and ingenuous, and not the least bit accusatory. Realizing this, he tried hard not to smile and make fun of my naïve intrusiveness, but failed miserably when he remarked, "Nah...You're plenty fun for being so uptight."

14

August, 1879

We left Vegas and headed south, stopping in Lincoln to call on Susan McSween and see how she was faring. She was thrilled to visit with me, but spent a great deal of time irritating me, attempting to turn my mind back east. Her agenda, though made with the best of intentions, involved a sermon that marked my path as one of wickedness, hoping to help make me see it as a hasty road to the devil's den, but I reminded her that that very same path was also my road to salvation, and if my salvation lay with the devil, then so be it.

Susan had been entertaining guests. One guest in particular was our old friend and veteran Regulator, Frank Coe, down from Colorado on business and toting his fiddle with him. Another guest, a U.S. soldier, piqued the devil in Billy. Finding himself in the near presence of this disagreeable guest, watching as the solider danced with Susan while Frank plied his instrument, Billy's demon was called to revolt, and he made it a point to crowd and torment the soldier something awful during the gaiety of the affair by deliberately bumping into him, knocking the soldier off balance, stepping on the toes of his boots even as he twirled me along. Billy's overconfidence had won out, as it was sometimes wont to do, and I was fraught with concern as I made efforts to express my disapproval of Billy's foolish misbehavior, quietly begging him to quit it, but he paid me no mind.

With the military and everyone else of territorial, hierarchical importance out looking for him, Billy had grown insolent in his weariness and resigned himself to a devil-may-care arrogance, reacting impertinently to the prejudice the law and military assigned to his case. Tired of running and, knowing the land and trails far better than the U.S. Military, Billy not only felt superior to the otherwise competent soldiers, but by now considered the military to be little more than a nuisance. The army knew only confusion when it came to their attempting to understand the terrain that Billy and others like him travelled with ease, such as the tracks which helped Billy evade and circumvent the bands of government issued men who searched him out. They were at a loss when it came to capturing the notorious outlaw, concluding his wiliness must be something wraithlike. And then there were the hosts of citizens in the towns and placitas whose loyalty lie with Billy and the Regulators, people who kept him safe, and so he concerned himself with the military not at all, his overall feelings toward them indifferent or a casual annoyance. Billy's ability to disappear seemingly under one's nose and before one's eyes, evading capture, earned him a new significant form of notoriety: Mestizo—a half-blood, half man, half coyote, or half man, half phantom, depending on the location and who one asked.

When the soldier grew tired of Billy's offensive actions, Billy challenged him to do something of it. Noticeably shaken by Billy's remarkable daring and intimidated by his reputation, the soldier timidly replied that he didn't have to do anything about it just now, using the unsettling confrontation with the notorious Kid as an excuse to leave. With Billy's aggravation satiated at present, the soldier left Billy feeling pleased with himself. I warned Billy to quit this brash behavior of his in the future, but he was resolved to the act of instigating and defying those of the law. Sometimes, and especially as of late, Billy was often a handful. He was simply incorrigible, and not even I could make him see reason. I supposed this should only be fair considering the exhaustive handful I had proven myself to be for him. The two of us made quite a pair indeed, both of us afraid of the other's shadow of death.

15

October, 1879

It was agreed upon by the lot of us that it would be nothing but thievery and stealing from here on out in order to make a living, cattle and illegal gambling practices to be precise. Back in Vegas, Billy had stood trial on both counts of these offenses with a handful of others, but he had been dismissed on both cases for lack of evidence, until another incident regarding stolen cattle ran him out of luck and holed him up in jail but good, and for which I had to procure for him a sum of three hundred dollars to make bail. Having the money wired from my bank account in White Oaks, which was now a popular gold-boom town, I had not yet confided in Billy that I had a fair amount of money secured there in my name, and when he became curious as to how I came by such a stately sum, I imparted a vague lie in order to dismiss any room for questions, offhandedly claiming that I had borrowed the amount from Jim Greathouse, an entrepreneur with whom we had befriended and whose property was also near White Oaks, making my monetary receipt convenient. This fib of mine wasn't such a stretch for Billy to believe as Greathouse often gave us supplies and credit as he was part of the underdealings in the territory himself and bartered in stolen cattle, among other things. He knew the notorious Kid was good for providing the delivery of stolen goods, and so there was a tremendous amount of trust on Greathouse's behalf in lending us whatever provisions we needed, knowing one way or the other things would come out square. Once I bailed Billy out we went back on to our wicked ways.

It was all too easy to drive stolen stock up from the Bosque Grande and leave them off with the Dedrick brothers, associates of Greathouse, who'd butcher them up proper and distribute them out amongst the hungry miners of White Oaks. The local rags had rightly fingered us as the culprits, albeit without proof, stealing John Chisum's cattle, signaling Billy as the ringleader and mastermind, making sure never to spare my name in an attempt to romanticize us as two desperados in love as it made for good fodder and entertainment among gossipers, boosting the sale of newspapers.

They reported our gang as driving one hundred and eighteen head, selling them off to a ranch run by a man named John Yerby who was known to rebrand rustled cattle. Our illicit deeds were deliberately directed at Chisum and his famous Jingle Bobs because Billy had yet to see a single red cent that Chisum promised him for fighting on his side and protecting him and his land during the late Lincoln County War. So then, just as Billy said, we would just take the payment out in stolen stock.

Now, despite the impossibility of rebranding the stolen Jingle Bobs with Chisum lopping at their ears for the purpose of making their identification unmistakable, it didn't mean fools wouldn't continue to try and steal his cattle or that outlawed businessmen wouldn't still purchase them. It was easy enough to cut them up and sell them piecemeal for food in which the ears, distinctive or not, did not factor, being hacked off completely and tossed during the butchering process.

One ought to have thought it preposterous to think that we would welcome trouble and bring attention to ourselves by risking capture, driving such a distinguishable herd of cattle, but Chisum's herds presented plenty of fair opportunities for poaching, and the cash they would fetch was too good to pass up. Nonetheless, Billy would take Chisum's cattle if only to tweak the old man, but of course Billy and his men never had been known to play it safe, doing what needed to be done if necessary. And I, of course, went along with everything Billy did.

Billy split the money made from the sale of the cattle among the men—he never gave me a direct cut of the income brought in, instead he took care of me, keeping me clothed and fed, providing me with a few dollars from his pocket as an allowance, or more if I asked, always giving in to my whims when I wanted something as it pleased me, but he appropriated one hundred dollars from his earnings to reimburse Greathouse some of the bail money I claimed he had loaned me. It wasn't until this point that I realized the gaping flaw in my plan. I would have to come clean about my bank account in White Oaks, and I worried over how this detail would irritate Billy. Having the money itself wouldn't anger him so much, but the fact that I had kept this significant information from him for selfish reasons might compel him to lash out at me. I decided to ignore the problem at present in order to hope for a better time in which to tell him before he prepared to give Jim that money.

Josiah, Jimmy, Minxie, Tom, Henry, Big Jim, Joe Bowers, and Jose Salazar were still with us, though Josiah's intentions were to move on over a dispute in the splitting of the funds from the sale of the stolen cattle. Jimmy and Tom considered being part of the Regulators such a prestigious badge of honor that they were only prepared to give up the honor upon the coolness of their dead bodies. They were nowhere near eager to leave the gang behind like smarter men before them.

A few new men had expanded our posse by now: Tom Pickett, Billy Wilson, referred to as "Little Billy," causing a bit of confusion between us two as I was sometimes jestingly referred to in kind out of affection and my affinity for behaving as influenced by Billy, and a real foul devil by the name of "Dirty" Dave Rudabaugh, whose aversion to washing should have been an infraction of the law all on its own. He smelled so awful that I could become anxious lest I found myself downwind from him whenever we rode or stood around in a placita. Sleeping near him on nights when the air would have otherwise blown peacefully about brought nothing but restless sleep as it carried his stubborn odor on the breeze, invading my nostrils and making it impossible for me to slumber.

As I found him repulsive, one might imagine Dave and I seldom got along with one another. I'd verbally lambast him, calling him a mockered sonofabitch over his considering himself a man despite such unsanitary, childish washing habits, and he'd give it to me right back, accusing me of considering myself a lady, participating where I didn't belong. Dave managed to get away unscathed with this light abuse of me as Billy found it, at first, comical, and then eventually only a minor irritation, rolling his eyes at our bickering. But God help Dave should he call me such a vulgar thing as a "whore"—Billy would suffer none of that, and at this Dave understood never to overstep that line. Even a disgusting bug like Dave knew better than to want to reap those consequences.

Apart from my insistence that he wash his disgusting self, there were the arguments and assertions that it was he who was in charge of the gang, and he disliked it even more so that I tended to trump him in nearly every decision made among a group of men. It hurt his pride as it would any man to have a woman outrank him. He wanted to be considered a match-wit with Billy, but it was I and O'Folliard who beat him to the quick. It wasn't that I held any true sway, having hardly a decisive say in matters as far as the group was concerned, but my opinions weighed heavily with Billy in private. In public, I knew how to manipulate Billy, using my charms to influence him which frustrated Dave to no end. Dirty Dave was simply a legend in his own mind and he knew it, too. It just didn't sit right with him, and because of this, his ire was never at rest.

The Regulators were now becoming a less than prideful sort among the citizens of New Mexico. A scourge, they'd call us, stealing cattle and drifting along, generally making life miserable for the territory's inhabitants as we tormented them with our unruly, errant way of life. It was unfortunate, but we had to make ourselves a living to get by. If they wanted to turn on us, we'd turn on them. It was unavoidable in the interest of survival. I administered this point of mine to the group, having it adhered to as correct, even by that damned, Dirty Dave.

Our outlook on the matter was unanimous: lie, cheat, and steal. And as far as Billy was concerned, God in Heaven knew that he had tried it out the right way, to make an honest go of things, but the wrong way was the only path that yielded to our needs and kept its promises, as all other promises made to Billy had been broken in the past by the very men whom he had trusted, the same men who created their own trouble and would have Billy put his life on the line in the interest of protecting them during their own selfish want of survival after the calamity of problems they brought upon themselves. And by now, one ought to be aware that in the end it was all for naught. Those men of self-importance had given Billy nothing but an insurmountable load of trouble and a severe lack of thanks. I blamed Billy for his lot in life, I truly did—I knew Billy had his own responsibility to accept for his sorry state of affairs, but what else could be said? He had unprecedented loyalty, and his "betters" used this against him to their own advantage. The boy truly believed he had done the right thing by standing up to the machinations of a mighty, tyrannical power. But now that all had been revealed and dealt with and the results less than optimistic, I suspected that Billy's pride had been irrevocably wounded in realizing how right I had been from the beginning of this conflict, resulting in his refusing to swallow the jagged little pill of acceptance and maintaining an opposition to caving in and proclaiming my wisdom on the matter. But I knew better than anyone just how sorry Billy was for his choosing to involve himself in the whole ordeal of the Lincoln County War.

We had stayed on at Greathouse's boarding Inn before moving on to the town of Picacho on the Rio Hondo. Fortunately, Jim was away on business, so I had been given a reprieve and had yet to worry over spilling out the truth of the bail money.

By late afternoon we arrived in Picacho, and there I always suffered the mis- fortune of running into that Mexican puta, Adriana. Upon entrance to the small town I took note of her clamoring around Billy as he strode in upon his horse valiantly despite the fact that it was well known that my place was to enter a town with him side-by-side. But she paid no mind to me, instead following him along until he dismounted, her hand clutching his leg possessively, running up the length of his thigh as he climbed down, then sliding her hands up along his body and wrapping her arms around his shoulders as he stood on the ground beside her. He hardly looked at her, but she was undeterred by this, raising herself onto her toes and leaning over to place her lips upon his cheek. Used to such attentions by women, he paid her no mind and remained busy, caught up in talking to his closest compadres. Pouty and aware that he had failed to notice her in the way she'd wanted, it encouraged her to slither her hand to his cheek so she might turn his face toward her own and kiss him on the lips.

Having no choice but to pay attention to her then, he said, matter-of-fact, "*Buenas Noches, Adriana. Tengo que hablar con usted más tarde. ¿Está bien?*"

Disappointed, she nodded, and without thinking much on her I walked over to Billy and he customarily slid his arm around my waist as he turned away from Adriana and easily fell back into conversation with the others.

Innocuously, I turned toward Adriana's direction and was met with a markedly nasty expression. I disregarded this and turned back around, pretending to listen to the men. My rebuff of her made her angrier, for I heard her make a grand production of turning on her heel and exhaling loudly.

16

October, 1879

As of late I had noticed a peculiar transformation in me. When I was not curiously fatigued, I was carnally restless. One late afternoon in particular I prayed feverishly that Billy would touch me as he often did when he needed me in that certain, passionate way in which a man needs a woman. I hoped his attentions would deter me from being the aggressor, lunging at him like some wild animal. Despite our current predicament as desperados, I still valued my assets and dignity. Behaving the consummate lady was still of an utmost virtue to me. But, it being so early in the day, it was unlikely he'd desire me with his usual late night desperation. Furthermore, there was his preoccupation in preparing to find the boys in order to relax and squabble with over a game of cards. I bit at my nails like a vulgar, unbred crofter, becoming more and more agitated. Of course I had felt such amorous feelings for Billy before, but never with an overwhelming, all-consuming longing. I didn't know I could ever feel for him more than I have already.

I sat on a rickety, splintered wooden chair in our room, my leg shaking un-controllably—impatiently, as I continued to bite at my nails, crudely and unladylike, as I watched him go back and forth across the room, my mind screaming at him irritably, begging for him to notice me—to come and have me even as he paid no mind at all, focused on his task at hand. He seemed to be looking for something, not wanting to forget or miss anything before he walked out the door. But he *was* missing something: me—sitting in a chair, growing needier for his attention by the minute. At last he found what he was looking for: his pocket watch. Once he found this mundane little article he came to me and gave me a sweet, simple kiss before he departed my company.

In the time we had spent at Greathouse's Inn before coming to Picacho I had begun to notice an inaccuracy regarding my courses and an occasional queasiness that often caused me illness. I wish I could say that I had simply failed to mention these facts to Billy, but the truth was I feared telling him what I believed of the implications. I tried to pretend that it was nothing more than nerves—I didn't want to cause him any undue worry or alarm, afraid I'd spook him away from my bed supposing the symptoms were false. I felt I must tread lightly. If I let him in on my secret, but turned out to be wrong, it might still present itself as a wake-up call. Billy might turn away from me in the interest of avoiding a true slip-up next time. This was always a fear of his, getting me into trouble or causing me a helpless illness should we be caught in the middle of nowhere and in need of riding out fast. But I must have been a month gone now, and the simple math indicated that all the signs were there: my breasts were fairly swollen and sore, and sickness plagued me throughout the days so that I often refused to eat, yet still my clothes were snug.

I needed to see the doctor and considered going to Jimmy for help in an attempt to avoid distressing Billy should it be nothing, but not only did I have the accompanying guilt that came with hiding such a precious consequence from Billy when it was he who had a right to know before anyone else, I also could not go about it without having Billy there to rely on as always.

The chance of a baby being true rendered me giddy and overjoyed and, above all else, I did not want to squander the possibility of learning of such a happy occasion and experiencing with anyone else. I wanted Billy with me when I found out the news, whatever it may be. I needed to share this with Billy.

I knew what I could do to help my predicament. I didn't need to tell Billy of my suspicions, only that I was not feeling well and make a request for him to call for the doctor. If it turned out to be nothing, which was doubtful, than Billy wouldn't be any the wiser. But if it turned out that I was pregnant, well...I couldn't imagine his not being happy.

Lying in bed, I asked him to go for the doctor. Billy's concern was somewhat considerable, as asking for a visit from the doctor could indicate a serious illness. But I put him at ease, explaining that it was only my stomach, and that it had been upset these past few days. I had explained perhaps the doctor could give me something to calm it.

He folded his arms and leaned against the door frame.

"Not laudanum, nor none of them remedies that have opium," he cautioned.

"Of course not. He wouldn't give that as a remedy no way anyhow. Some seltzer or mineral water, I would think," I assured him.

"You be sure a'that," he warned again.

"He'll perhaps advise a remedy of soda water, or offer me some ginger powder.

I don't know where I could obtain either medicinal benefit here without the aid of a physician."

Arms still folded he smiled at me.

"All right niña. I'll go for him. You just stay put there in bed."

He came to me and kissed my forehead before turning to go.

Billy waited in the hall while the doctor examined me, and I confided in the doctor that I suspected I was with child and gave him a summation of my symptoms to which he agreed that I was most likely correct to assume this was my case.

I had to lie back on the bed and allow him access to myself in a most undignified fashion. We both were discomfited by the action, but what else could be done? I wore a simple shift which slid down my thighs as I lay there, knees bent and legs apart so the doctor could view me. He first placed his hands upon my breasts, and my abdomen, applying pressure, and then, not having the proper tools with which to examine me medically, used his fingers to investigate me inside and out with one hand while still pressing upon my abdomen with the other. It was over in what must have only been a matter of seconds, but seemed to stretch on for an eternity given the uncomfortable nature of the visit. I quickly closed my legs and pulled my shift down when he was through.

Having a difficult time maintaining my gaze, he explained that my "feminine region" had a purplish tint and appeared swollen, as did my abdomen.

"Without testing your urine I cannot give you more of an accurate reading, but by your symptoms alone and the body's telltale signs, I can be almost certain that you are indeed with child."

He reached down to pick up the black medical bag he had brought with him, though he did not seem to need it. Clearing his throat and appearing more at ease now that he was not poking at my private regions, he advised me of a first-rate midwife in White Oaks whom I should consult with, but advised that I could not travel to her while in a delicate position. If she would not come to me, he assured that there were women enough here who had experience in birthing whether it was because they had given birth or assisted in its process. I thanked him and let him be on his way, allowing that he could speak with Billy on his way out.

So then, it seemed now I would have a baby and would need to stay put. The idea of staying behind didn't bother me so much now as one would imagine. Protecting Billy's baby was the only thing that could keep me from running off and following him.

After the doctor had gone from me I made myself comfortable by leaning back against a bevy of pillows fit for a queen and laying on my side, drawing my knees up to my chest and twirling my hair around my fingers. I lay there, content and relaxed, listening to the muffled voices outside the door as the doctor spoke with Billy, telling him that I would have his baby. At the thought of becoming a mother to Billy's child my natural regality rose as I thought I might have to plead with Billy should I need to, my regality suddenly taking precedence over my being. I had suddenly grown nervous at the idea of his learning the blessed news and was afraid he'd be upset. But when the door opened and he came in, his smile was the widest I'd ever seen it. He came to the bed and sat down next to me, taking my hand in his.

"Can you think it's true?" he asked of me, his divine blue eyes begging me to say "*yes*".

I smiled at his overwhelming enthusiasm and found it curious that I felt more joy for him in that moment than I did myself. I was relieved by his excitement and felt happiness at seeing how thrilled he was and glad that I could fulfill him in such a way, that I could give him a family again.

"I believe it must be, Billy. I've believed it for a short while now, since I realized—"

"—You've known?"

"Well, I wasn't so sure. Not without a doctor's say so."

"You didn't say nothing to me."

My hand held carefully to his as he dropped his smile for a moment, registering a slight look of perplexity. His expression seemed innocuously questioning.

"I didn't want to worry you until I could be certain. You understand, don't you, Billy?"

He smiled again and brought my hand to his lips, kissing the palm before leaning in to kiss me gently on the lips. He was beside himself with elaation, looking at me while he giggled at what seemed like nothing, the way a young girl might do, his smile reaching his eyes as they twinkled more brightly than I remembered. Seeing this side of him made me giggle as well, disbelieving what I was seeing in him as I knew he had feared this moment so often. I was amazed that he could be so candidly happy, so winsome. I had suspected that news such as this would thrill him.

I leaned into him and playfully whispered as though there were someone else in the room to keep the secret from.

"The doctor agrees that I'm more than a month gone now."

His face lit up in astonishment, and like a child lost in wonderment he said, "A whole month? Imagine that!"

"*More* than a month."

He put his hands to my belly and then his lips.

"My baby's been right here inside you all that time? I wish I could'a known."

"And how come?"

I smiled sweetly at him as he grabbed onto my hand.

He looked at me, surprised. "How come? I could have been this happy all this time. Why wouldn't I want that? I'd have known it would have been the three of us."

I laughed, delighted by his innocent exuberance and held tighter to his hand.

"Life doesn't get better than this," he professed.

He was so full of awe. I had never seen him in such a state and decided that this would be my new favorite side of him. There was no sign of the treacherous Billy the Kid in him at this moment. He had been replaced in by the young, untroubled boy I used to know, and by an adoring man bound for fatherhood at that! To look at him now, no one would ever guess that those eyes, tempered now by love, had stared into the darkest depths of hell, and that the man who owned them had done dark, bloody deeds. If a stranger were to look upon him in this instant, they would only have seen a good, loving man whose soul was flawless and unscathed.

"I can't believe it," he gushed. "Elucia Howard with my child in her..."

He was resting his head gently on my belly when he sat upright with a start and looked at me nervously.

"Will you marry me, then?"

His eyes searched my face with worry, as if there was even the slightest chance I would say "no". I could only stare at him with amused bewilderment. He was truly beside himself and was so overwhelmed with the joy only a proud father-to-be could have that he seemed lost. Where was the confident, arrogant Kid with all of the answers? He had never endeared himself so much to me as he did now.

I should have been delirious over his question. I should have squealed with triumph and cried out, declaring "yes!", but his demeanor caused me as much puzzlement as it did pleasure, and I was taken aback. It felt as though ages has passed before I said, "Don't be a fool! Of course I will marry you, Billy!"

He gave a toothy grin as he leaned in to kiss my lips with chaste warmth.

"What is it he said to you? The doctor?" I wondered.

"Oh...he just congratulated me and told me I would be a father—that you were with child. He called you my wife. Can you believe it?"

His face lit up again as he laughed amusedly, and I smirked.

"Yes, I suppose I can. One of the first things he did when he assessed me was to look at my finger and see your mother's ring there."

"Then it's a damned good thing I put it there!"

"I'll say!" I smiled. "Did he say anything else at all?"

"No, not much. I guess we didn't have a whole lot to talk about. Anyway, I was eager to see you."

"I should think otherwise, that you'd both should have had much to talk of, what with you both being the only two men in the world to have ever seen my naughty bits."

His face reddened and he looked down at his lap, trying to stifle a laugh.

"I gotta tell ya, Billy...that was the most uncomfortable experience I've yet had to suffer through."

Laughing, he said, "I'm real sorry about that Bonita."

"Yeah, you seem real sorry." I retorted, playfully.

Still laughing, he told me that I would change my mind about that nine months from now when I had a handful of people staring there, begging for them to get it out. I laughed at that until my eyes watered, but then I thought on the truthfulness of it and began to whine. I gave him an affectionate shove for reminding me of such a thing, but I couldn't truly be angry or complain, happy as I was.

"He didn't tell you about the midwife in White Oaks, then?" I asked.

"No. What about one?"

"He recommended her, but I'm unable to travel that distance. I would suggest writing a letter, but I think it would be more appropriate to visit with her in person and have her come here."

"If the doctor recommended her then I'll have to go on ahead and do my best to convince her to come. But I don't have to go now, do I? Can I stay with you for a little longer?"

I brushed his hair from his brow lovingly. It had grown a bit longer since he had last gotten it cut.

"Of course, Billy. I would expect you to."

Now! Tell him now about the money, now! I thought. *While he's happy...*

"You can promise to pay her well enough—if she'll come."

He looked at me funny a moment, a strange little smile on his face.

"Well, ain't that a funny thing for you to say?"

I stared back, innocent. "What is?"

"We can *'promise'* to pay her well enough?"

I stared at him for a minute and said nothing as he stared right back. It wasn't a terrible thing, my having that money in the bank. If anything, it should please him. But I had kept it from him for so long and lied about it when I paid his bail. If it weren't for that, I could stand telling him the truth much easier.

I took in a breath.

"I have money."

"Yes, I know that you do, but that's a'ways back in New York and—"

"No, I have it here. Where we are."

He stared at me, saying nothing while his eyes registered confusion and altering thoughts, revealing at first incomprehension, and then concluding in disbelief. The only word to come from his mouth as he continued to stare, disbelieving, was, "What?"

"Right there in White Oaks. In the Exchange Bank."

He let go of my hand and jumped up, turning away from me. I sat there and waited quietly to see what he would do next. He didn't seem angry, only baffled. Maybe stunned—he was obviously thrown. Rubbing at his chin he turned back.

"How? Why'd Jim give you that money, then? Jim had given you that money, you said so. You knew I was putting money aside to pay him back, but you still said nothing."

The statement was inquisitive, not bitter, and with a firm sense of honesty I replied, "No, Billy. I gave me that money."

"You made that bail?"

I nodded. "I'm sorry—that I lied. I was afraid you'd press harder for me to use my money and leave if I told. I had my reasons for waiting to tell. I wanted it to be *ours*, honest!"

"How much do you have?" he asked, taken aback.

I put my head down when I answered him. "I had over fourteen-hundred—"

"Fourteen-hundred dollars!"

I nodded again.

"Jesus Christ! You had all of that and you never *told* me?"

I began to feel guilt-ridden and didn't answer him. After reasoning all that time with what I thought was practicality for not telling him, this moment, a moment that made me feel more connected to him than ever before, made me feel remorseful for not sharing the truth with him from the beginning. When I didn't reply he again asked me how I had gotten that money. I told him about the land I sold to John Chisum during the war and how he paid me what I had asked and more.

"You sold him that land during the war? Even while Seven Rivers was in an uproar and against us because of him and the land he took over?"

"I didn't care about that, I was thinking of myself. I was thinking of us both. I can't apologize for that."

"I'm not asking you to."

Worried that he was upsetting me in my condition he came back over and took my hand again.

"It's okay, I'm not angry—there's no good reason to be. It's good news. It's just that it's a lot of money and you took me by surprise. I don't think I'd have given you a hard time about it like you thought I would—about you using it to get back home. I think I would have felt much better knowing you had it if something should have happened."

I looked at him with a small smile.

"I'm glad you told me, t'tell the truth. I guess I might've looked pretty silly giving Jim a'hundred dollars for nothing."

He made me laugh as he leaned in to kiss me.

"So how do I go about getting this money without you there? It's in your name, isn't it?"

"Yes, but I can arrange for checks to be sent here to me."

"Well...ain't *you* the smart one?" He smiled, pleased with me.

Picacho was a small, rustic town. It was perhaps not entirely conducive to a woman of my delicate condition, but nonetheless, Billy and I were joyous and inseparable. We had kept our secret, spending our time locked away inside of doors, whiling away the hours talking and planning a future of solid roots where we prayed uncertainty would become a recollective demon of imagination. Our illusory idealistic life would have insecurity exempt from the new life we would map out for ourselves.

But, during these times, the winds of change would soon find him pushing to move along—it was inevitable, and under the circumstances, he must leave me behind to which we both agreed. I would not sulk—not when the stakes were so high and I remained contented. Naturally, I worried it would be inevitable that he would eventually need to go, but I could stand it. He would be back for me.

We kept up appearances, careful not to lock ourselves away for too long. I tolerated my attire, as snug as it could be, but it was not altogether uncomfortable. I did not want to raise any eyebrows by presenting myself as an oddity, adorning myself in ample skirts and blouses. It would have seemed nonsensical considering how I'd been outfitting myself these near past two years, so for the time being I kept up my cowpoke charade for as long as I could stand it until, soon enough, I knew, the others would move on and Billy and I would make our excuses to stay behind. I could then relax into my newfound role, wearing all the billowy attire I could get my hands on.

17

October 1979

Billy and the others were off gambling in one of the town saloons, so Jimmy and I decided on a walk as the day proved pleasant enough. We wandered casually through the dirty, muddied streets having an agreeable visit when suddenly he shoved me aside forcefully. I felt a solid blow my side and yelped, thinking for a moment that I had been mule kicked powerfully. My hands yielded to the lateral pain in my side, and as I pressed them intensely upon the great ache in an attempt to stabilize the agony, I sunk down to my knees in a state of confusion. I heard a commotion, recognizing only Jimmy's voice as he yelled, screaming. I lay down and curled up on the damp earth, gasping for air while I held my side, knees drawn up to my chest as my other hand clutched at the mud, scraping great clefts of wet earth as I tried to understand my agony.

Through watery, bleary eyes, I raised my head as far as I could, my eyes slick, and I thought I saw Jimmy wrestling a figure to the ground, striking out at it with curled fists. I pulled my hand from my side and held it to my face, finding it sheathed with a dark maroon.

There was an uproar that had gathered, but the shouts were disjointed, and so I closed my eyes against the tumult when I was suddenly seized by another sudden, sharp pain in my insides that caused me to yell out and tear up. I clamped my body tighter against the pain but couldn't stop the sound of my own shrieking. When my strength gave out my voice died with it. I remained there on the ground, breathing intensely, sharply. Panting like a dog in an attempt to cling to life.

A strange thought occurred to me: *I didn't recall the ground being so wet when I first lay down upon it.* But I had been lying in a spreading pool of my own blood as it burgeoned out all around me.

An all at once familiar yet strange voice called to me, screaming my name in what sounded like terror. I was being lifted, and through the cacophony of sounds that surrounded me, I heard that same terrified voice tell me to hold on, but I was too dazed and hadn't the ability to answer. I felt desperation in wanting to respond. I could hear voices shouting *Jesus Christ* and *goddammit!*

Outside of the pain, I was aware of nothing other than being laid down on a table in a room I did not recognize. I had been taken from the street into a safe place in which I could be tended to.

Now I understood the voice that had been shouting to me: Billy. Billy was there, holding my hand and leaning very closely to my face as he spoke to me, trying to get my fluttering eyes to focus on his in an attempt to calm me, but it was no use as my eyes would loll this way and that. For once I had trouble concentrating on those beautiful blue eyes of his—his eyes, so clear and luminous, the eyes I would dream of, making any excuse to gaze into and search. But they were indistinct to me now, my own vision blurred and confused. An odd, heartbreaking thought passed through my mind. What if I were going to die here? How could God be so cruel as to punish me in such a way? Those cerulean irises were the only thing on this earth I forever prayed to see.

Though my sight continued to waver, Billy's soft voice in my ear began to calm me, and but by the grace of God my sight cleared and my eyes locked onto his. As he held my hand he showed me a face that was brave. I picked up on his kind lie and I fixated on his smile even though I knew that it was forced. It's strange, but that small detail, real or not, helped me deal with my own crisis.

"You're all right, sweetheart. You're gonna be all right..." he said.

There was a slight, troublesome laugh in his voice for my benefit, like it weren't nothing. He stroked my forehead gently with his finger tips and brushed the stray locks of hair from my sweated brow.

I didn't recognize the sound of my own voice—my throat dry and rough—when I asked him what was wrong, what was happening to me.

"You're gonna be fine, sweetheart. You just got a little hurt is all."

"*Billy*..." I sobbed. "Was I shot? Please don't lie to me! I was shot, wasn't I? I think I might die..."

Through fitful breath, uneasy and halting, I told him I was sorry.

Tears filled my eyes before spilling down the side of my face. I plead with him to forgive me for dying on him. He shushed and calmed me, assuring me that it wasn't true—that I wasn't going to die, that he wouldn't let me. But even in my confusion, I could see the panic displayed on his pallid face.

Then, an acute pain, sharper than the pain I had become accustomed to, pervaded my side. I screamed murderously. I screamed so powerfully, deafening the hardened men, causing them to cover their ears or leave the room entirely, but not Billy—he stayed right there by my side.

A Mexican frontier doctor had inserted an extraction tool into the mauled tract of my wound, attempting to remove the bullet that had embedded itself into my body. I didn't know it had been implanted there, becoming an even greater source of agony.

"What the *fuck* are you doing to her?" Billy shrieked.

"La bala está en profunda, señor..."

"I don't care if it's lodged half way t'China," Billy hollered. "You get that thing out without painin' her!"

"Billy," Tom offered. "He's trying to help her—he's doing the best he can—"

"—He can do better!"

I felt that I might pass out, and I prayed that I would, but Billy would slap at my face, yelling at me to stay with him.

In my excruciating haze I saw the door open. Josiah had come in to see what the trouble was.

"What is it? What happened?" he demanded.

"She's been shot, and this fucking beaner is slaughtering her," Billy screamed.

Josiah, who had begun studies to be a doctor himself, shoved the Mexican out of the way and went to work. Carefully, he rolled me onto my uninjured side. I winced, but I was becoming lethargic already, with hardly any energy to cry out. He felt around my lower back by the wound.

"It's all right," Billy soothed. "Doc's got ya now."

"Near as I can tell, she's lucky. Don't think anything was hit, but it didn't exit," Josiah explained.

"*What*?" Billy asked.

By now Charlie, Minxie, Henry, and Jose, had filed into the room. The streets of Picacho were abuzz with the controversy that enveloped my name.

"The bullet," Josiah went on. "It didn't exit. Who was with her when this happened?"

Jimmy spoke up, "I was, sir."

"Did you see what type of gun she was shot with?"

Jimmy produced the piece. "This one. I grabbed the piece and took it."

Josiah examined the piece, a small Derringer. He let out an arrested breath. "No wonder she got lucky. She couldn't have been shot close enough or else the damage would have been considerable."

"No, she wasn't—that's true. Adriana shot her from a good fifteen feet. If I had to guess..." offered Jimmy.

Around the small of my back and on the utmost left side of me, he gently ran his thumb over a small, shifting lump that resided there.

"It's right here, right under the skin. You can see the bead. I'll need to cut it out, but she won't quit bleeding. Why's she bleeding so goddamned much?" Josiah said to himself.

Billy's eyes widened with terror. "*Bleeding?*"

"Yes, Bill!" Josiah yelled, short-tempered. "She's still bleeding. *Too goddamned much!*"

"What's it mean?" Billy asked, alarmed.

"It means we have to stop the bleeding!"

Josiah carefully rolled me onto my back. Using his hands, he applied pressure to the gunshot wound. He looked to Charlie and, pointing, ordered him to place a poker in the stove until it was scalding.

Charlie stood a moment, transfixed.

"*Move!*" Josiah yelled. He turned to Henry and instructed him to run and get a bottle of whiskey, any alcohol with which to cleanse the wound. Henry hurried out of the building in search of alcohol with which to sterilize my injury and the implements Josiah would use upon them.

Charlie went to the pot belly stove and propped the poker in.

"What are you gonna do?" Billy asked Josiah anxiously. If Billy's wits had been about him he would have known exactly what Josiah intended to do, and at this, Josiah did his best to accommodate Billy's distress.

"Stop the bleeding."

Sauntering in just as serene as you please, Dave chuckled smarmily and said, "Well, well...look who got herself done in."

Billy glared at him violently and Dave drew back and threw his hands up in a show of submission as he disingenuously replied, "I'm sorry." He gave a light chuckle and displayed a slightly pleased, self-serving smile.

The entire time I lay on the table Jimmy stood in the corner with his hands fretting his hat brim as he was known to do when worried, ashamed and afraid to come near me. If I had been aware of this and in adequate health, feeling first-rate, I'd have gone to comfort him, but as it were, I was laid out with my body vulnerable and uncertain. Minxie stood by with worry but remained prepared should any quick action be asked of him. Henry burst back in with a bottle of whiskey and Josiah turned to Charlie.

"Charlie, the poker!"

Charlie grabbed for the iron and brought it to Josiah, its tip furiously scorched with heat.

Josiah sucked in a breath. "Hold her down Billy..."

Billy looked at Doc with apprehension.

"*Do it!*" Josiah demanded. "And don't go easy on her! Keep her down no matter how she cries..."

Billy looked at me and stroked my hair again.

"Darlin'...Bonita? Hold my hand and squeeze it as hard as you can. Keep looking into my eyes—look at me."

I had no understanding of his urgency, but I registered his assertion. Feeling a stinging sensation I cried a little as Josiah poured the fermented, alcoholic concoction in and over my wound. I tried to comprehend why Billy still seemed so nervous and fearful for me after I had already been stung by the liquid when I felt a searing pain in my belly. The agony was unbearable. I kicked my feet and nearly took out Charlie's eye with my spur, and with a high pitch, I screamed my voice raw. I prayed fiercely that I would die.

"Her feet! *Hold her feet!*" Josiah commanded. "And remove her spurs for God's sake!"

Charlie and Minxie quickly removed my spurs and grabbed hold of my boots and held my legs as firmly as they could to help keep me steady on the table for Josiah, attempting to keep me from struggling and flailing about. Billy placed his arms firmly upon my shoulders to hold me down, but I made the task easy for him. By the time the wound had been seared properly, whatever verve I had left in me was gone. I shivered from exhaustion and sweat, and felt up to giving in. My eyes began to flutter uncontrollably again, and I felt surreal and strange.

I was vaguely aware of being rolled back onto my good side as Josiah gingerly positioned me. I felt the sensation of liquid pouring over my skin before feeling another sharp, fine pain in my side from the back. Josiah had sliced open my skin with a clean knife to release the lead that had come to rest there just beneath the surface. When he cut into me I hadn't the strength to cry out. I had only enough strength to whimper as tears glided over my face.

∞∞∞∞∞∞∞∞∞∞∞

"She's out!" Billy yelled. "Goddammit, she's out!"

Panicked, he wondered if Lucy were dead.

"She's okay," Josiah gently assured him before explaining, "She's lost a lot of blood. Her body's been through a lot and she's exhausted. She needs the rest, so it's to be expected."

Josiah looked at Billy's stricken face and said, "Here, place your hand on her belly."

Billy did as Josiah instructed.

"Feel her breathing?"

Billy's face broke into a relieved smile. "Yes, I feel it! She's breathing"

Josiah pulled out the offending ball and examined it closely.

"It's small enough, dammit. This is lucky..."

He kept rolling the ball with his thumb and two fingers, rubbing away the gore as he scrutinized it.

"What're you looking for?" Billy asked, distraught.

"Her shirt piece. I want to find that."

Josiah leaned down to peer into the small wound again. Without looking up he directed someone to grab for him something fine enough to probe the wound with.

Jimmy stepped forward and stuck his neck out. "I got this..."

In his hand he produced a very thin bladed Mexican fighting knife. Josiah took it from him and examined it.

"You ever use this much?" he asked. "Looks clean enough. Get it in the stove then bring it here."

Jimmy quickly stuck his knife in the pile of scorching wood, burning his hand when he tried to pull it back out. He brought it to Josiah who poured alcohol over it before he began probing the incision he had made. All the men, save for Dave, who bit at his fingernails, spitting out the gnawed pieces and looking bored, watched Josiah intently and his task at hand. Finally, Josiah stood up straight.

"Here!" he hollered triumphantly.

He matched the small piece of fabric to the front part of Lucy's shirt where the bullet had torn its path.

"Got it, it's all there," he said, pleased.

After Josiah carefully rolled Lucy onto her back again his eyes became enlarged at a curious sight. Blood! *More* blood! It flowed from that sacred place on a woman, spreading out and further staining Lucy's already soiled clothing and the table. Billy took stock of Josiah's alarmed expression and followed his gaze.

"What the hell *is* that?" Billy wondered aloud, terrified.

Josiah's stare at Billy was markedly disturbed. "*Jesus, Billy...*"

Sternly, the two stared at one another as the others gathered round desperately asking what the matter was, but Billy and Josiah continued their silent tête-á-tête.

"Billy..."

The implication was clear: *Is she pregnant?*

Billy's face disclosed a look of horror and misery before manifesting into an air of furious anger. Billy ferociously glared at Jimmy.

"You was with her, weren't ya? What the fuck happened, *Moffey*?"

Jimmy immediately broke out into a cold sweat, panicked—his collar sticking to the back of his neck. He saw what had happened, it was true, and it seemed to occur almost in slow motion. But Billy's tone terrified him so that Jimmy couldn't speak. There was an undercurrent of blame in Billy's words, and God help the man who'd allow such a horrendous thing to happen to Billy's chica preciosa, his "mi amor".

Billy wanted facts and he was undeterred, his eyes burning holes into Jimmy's, blaming him for allowing such a perilous thing to happen.

Jimmy's lips quivered as he mentally, painstakingly ran through the vocabulary of his mind's eye searching out the best words in his lexis, but even if he had found and settled on a perfect word, there was no satiating Billy. Jimmy's voice would have been unable to produce a fine enough word. Feverishly, Billy moved closer, his eyes a hardened, stormy blue, and the look upon his face frightened Jimmy more than if the devil himself had materialized before him.

"*What the fuck happened to her!*"

"Adriana..." Jimmy stammered in a whisper.

It was all Billy needed to hear—to know. Billy's eyes glared dangerously at Jimmy, but the look was not meant for him. Without comprehensive thought and looking wretched, drenched in Lucy's blood, Billy looked like a wild man, turning toward the door that led out onto the street, the other boys either too dumbfounded to try and stop him, or using whatever good sense God had given them to not get in his way. They all stood back and stared after him.

Out on the street, Billy asked the curious onlookers where Adriana had gone. To the jail—*A la cárcel*, was the repeated chorus of the Mexican patrons near enough to hear his inquest. Billy doggedly closed the gap between himself and the jail to search out the blackened soul he would drag with him into perdition like a hound from hell.

When he reached the small sheriff's office he pushed past a man who had been standing idly by the entrance, proceeding to then push past a small swarm of armed men standing outside the open cell in which Adriana was being kept. They hadn't been prepared to stop him. Billy may as well have been a specter passing through, which might have sent unnerving shivers down their spines if he hadn't moved much too quickly for them to take notice.

Like a shot he was in the cell and Adriana stood from her cot and foolishly lifted her arms to him as though he might embrace her like a lover. But when he reached her he pulled back his right arm and then swung it forward with all the force he could muster, his fist connecting to her mouth with the strength of a fast moving, iron horse.

Falling backward over the cot, she hit the wall and smacked the back of her head, shock rendering her senseless for a moment. She touched her lip instinctively and, pulling back her fingers to look, saw the blood Billy had spilled on her as the men dragged him out of the cell. They held fast to his right arm as he attempted to wrest his pistol from its scabbard. Billy's rage was so complete that four men had to hold to him firmly, the combined strength of them necessary to keep him from murdering the girl outright.

"¡Billy, no!" hollered one man.

Without taking his eyes from Adriana, Billy demanded he be let go and fought hard against the hands that held him back.

"¡Ella no está bien! She is no right in the head...Leave her be, it's not worth it!"

The men were able to pull him back and away, Billy panting with anger and exhaustion from the fight, the anger in his eyes for Adriana absolute.

"You don't want to kill a woman..." one of them said.

Still in her cell, Adriana stood up from the cot to look at Billy with an expression of defiance. "¿Es que su sangre? It is her blood, is it not? Is she dead?"

At those words, Billy moved to get at her again but was once more overcome though he struggled. Bested by the power of the men holding him back and emotionally worn out, he merely looked at her having no words to spare, painfully aware that the ceremony of this entire ordeal did no justice to Lucy's suffering. Being here only wasted his time with Adriana and kept him from her, and she could be breathing her last. The men who had kept him from making the grave mistake of killing Adriana began to loosen their grip as Billy seemed to regain his bearings. He stood up straight, resigned, and they let him go so he could get back to Lucy. Before leaving, he casually walked to Adriana, and the two faced one another through the bars. Billy, out of breath and exhausted, and Adriana smiling, hopeful. As they looked at one another, desperate and aggrieved, Billy spit in her face before turning his back on her.

"¡Dios mío! Usted cerdo asqueroso! Usted ama a mí, vuelvo a tu puta!"

18

November, 1879

Lucy had been carefully moved to Herman Guzman's where she was considerably looked after, and Billy sat forlorn on Herman's back porch as she slept. Lucy had been given chloral hydrate to help ease her pain and cause her to rest. The women who occupied the house and a few from town tended to her constantly, and though he had badly desired to sit with her and hold her limp but blessedly warm hand as she slept, the shame he felt made it difficult for him to sit by her while she lay there sleeping without her permission. He made it a point to remain near and had asked to be sent for immediately when she would regain a short consciousness prior to being put out again, but so far, since she had been mended, she had largely remained in a listless slumber and was never quite awake nor clear minded enough to notice him during the brief moments when her eyes would flutter open.

He slumped against the house, still in the clothes stiff with her blood, refusing to change them. He hung his head low with his knees drawn up and his arms around his legs. He blamed himself for what had happened. He would not change his soiled, bloodied clothes or wash her dried blood from his skin, from his face and his hands. He wore Lucy's gore like a much deserved albatross. He would not wash away the reminder of his sin.

Jimmy watched him sitting there despondently—a low soul, indeed. He approached him cautiously, apprehensive at daring to confront the man who might kill him as soon as look at him for what he'd done. Jimmy felt responsible, and he was certain Billy blamed him all the same. He wasn't paying attention. He didn't look out for Lucy. He didn't do for her what he was certain Billy would have. He didn't protect her. But he summoned his nerve and sat down beside him. Billy did not seem to register his presence.

"Billy..."

Billy looked at Jimmy, his distressed blue irises bright and intense against the thick red vessels in his eyes. At first, Jimmy was taken aback by this sight, forgetting to speak as he lost his sense of self, bewildered at seeing Billy in such a state. Never before had Billy looked so remarkably infernal. Yet the Kid looked on at him, expectant. For a fleeting moment he thought to stand and go, but he wouldn't let his shame and anxiety excuse him. He sat there next to Billy and remained silent for a short time, sifting through his mind for the words that would make the most sense but suffering a great difficulty in finding them.

"I'm sorry, Billy..."

"What for?"

This response threw him, for Jimmy felt certain that, given Billy's penchant for Lucy's safety, and the tension that lie between them where she was concerned, he would have nothing but blame for him.

"For letting Lucy get hurt. I swear I didn't see it. I didn't see that girl coming."

Billy looked away from Jimmy and stared forward in a daze. "Why should you have known about it?" he wondered out loud.

Jimmy's brow furrowed. He hadn't expected to find Billy so merciful and wholly beaten, but of course it made sense. The terror of seeing Lucy's life at stake would have been more than Billy could bear. That alone would have been enough for him. But, though her life was spared, there was still the loss of life her traumatized and weakened body was unable to sustain, a life he had made with her. It had sent him over the edge. Gone was the intrepid spirit that was inherent in him.

Jimmy opened his mouth, taking in the breath that would allow him to persist in this conversation, to try and connect with this man who was so obviously lost, whose pain reflected that of his own, though Jimmy was humble enough to understand that it would be impossible for him to feel as deeply as Billy did in this moment. He felt strongly that he hadn't even the right to imagine that he could be cut as deeply, despite feeling a tremendous tear within his own gut.

But before he could say anything, Billy spoke in a broken voice. "This is not your fault."

With that, Billy stood and made to walk off.

"Don't you feel you ought to wash up and change those clothes?" Jimmy asked.

Billy looked down at himself, but he was only going through the motions, acting instinctively in response to Jimmy's question and not really regarding his own appearance. Absently, he ran his hands down the stiffened front of his shirt. When he looked back up he said nothing, turning to go without knowing where, wanting to find solace.

ooooooooooooooo

Herman's wife Lily spent the most time with me, her daughter Abigail helping to bathe my body and tend to my wound, cleansing and dressing it. I had been laid up for nearly a week, and I made it clear that I would not see Billy and would not relent on this decision. Yet still, he spent his time nearby, desperately wanting to see me. I was told that he had been anxious and fitful, wanting to talk with me and be by my side, but I still refused him. I didn't want to see him—to look at his face and be reminded, once again, a bullet had robbed me of him.

Lily and Abigail plead with me to let him in, beseeching me to end his suffering as they were understandably sympathetic to his case, talking of and conjuring in my mind images of my beloved's anguish. They assured me that he so very desperately wanted to be with me. They told how he had kept a close vigil during the days that I had lain ill in bed, and how my keeping him at arm's length was of no consequence to him—that he would wait, though it hurt him deeply to do so.

My insistence that he be kept from me truly made me sorry. I wanted nothing more than to have him with me. After all, it had become a natural instinct in me to want for him when I suffered, but in a twist of cruel irony, it was the very idea of seeing him that would cause me further irrevocable torment. I had lost him. I had been so close to having every happiness I'd wanted, and now he would make it so there would be no opportunity for there to be such happiness again. I knew him well—he would not allow fate another chance to bring us together in that way again. He would reject me now. He would never again tempt harm to find me in that way. He would blame my misfortune on his dealings with other women. He'd keep his distance, fixing it so there'd be no chance of one of his lovesick madcaps rushing at me again with a bullet, and no chance of my succumbing to the loss of a child given to me by him. But I wouldn't be angry with him because of this. How could I be angry when I knew his reaction would be out of concern for my welfare?

But no, I wouldn't see him, because for four wonderful days when I looked at him, I saw the future I had wanted since we first met, and my happiness had transcended words. Now, all I would see in him was forfeiture and a prolonged sense of futility in our relationship.

But it wasn't long before he disregarded my wishes. I knew soon enough he'd force his way in, and when his wits finally came to an end he came through the house in a rush, pushing past the occupants who begged him to be reasonable and calm, to first try and let them coax me into seeing him, or to at least give me the time I needed and continue waiting patiently until I felt ready to see him.

He came through the door of my room like a gale force and I turned away from him as he flung himself at my bedside, hands clasped together as though in prayer, begging me to look at him and let him be with me. I cried, wanting desperately to all at once end the hurt he felt at my rebuff and to let him comfort me, too. I still was not ready to face things with him, but I gave in despite my feelings and turned to him, compelling myself to remember that, no matter what, I wanted him in my life, and so I broke down my resistance sooner than later to let the healing begin so that we might find our way back to one another regardless of how we might have been changed.

∞∞∞∞∞∞∞∞∞∞∞∞

The law wouldn't make her pay for what she'd done.

What Adriana did to Lucy was ruled an accident and so she was not tried. All the same, however, the townspeople judged and shunned her, but their informal verdict of guilty seemed to have little effect on her.

It was a beautiful and fairly warm November day. She strolled along the promenade, her contemporaries giving her a wide berth as they passed. Jimmy stood across the street, arms folded indignantly as she went about her business. He glared at her proud disposition, the bruise Billy had put on her face evident and visible from even this distance. Planning to appeal to the spurned women in her, he crossed the street and approached her under the guise of sympathy.

In a pleasant, courtly tone he called to her. "Adriana..."

The girl turned to look at him, her countenance registering indifference at first, then piquing with interest as she recognized Jimmy and wondered at his affability.

"¿Sí?" she asked of him.

He removed his hat as a gentleman would do and smiled as he closed the gap between them.

"Hidee," he smiled. "Heard things got a bit rough the other day between you and Billy."

"*Sí,*" she replied again, nodding in affirmation though her expression disclosed a quick look of fury. Jimmy decided to play her for all she was worth.

"I just thought it might be okay to tell you that, well...if you don't mind my saying so, you got a raw deal. That boy just didn't do you right."

She smirked pleasantly at his reckoning, pleased that he understood.

"You still love him?" Jimmy asked.

Frowning, she nodded and again said, "*Sí*".

"Well now, then. You ought to get over something like that. What you need is a man who's gonna treat you right. If you was *my* girl..." Jimmy let the sentence drift, feigning reticence and giving a slight, modest laugh.

Adriana only continued to stare, but she smiled at him.

"He was wrong to do you that way, and I can tell you he's got a real bad temper."

"Yes, he's a bastardo."

"Sure thing, he is. Why don't you and I go off someplace and talk it over, see what we can do to fix things. You want to fix things, ain't that right?"

"Yes, but I want the...una disculpa—an apology." As she said this she touched the bruise Billy left on her face.

How proud this one is, thought Jimmy.

"Well, maybe I can smooth things over enough to make that happen. I sure wouldn't mind a chance with a pretty gal like you, and I'd like to see you get that apology. I wouldn't allow any man to treat you that way. Tell you what. If you do me the honor of spending the day with me, I'll see to it that I make him give it to you."

She smiled at Jimmy and, almost as an afterthought, said, "You look like him."

"Is that a fact?" Jimmy replied.

Adriana nodded. "Perhaps this is why the little bitch likes you, too."

Jimmy bit down on the insides of his cheeks, forcing a tight smile and holding his hands behind his back, squeezing his fingers together to keep his hands from reaching for her neck.

"How is the little bruja? I hear she almost died." Adriana smiled, reminded how she almost did in the girl Billy seemed to live for.

Again, Jimmy held his tongue, but just barely. Adriana was proving a tough challenge for him.

"Bruja..." Jimmy feigned scratching at the side of his head. "That means "witch", don't it? Yeah, you sure did her over one good," he confessed.

Adriana laughed, pleased.

"So what're the odds you'll let me take you off with me today? There's a real pretty spot that overlooks the Hondo. You can see it real fine on a pretty day like this."

They smiled at one another and Jimmy offered his arm to her.

They both sat atop Jimmy's horse as he led the animal up a steep rise next to a ravine on the Rio Hondo. Dismounting, he held his hand up to Adriana and helped her down before leading her to the edge of the gorge so they could look down and wonder at the view. Jimmy stood behind her, and when she turned to him to ask for a blanket so they might sit together a while, he responded by reaching for his gun and placing it between her eyes. He cocked back the hammer, ensuring that it was the last thing she would ever hear before pulling the trigger. She fell where she stood and Jimmy callously kicked her over the side, not bothering even to give her respect in death. He watched and heard the weight of her as she tumbled down, hitting each protrusion on the side of the ditch until her dead body fell out of sight among the brush along the full length to the bottom. Her corpse would quickly be eaten away by the environment and torn apart by scavengers, hopefully before anyone would bother to miss her, and he thought this a fitting end to the life of a pointless cunt.

19

November, 1879

Josiah had been gone a few weeks now, taking with him his family to Texas. I was sorry to see him go after all he had done for me, and because of this, I was even sorrier for the falling out he had with Billy over the resources of the cattle.

A short while after the case between us, Adriana seemed to have disappeared from the town. Her assault of me had been ruled an accident, and though the residents of Picacho were of a different mind concerning her guilt and had decided to alienate her, her absence had nonetheless become an apparent and curious occurrence after a while.

It had been fortuitous, then, that Billy moped hopelessly by me and had forced his way into the bed chamber I occupied while I lay ill, as those who witnessed his desperation to end her had cleared him as a suspect in her disappearance as the town knew he would not leave my side.

His accepted innocence in the case of any possible, nefarious wrongdoing to rid Picacho of Adriana was a new concept to Billy since, whenever he was involved in a dispute, he was always the first to be blamed in any mysterious or ill-fated happenstances involving his enemies. And where Adriana was concerned, after what she had done to his *chica favorita*, he would have, otherwise, been the first thought to transpire as a suspect in the Sheriff's mind. But with Billy considered cleared of any offense, it was speculated that after being spurned by the town, Adriana had perhaps simply and quietly gone off to another place where she was an unknown and might begin again. But her family disputed this possibility, citing that Adriana would do no such thing. *Oh...But the things Adriana would* not *do*...I thought sarcastically. I wondered if they believed she was incapable of murder, too. Families are a special type of marvelous obtuseness. A family member could no wrong despite doing it right under their family's ignorant noses. No matter...she was no longer our problem, and we all endeavored to quickly forget about her and move on, happy to have her gone.

While I lay in bed recovering, Billy never left my side, flitting about here and there, this way and that, making sure I was comfortable. He outshone my female attendants and put them to shame with his intense fostering of my wellbeing, seeing to it that I had everything I needed and more, spending his time entertaining me to ensure that I would not fall bored. He doted on me every second of every day, and when I grew tired and needed to rest he would cautiously lie beside me, minding my injuries, and put his arms around me knowing this always made me feel secure, lulling me into a fast, recuperative slumber. But once I was well enough and out of bed, Billy began to pull back from me as I had suspected he might. When he felt assured that I was mended and quite all right, he began his campaign to avoid me.

One evening I spied him standing alone by a small animal pen that housed a sow with suckling piglets. He was bent over the wooden posts, staring blankly, lost somewhere inside of his head.

I approached him, realizing that he might not welcome my presence since he had been keeping his distance from me for nearly a month's time at least.

"Billy," I began. "will you talk to me now? Hasn't it been such a long while for us?"

Though startled to hear my voice he did not look to me. He merely said, "Cariña...I don't want to talk to you. I can't talk to you now."

And then, without ceremony, he walked away from me, head down and eyes averted. I knew he was hurting, and I didn't begrudge him his austere position toward me. But I was hurting, too. I understood him. I only wished he would spare the time to understand me. To work matters through with me, or at the very least remember that he was not alone in this, that I was affected too—perhaps even worse.

As if to punctuate his departure, my healing wound suddenly stung me and began to itch as it often did as of late. It was still sore and tender and I had to treat it with care. I looked up at Billy's receding figure as I tended to my discomfort and could not help but realize the concurrence between his turning to leave me and the subsequent, abrupt pain in my side.

He very rarely shared a bed with me these past weeks. I'd lay awake at night, almost unable to sleep without him. On occasion, he'd wake me after I had finally drifted off, coming in sometime during the early morning hours. I'd feel the weight of him as he lay down beside me, and I had thought to refuse him this—sharing my bed. But it would have been out of spite, a vicious attempt, or hope, to force him into missing me by punishing him. But I could not provide reason enough for which to punish him. He was not isolating himself from me because he no longer loved me, but because he loved me too much. He *needed* to push me away. He felt eternally responsible for what happened to me, making him that much more determined to force me out. I endured the declination of his affection for me as he became crueler in his efforts to erode my resolve to stay. The penance he bestowed upon himself was emotionally and significantly taxing on me as he went about with other women more flagrantly than ever had before, growing bold in his determination to force me to acknowledge and understand that I had lost him and so there was absolutely nothing here for me.

But it was *he* who did not understand, who *never* understood, that what kept me here was bigger than he. Yes, my love for him was paramount and made him an exceptionally predominant reason for my desired emancipation from the east in favor of the west, but the freedom the territory of New Mexico gave me was supreme and would continue to trump any reason to turn back, though admittedly, it would seem empty without him directly by my side. But, aside from my love for Billy, nothing gave me a greater purpose to stay than my liberation. And so, with or without him, I would press on and fight for that. This territory was now my home. Though it was true that I considered it home because of Billy and wanted nothing more than to have him with me always, I had come to love it despite him.

Billy made every effort to shun me, and of all the things he had done to wound me and make it clear that he fully intended to avoid and discourage me from having a reason to stay, the cruelest affront came about when I entered the room we shared and I found him there with another.

I left the room, and though I would have stubbornly held back any tears, they did not come anyway. I wouldn't let this fresh cut break me. And of course I knew he had always lain with other women, but he had never done so in such a disrespectful manner, bringing a whore to our bed. It would seem his intent was to make war with me. But I wouldn't retaliate. No matter how appalling his determination to offend was, I knew what truly lie underneath his deceitful, punishing actions—the hope that he would finally break me, and I would not allow him that satisfaction. I know...it must have pained him to stoop to such a vile measure. It must have been a self-validated belief of his: to feel certain that he would desperately need to push the limitations of my confidence in order to, as he no doubt believed, save my life. I would never forgive him such callousness, regardless of his principled intentions, noble within his own mind. And it was all for naught—he would never persuade me to run.

We left Picacho for Patricio and it was learned that the boys were now considered a vile scourge across New Mexico. Our saving grace was that nobody, no one, wanted to come face to face with the infamously dangerous remaining Regulators.

Sherriff Kimbrell of Lincoln County himself was terrified of the Regulators and refused to fulfill his sworn duties, and so rumors abounded of a man with tremendous grit by the name of Pat Garrett who was being petitioned to run for Kimbrell's position by powerful citizens, among them Chisum and Dolan. Billy had known Pat as an acquaintance out of Sumner. They'd gamble together, referring to each other as Big Casino and Little Casino respectively, as Garrett stood well over six feet and Billy well under that. Billy dismissed Garrett as a man out to make a name for himself, but we all knew, even Billy, that Garrett knew exactly what Billy looked like and knew well his haunts. If Garrett was sworn in, we'd be in for a whole new, far more serious game, and because things were serious enough as it was, it should have been plain as to just how much worse things would become. From this point forward, we'd need to be much more careful of our whereabouts and in whom we trusted.

In Patricio, I found the Painted Ladies setting up their makeshift tents on the fringes of town, and so I spent my time carousing with them. Billy, of course, continued to avoid me, but this did not stop him from sending his cohorts to check up on me whilst I was in the company of the whores he called "troublemaking trash", as if those seemingly ladylike, urbane whores he went with were anything but. Men amazed me with their selective blindness. Wasn't it one of those "genteel" whores of his who caused this mess between us and nearly laid me so low?

The Ladies attempted to bring me aboard, saying I could turn a pretty penny, being the Kid's girl and all that. They tried convincing me by assuring that I'd fetch a handsome sum. What man, after all, they'd say, would pass up the chance to lay with the infamous Kid's lady? I politely declined, but this did nothing to stop men from propositioning me nonetheless when I spent time in their presence or loitered in the tents they occupied, playing cards or having interesting conversations. My guns made me easy enough to spot—everybody knew who I was by those guns as they were eminently renowned. And as I hung around the tents cavorting with my famously slutty consorts, the men who would frequent the girls (some of whom who were considered favorites to the men in each town) would beg to lay with me when they learned of my identity. They were so desperate to boast of having "Billy's niña pequeña," his chica favorita, that the more I said "no" the more they would negotiate, raising their offers. I had one man offer twenty dollars to be with me, and another pledged fifty. I was disgusted yet flattered all the same.

Jimmy made it a point to spend most of his time with me, lending his angelic advices in my ear, advices which were really those of Billy, as he instructed Jimmy to watch me and report back what he knew. The truth was, when possible, Billy never took his eyes from me, and when it wasn't possible to watch me himself, he had his eyes and ears spread out among the men to ensure that I was okay. I was constantly under surveillance.

I assured Jimmy that I would not falter and succumb to the livelihood of the Painted Ladies, an assurance I'm sure he happily reported to Billy Bonney, knowing full well that anything less than good news where I was concerned might cause Billy's temper to flare and take on a "shoot the messenger" quality.

I had no doubt that Jimmy reported back to Billy the generous sums of money I was offered to lay with these strange men. My presence alone ensured that the Ladies still did a smart turnover despite the fact that I laid down with no one—my mere existence with them bringing on excitement. The Ladies became ever more insistent that I stay on with them and help make them a fortune, promising that I could keep the lion's share of my haul if I decided to go to work. *Ha!* I thought. *Damn right!* If I was gonna sleep with any strange, disgusting men, I was gonna keep *all* a'my money!

Billy could not resist, unable to ignore me whenever I kept such low company, and he would interfere with my fun and business among my friends by sending one of the others to come fetch me away for some invented meeting or another. It was clear that he was jealous of the attention strange men lavished upon me, though, too, he was also extremely upset, and I admit that his jealousy caused such a pleasant stirring within me. Despite our rift and the position he took to stay clear of me, I sometimes had to catch myself in daring to beg him to lie down with me. I would bet everything I had invested in that bank in White Oakes that if I had asked him to, the sheer knowledge of men offering to pay for my services and the resentment he felt over it would have forced him to take me to bed.

From time to time I'd catch Billy shooting disapproving glances at me while I spent my time in the company of the Ladies, but I paid no mind. If he planned to shut me out then he'd have to get used to my doing as I damn well pleased whether it upset him or not. He attempted to fool me by using Jimmy as a means to relay his council to me, but the fact was I knew Billy so well that I knew when he was speaking to me through someone else's mouth. It was proof positive that Billy's feelings for me had not wavered. This was exceptionally evident by his need to protect me despite his cool distance. While I admit that this pleased me greatly, his concerns would have made a greater impact had he allowed our relationship to go on as it had been before the incident with Adriana. As it were, I would not allow him to rule me from afar as I once did—not under such selfish circumstances. I would not allow him to freeze me out, yet continue to direct me despite my knowing that he only did so because of his love for me. I would be my own mistress, giving myself ample opportunities to show him just how serious I was when it came to my liberation with or without him.

The more Billy ignored me, the more time I spent with the Ladies and Jimmy. Billy was remarkably perturbed over my choice of friends and he made it all too apparent. But still, his resolve would not break. Whenever I was with the girls and he would pass by he would aim such a look of disdain at me that it would nearly knock me off my feet. His look would render in me a residual need to give in and please him by running to him and pleading for his forgiveness, but I shook this off and reminded myself that it was I who was winning out. I was getting to him and I would not fail. Other than using Jimmy as his delegate, who was of the same mindset as he, agreeing that those girls were a bad influence, Billy continued to evade me unless it was absolutely necessary he be near me.

On one occasion we sat outside our usual haunt in Patricio, The Old Ruidoso, while the men played a friendly game of cards.

Little Billy Wilson lamented that a girl he had gone around with confided to him that she was pregnant with his child. Wilson declared that this could not be as he hadn't been with that girl in months.

"She's a real sportin' kind of gal, that one," Dave said.

Wilson snorted in agreement.

The day had grown dim and was quickly slipping into night. As they discussed Wilson's dilemma, Jimmy, who sat out, rested Indian-style on the boards and I leaned back against the wall of the building, arms crossed, listening to the boys grapple with Little Billy's predicament.

"It ain't possible," Wilson complained. "I ain't been with that girl since. Well since I don't know when."

"Since the last time we was in Patricio," Henry said, laughing.

Billy had the deck and sat playing with them, cascading and shuffling them overhanded. He riffled them and then tapped them against the wooden table.

"Well," he spoke up. "I know a little something about women."

"Yeah? That a fact, Bonney? Go on then," Tom Pickett said sarcastically.

"First thing, if hanging around Lucy's taught me a thing or two, it's near impossible for them to get knocked up because they're constantly bleeding a river full."

They all laughed at Billy's joke and I piercingly squealed in embarrassment.

"Oh, *Billy*!" I shrieked. My hands made into tight fists. "How could you *say* that?"

Billy dropped his head to the table in stupidity and breathed a heavy sigh as I took off running to our room, nearly knocking Jimmy over as I passed him. When I reached the door I heard Pickett say, "Way to go, Bonney" before opening and slamming the door shut and locking it. Mortified, I ran to the bed and landed face down on it and began to bawl my eyes out.

∞∞∞∞∞∞∞∞∞∞

Tom looked disparagingly at Billy and shook his head. "Jesus Billy..."

Feeling guilty but feigning indifference, Billy replied, "Aw, well...I forgot she was there. She'll get over it."

"Maybe it's yours, Bill," Henry teased.

"Hell no, it ain't!" Billy swore. "I ain't never laid with that girl. Who knows what ailments she carries about. She probably got the French Pox for all the devil knows. I think it's you, Henry, who should worry about all that."

"You been with her?" Wilson asked Henry, visibly upset.

"What's the difference?" Henry asked. "You don't give a Red Indian cent about her, and she's soiled property anyway. You as much as said so yourself."

"I don't know why she's picking on me so much. Why's she want me to be the daddy?"

"Well," chimed Joe Bowers. "I'm afraid when a lady says a certain man's the father, then he ain't got no choice but to believe her."

"Naw, that ain't true," explained Billy. "I know enough to know that women can trick a man by accusing him of such."

"Nobody can argue that a woman ought to know who the daddy is," replied Joe.

"Ain't no way. They can be just as confused as they make us out to be," said Billy. "Y'all know they lay around plenty. They ain't all a scented lily. Hell, they'll use it to their advantage for the same reason you just said, Joe, because she'll expect a man to believe her on the principle that it's suspected a woman knows who the father of her child is."

"That a fact?"

"Yep, that's a fact." Billy shook his head. "If a gal wants a man, she'll trap him by pointing her expectant little finger at him."

"You learn that from Lucy also?" Joe winked, wisecracking.

"And if I did?"

"Well hell...maybe your little Lucy used her tricks on you then, Billy," Dave said.

Billy squinted at him, eyes threatening.

"Watch it, Dave. Lucy ain't like that. That little girl says it's mine there ain't no question about it. Now shut your goddamned trap before I shut it for you forever."

Billy's face reddened with anger, his eyes glancing fleetingly around the table. "Are we gonna play cards or what?" he asked, annoyed and attempting to change the subject before he had to add another killing under his belt.

"Well, somebody's high-strung, ain't they?" Dave said in reference to Billy's remark.

Pushed by Dave, and with his nerves still raw and stinging over the loss of his and Lucy's child, Billy summoned all he had not to draw on Dave and drill him through the head. He threw down his cards. "I don't wanna play with you guys no more."

Billy stood up to go but the men pleaded for him to sit back down.

"Now look what you did, Wilson, bringing up that whore," Henry accused.

"I ain't done nothin'. It was Dave. Jesus Christ, can't we just sit and play a decent, friendly game of cards like men? And you, Henry, watch where you're stickin' your little pecker next time."

"Fuck you, Wilson. I don't care about your whore and I don't want to play with you neither. I'm out, too."

Jimmy sat there, confused by the absurdity of the fracas before him. Billy pushed past him as Lucy had done, nearly knocking him over as if he weren't even there. Jimmy remained quiet, looking wide-eyed at the display of hardened men behaving so much like females.

"You're all just a bunch'a goddamned women at heart," said Joe, before throwing his cards down on the table as well.

As the men sat henpecking one another, Billy went to the room and, expecting the door to opened easily, pressed the lever and kept walking, banging head first into the door as he found it was locked.

"Open this door, Lu!" he yelled through the wood.

"No!" was the muffled reply.

Billy could hear the men arguing amongst one another and he rolled his eyes at being stuck in the midst of all of this.

"Lucy! Open the goddamned door and let me in!" he shouted.

He heard the sound of Lucy's feet hit the floor as she leap from the bed and crossed to the door to unlock it. He recognized those little angry stamps of hers and had to smile. Letting Billy in, she went back to the bed and fell down upon it.

oooooooooooooooo

Still lying on my stomach I demanded to know, "How could you say such a thing?"

"I'm sorry. It was meant as a joke, as unkind as it was. I didn't mean anything by it."

"Well, whether you meant anything or not, you've made me embarrassed."

"I know it."

"Don't use my personal mysteries as fodder to make your men laugh," I spat.

Billy leaned back on the bed next to me and began petting my back. It was the nicest he'd been to me in a long time, and the pleasantness almost made me want to forgive him.

"I'm sorry sweetheart. I didn't mean to make a joke out a'you."

I sniffled in response.

"Niña, believe me. I'm sorry."

"It ain't easy, being a woman among men, you know." I wiped at my nose.

Billy kept rubbing my back to try and calm me.

"I don't know why I was so disrespectful," he confessed. "If it makes you feel any better, all them culos are proddy and at each other's throats."

"Why should that make me feel better? The damage to me has been done, hasn't it?"

Billy sighed in defeat.

"Why don't you and I turn in and forget all about it. You know them boys don't think a penny's less of you."

Having him stay with me filled me with elation. I knew that if he stayed, if I laid here with him tonight, he'd wrap his arms around me like he used to and be so very loving, but I said "no" wanting to rebuff him. I refused to make things easy for him after all he'd done, and for his horrible mistakes.

Billy continued to rub my back, unconvinced by my rejection. The more he touched me, the more I wanted him to stay. He stared at me lying there, tears falling from my eyes for what he'd done. By my distraught reaction, I'd wager a pound of nickels he knew better than to think I was only angry over this one indiscretion. In fact, I'd bet he knew I was angry at the way he'd been acting incorrectly toward me.

He lifted my shirt and lightly drove his fingertips across my skin on the small of my back playfully, even as he listened to me sniffle. Usually, I gave in to him when he did things like this, and even now I trembled under his touch, turning my face into the covers on the bed in an attempt to fight him. He knew how to touch me right. I'll just bet he meant to keep up his little charade of pretending to want nothing more to do with me, but for tonight, right now, he wanted his girl. But I wouldn't let him play me like some goddamned fiddle!

He told me once that intimacy with me was different from anybody else. Other girls made love to him like it were a game. They'd let him have them and believe that they could please him, could possess him by making him choose them and want to come back. They were all the same, he said. They knew nothing of him, who he truly was. What they wanted was the Kid. But, he told me, he knew I loved him sincerely, that I loved that poor boy from the streets and knew him by no other name but William. I made love to him because I needed him, and he needed that from me.

He told me when he first saw me he was love-sick, but understood he was born with the misfortune of never being able to have a girl like me, that he would have to love me from afar. And he knew then, without knowing me as well as he would eventually come to, that no matter who he courted, or married, they wouldn't compare to the girl that was Elucia Howard because she would never leave his mind.

When John had provided him the good fortune of assigning him as my instructor, and I surprised him with my enthusiastic keenness to know and understand him, he was a man spoken for, regardless of whether or not I could be his. In his mind he knew without a doubt that his heart would always belong to me. And that afternoon back in Lincoln, a day that seemed so long ago now, when I let him into my bed to make love to me, he knew for sure he was an absolute goner. He said it was ridiculous to believe that he could ever truly not want me, and he knew that I damn well knew this no matter what his actions toward or against me might be.

Perhaps now it might be understood why I could tolerate so much from a man like that.

He now placed both hands on either side of my waist, gently and salaciously squeezing me there. I didn't make an effort to stop him. I remained still in his hands, but though I didn't attempt to get free he heard me begin to weep. Gently, he rolled me over onto my back and looked into my dewy eyes.

"Billy, I know what it is you want, and I don't want it. Don't make me do it."

I was pleading with him to let me go because I would not be able to resist him if he continued on, and I knew he must know this.

"I want to respect that because I know I don't deserve you—not tonight."

But he climbed on top of me anyway and straddled my waist, and as he did so I turned my face away from him, and I know he watched as my tears fell more fervently. Like a child, I rubbed at my eyes, but despite my contrary reaction to him, I knew he could tell by the warmth of my skin and the bumps of my flesh, and the slow rise and fall of my belly, my breathing becoming shallow, that I was imparting the certainty of my desire for him. I reached a curled fist up to my lips and placed the knuckle of my thumb between my teeth, trying to fight the enjoyment of his hands on my body.

"Billy...if you ever loved me," I beseeched, "you'll let me alone."

Saying not a word, he slid his hands under my shirt and along my stomach. He began to unbutton my shirt, leaning down to kiss my exposed belly.

Very quietly I again begged him, "*No*. Don't." My protest tearful, I plead, "Don't make me do this."

I kept my face turned away from him, but he leaned down to my ear and softly asked, "Why should I quit this? You and I both know you want this as badly as I do."

"But tomorrow things will be—"

"Forget about tomorrow, this is about right now. I am not the Kid. I am William Bonney, and you're Lucy, just like we were all that time ago when I would come to your bed. Just for tonight, the love we have for each other is innocent again."

I loved him for saying that. But to lay here with him tonight would only make it hurt much worse for me tomorrow. Perhaps *he* could make love to me and then return to that cool manner of his, but *I* would spend tomorrow devastated and lonelier than ever for him. I had learned to accept his mistreatment of me during this past near month, to accept his cruel withdrawing of the intimacy that I so badly needed. I had learned to live without the hope of it. And though I wanted desperately to feel him again in the way I was meant to, I couldn't do that to myself—it would be the cruelest punishment of all as it would be a punishment that I would foolishly place upon myself. With tremendous difficulty I forced myself to be just like him—mean. Mean, so I could make it easy to push *him* away. I made it even easier by forcing myself to think back to that day when I caught him soiling our bed with that whore, a poor practice in which there was an unspoken, understood rule that such behavior would be inexcusable and not tolerated.

I bolted up and did my best to force my eyes to purposefully meet his, but failed miserably in holding them steady.

Hurriedly, I wiped the mist from my eyes.

"I don't believe I want to share this bed like so much of the trash you've been keeping with lately."

Now it was Billy who sat up like a shot, his expression first displaying surprise, and then snapping back into that meanness he'd made an art of.

"You didn't mind lying next to me like so much trash before."

Oh, he wasn't going to let me rebuff and hurt *him*, was he? No sir. I had made it plain that it was war, and he was going to show me that he was up for the game.

I turned to face him, mad as a hornet. "I ought to punch you right in the mouth for that. That's twice tonight you've provoked me."

"I'd like to see you try it."

I turned away from him.

"And just where, then, do you think you're gonna go?" he asked.

"Wherever it is that I want. Wherever you won't be!"

Feigning apathy he said, "Fine. You go on ahead and do as you please for all I care."

"And I intend to, too."

"That so?"

"I know what you're trying to pull, Billy. You're trying to make me believe that I don't know you so much anymore. Bringing that girl into our bed was not only meant to horrify and offend me, but a mean trick to fool me into believing that you're no longer the same Billy, because the Billy I know would never have been so cruel as that. Well, Billy Bonney, I can play the game as well as you. Perhaps you'll find you know me not at all as well."

"Okay then, stranger. So where's it you intend to bed down, then?"

"I think I'll go and stay with Jimmy. He cares enough for me."

I got up off the bed and made for the door, but Billy was quick and behind me before I took two steps. He grabbed me hard by the arm and held me.

"Like hell you will!" he barked.

"Get your hands off me, you hoedown havin' hayseed!"

"Oh, really now?"

"What the hell is it you care for who I lay with?"

He stood silent, his eyes piercing me with the anger his tongue could not express.

"Well fine, then," I smiled. "If Jimmy doesn't suit your fancy, perhaps I'll go off and find the Ladies and stay with one of the men who've propositioned me—"

He raised his hand to me, an action he'd never taken before. We stood, respectively shocked by his reaction, when he shook me and said, "Like some goddamned whore? I thought you just said you hadn't the intention of acting like trash!"

"It's just like you said so many times to me before, Billy. Without you, I'll have to make my way on my back. Well, it seems you've abandoned me and so then I have no choice."

"Yeah? Well I'm sure it's lucky for you then that you'll turn a pretty penny for sure because of *me*. You think I don't know what they've been selling you? Trying to get you into bed by dangling dollar signs before your eyes, telling how much they're willing to pay because of who you are—because you're with *me*? They'll make you a whore, and any money you make you can thank me for!"

"Well, I thank you, then...for the money. As for the stigma of whore, it's unlikely they'll have anything to do with it as you've made me one already. Are you not the first to recognize that all the bad things I am now are because of you?"

He let go of my arm and half-heartedly raised his hand again as that primeval part of him reemerged, but I stood firm. He dropped his hand, but his face was pure fury. He was practically frothing at the mouth.

"And those girls," I declared. "They've been better friends to me than you have as of late, you...you damned old Owl Hoot! And I ain't with you, if you recall. You made that decision for us both. Now let me be so I can be on my way!"

He stepped back and surveyed me. His face softened slowly as he considered me. I had stung him. Suddenly, he was *my* Billy again, and it took all I had not to go to him and throw my arms around him and let him take me to bed after all and let us forget this.

"I never made you a whore, Lucy. I don't love whores. "

Expecting me to walk out the door now, he turned and began rubbing at the back of his neck like he often did when upset. With his back to me I ran to him and threw my arms around him before quickly letting go and leaving through the door.

Hardly anyone was on speaking terms the next morning at breakfast. Henry and "Little Billy" Wilson frowned at one another, Joe Bowers smoked his rolled tobacco and kept to himself, Jimmy sat by me but stared wide-eyed out into space, Big Jim was perfectly relaxed but kept his thoughts to himself, and Dave was his usual, contemptible self, hollering out the window of The Keeper's Inn at ladies passing by like some sort of barn animal. Minxie, Tom Pickett, and Jose sat aside talking between themselves, and Tom sat by Billy like so much the fool he was, waiting for whatever it was Billy asked him to do. Billy and I avoided glancing at one another completely, both of us resigned at present to hold the peace after leaving the previous night on a note of concession.

Harper Dealy walked in with Hattie and Maya, the latter of which Billy detested for that opium den incident. He frowned at their presence and scowled when they waved to me. I waved back and caught him look to me as I done so. I excused myself and walked over to them, deciding to sit down with them and enjoy a little female company for once. I refused to look back at the boys, but I could feel the heat where Billy's eyes burned into the back of my skull as he looked on disapprovingly, but I would be lying if I didn't admit that I took pleasure in disgusting him so.

After breakfast, with the chill in the air biting at me, I went back to our room and dressed in a warm pull-over that Billy had bought for me to wear during the cooler months. I then took a walk to the Kavanaghs as their cat Mittens had a rather large litter and I wanted to sit and admire her kittens and pick out one for myself as I was told I could do. The Kavanaghs offered to keep it with them and care for it when I was gone.

I sat out in the back yard holding the kitten I had chosen, a fluffy white thing with a black nose and black paws. I sat peacefully, minding my own business and playing with the small kitten when the shadow of a figure crossed over me and caused me to look up. My belly seemed to fall out from under me as I observed who it was the shadow belonged to: none other than Finnegan Flynn himself.

"Well, well. What you doing sitting out here without your man to protect your scrawny little ass? He know you're out here?"

I didn't say anything. I only continued to look up at him.

"What's the matter?" he asked. "Cat got your tongue?"

He laughed at his own ridiculous joke and it was then that I noticed he was not alone, but with Ru and Engle.

I tried to remain composed though on the inside my nerves were buzzing. I held onto the kitten, afraid to put it down and let it go for fear that my hands would be free to shake.

"What's it you got there? That a cat?" Finny asked.

Still I said nothing.

"Damn girl, ain't you got manners? When somebody asks you a question, you answer."

I put my head down and was aware of how very alone I was back in the yard with these three loathsome men.

"I ain't forgotten about what you done in that court a'law. Fact is, I still owe you for that. Lucky for you, what I got to give you won't be so bad, seeing as how I got off scot-free. It ain't wise lying like that to the law, you fuckin' slut."

That got me.

"I didn't lie about nothing, Finn, and you know it! Why don't you go on and git, leave me be. You got away with it, so why don't you let me alone?"

"I intend to, sister, 'cept I want to see what you got there in your hands."

Instinctively, I pulled the tiny kitten closer, but he reached down and forcibly grabbed her from my arms. I wanted to hold on, but he yanked so hard I was afraid it'd hurt her if I didn't give in and let go. Before I knew it, he'd grabbed the poor thing by its neck, its tiny mews protesting in pain, before slamming it powerfully into the ground. I heard bones snap and the dear little thing lie limp upon the ground.

"Well then, I guess it ain't a good day to be a kitty, now is it, darlin'?"

As he and his boys walked away, laughing, he mindlessly kicked at it. I reached out for the small, lifeless animal, lifting its limp little body and holding it close to mine. I began to cry for it. Finny was so cold-blooded and cruel.

As I sat there I cried so hard that it pained my insides. Jimmy had come by and found me, and when he saw my mood, he ran and sat down in the dirt by me and took me in his arms. I still held the dead kitten even as Jimmy held me. He asked me what happened and I told him.

"Why is he so mean, Jimmy? How could a person be so *mean*?" I sobbed.

Jimmy, who continued to hold me tightly in his arms and rock me back and forth in an effort to sooth me replied, "Who knows. Maybe because his momma was a whore and his daddy beat them both. His daddy killed his momma in front of Finn. I suspect that there's little left in this world that Finn's got any feelings for, now."

After hearing Jimmy relate this drama to me I was still unable to summon any compassion for such a horrible creature that was Finn. All the sympathy in the world would not change Finn from the evil incarnate that he was.

"Lucy, we need to let Billy know what Finn did, that he came by here and—"

"No!" I ordered. "Billy doesn't need to know about this."

"Lucy, if we don't tell Billy that Finn came and threatened you, and he finds out on his own, we're cooked. At least I am."

"No, Jimmy. If Billy finds out he'll kill him, don't you understand that? As horrible as it is, Finny did nothing more than murder a cat—it isn't worth the risk of Billy blowing Finn's brains out and getting himself in deeper with the law than he already is. Promise me you'll keep this just between us."

Jimmy stared at me for a few moments before hesitantly nodding his head in agreement to calm me.

"Okay, Lu, I won't tell. But I promise you, if he so much as comes near you again, by even one hundred feet, I'll run and tell Billy. God help us if he finds out about this."

I turned my head, nuzzling my face into Jimmy's shoulder as he still held on to me while I cried. The memory of what Finny did to my kitten and the feel of its wilted body, so fragile in my arms, felt so emotionally excruciating. Yes...I've seen bad men die, and I've seen my friends shot down, but such a small little thing never did anything to anybody. I wished I had not seen what he had done. I wished I had not come by at the wrong moment to admire such helpless, loving little animals.

My head still against Jimmy's shoulder I said, "Billy sent you to come find me and see what I was up to, didn't he?"

Jimmy waited a beat and said, "Well, he asked the group of us where you were, if we might have seen you. I told him I'd come look, figuring I was the best one for the job, if you agree. I'm sure glad I did, though. Seems to me you oughta not be so alone anyway."

I didn't say anything. I just lay there against him.

"Lucy," Jimmy softly spoke. "why don't we go on ahead and bury your little kitten? We can give her a proper burial if you want."

His consideration and the seriousness of his tone made me chuckle, the sound of my laughter muffled against Jimmy's shoulder.

"Okay, Jimmy. Just promise me again that you'll keep your promise and say nothing."

"I promise. I ain't gonna break your heart any more than it's already been today—not unless I have to."

We buried the kitten and Jimmy stayed with me the rest of the day. I did not make it a point to tempt Billy's ire by running around with the Ladies or doing anything that might catch his discontentment. Instead, I just stayed right by Jimmy's side.

20

December, 1879

When we had ridden into Patricio it was clear that my horse was done for and that I needed a new one. Looking for something to do, Jimmy and I went ahead and visited with the pinhooker by the livery and, upon settling on one that I liked, I still needed to get Billy's endorsement and have him validate the sale for me since he was the one with money. He knew I needed a new horse and so, as it was a necessity, Jimmy and I went to him so I could tell him that I had picked one out.

All three of us walked back to the pinhooker and I showed Billy the horse that I liked. The pinhooker wanted sixty dollars, and Billy looked the horse over, studying its gait and finding it satisfactory, along with observing its temperament and determining that he had a gentle enough disposition.

Billy insisted that he view the horse saddled, and he was obliged. Billy sat atop the animal and went a few rounds with him, pleased with the results. He asked the pinhooker if the horse was trained, stating that it seemed so, to which the pinhooker replied that the horse was indeed competent.

Billy asked the age of the horse and was told that it was three years old. It was a gelding, and Billy took a look at the teeth and found that the horse was likely a bit older after finding that it had canine points. This did not displease Billy, as in many cases a pinhooker was likely to guess a thing like a horse's age wrong, and to Billy, the age and other attributes of the horse seemed square enough.

"Tell you what...he seems a mighty fine horse to me," Billy said. "but I'm gonna give you thirty dollars and this little girl's old horse. She's broke, but she'll fetch you something."

The pinhooker looked Billy over, nervous.

"Well, sir, that there horse is sixty dollars, see—"

"It's thirty, plus a trade."

The pinhooker rubbed his hands along his pants, knowing full well who Billy was and afraid to press the matter.

"All right, mister," the pinhooker conceded. "I'll take the thirty and your trade."

The pinhooker was clearly ruffled, but just the same, it was clear he'd rather not argue.

Billy also got that pinhooker to promise that he'd throw in a new pair of shoes. The pinhooker had a few other horses to shoe and take stock of first, so Billy offered him ten dollars as a deposit, telling the pinhooker to hold the horse for twenty-four hours and to make sure it would be good and ready by the time we came back for it. Unhappy but anxious, the pinhooker accepted the ten spot with his head down.

"So then," I asked. "you like the horse? I can have it?"

"Yes, you surely may. I think it seems a fine enough horse."

The next day Billy and I went together to make good on the sale of the horse. It truly was sweet and already I had made an attachment to him.

"I want to call him Topper," I declared.

"Topper?" he asked curiously.

"Yes, Topper. It was the name of the poet John Keats' beloved's favorite cat. At least that's what I've heard. I'll bet you didn't know that!"

"You certainly got me there. No, I did not know no such thing. Every day I learn something new by you, don't I?"

He looked at me and smiled genuinely, and suddenly I was remembering the way we used to talk all that time ago when I was affianced to John. He seemed just like he did then, sweetly indulging me whenever I offered up a piece of trivia or bit of information that was of no particular consequence to him other than to please me by showing interest.

"Okay, Topper it is then," he agreed.

We went to the livery to put my new horse up and to take my old mare back to the pinhooker. After we had completed our arrangement with the man, Billy asked if I was hungry and I replied that I was, and so we went to The Keeper's Inn for some supper. Because it was just the two of us we ate in what amounted to near silence, yet it was pleasant nonetheless as the silence between us was comfortable enough, if regrettable. I took this time to thank him again for my new horse and again he smiled at me in that way he used to, telling me that it was no trouble and reminding me again that whatever I needed he would get.

As we sat together, our tongues taciturn, the reticence only served to prove with absolute clarity that we held an ardent affection for one another despite the lack of speech—that words spoken between us were unnecessary to keep us undoubtedly connected. *How funny.* I thought. Through no words having been spoken between us, the profundity of our feelings for one another seemed all the more overt. Despite the way things were between us, we still seemed to enjoy one another's company when we weren't looking.

"D'you remember that day when John let me take you out in the buggy? You wanted to go for a ride and he was busy, so he asked me if I wouldn't mind?"

I looked at him, surprised to hear him speak.

"Yes, of course I do. That was a fine day."

I smiled thinking back on that day. We had ridden along the outskirts of town. I wanted to get out of the house because I needed the fresh air. Billy and I had become fairly acquainted by then, and being with him, sitting so close in that buggy, made my heart beat so fast. I hadn't known him well enough then, but his body so close to mine did something so pleasant to me that I couldn't keep from smiling, but I was so nervous that I could hardly look at him.

"What made you think on that just now?" I asked.

He shook his head in contemplation and chuckled softly.

"You were just so quiet, like you are now. It feels a little like it did then. Doesn't it?"

I thought about it.

"Yeah. I suppose so." I smiled at him.

We had pulled the buggy along the side of a fairly unused trail where tall grass grew, Billy playfully fibbing me that a family of kangaroos lived there. Now, I knew this would be impossible, but who was I to tell him he was mistaken? Maybe there *was* a family of kangaroos there, stranger things have happened. He told me I had to watch long enough, assuring me it was just the sort of thing I should enjoy.

"It's the reason this trail is hardly used anymore," he asserted.

I nodded at him seriously, wanting to believe it were true.

So we sat there together in silence, watching for imaginary kangaroos, nothing but an excuse for him to lay his arm around me across the back of that buggy in an intimate gesture.

"I never did see a kangaroo," I chided.

He laughed. "You weren't supposed to."

We both laughed at this as I tried to finish my dinner, unable to do so until I settled down.

That evening a dance was held, and I sat off and alone, Billy never once looking in my direction. The moment we shared earlier must have been too close for comfort, I realized. I knew he found himself falling right back into the two of us, so he was intent on correcting that mistake now. Billy never attended a baile without taking me around more than a few times, much to the chagrin of the other girls. But tonight, he was all theirs.

I was asked to dance a few times, but I declined. I was too sad to want to participate, and seeing as how Billy was back to making efforts to avoid me, I went back to the room in which Jimmy slept to lay down. I thought about the wonderful afternoon I had shared with Billy and was sorry he felt things had to be so awful between us.

Lying there a while, I had finally fallen asleep, something I prayed to do as of late to take me out of such depressing circumstances, but I had a terrible dream:

Billy was way up high. I imagine it was a scaffold he stood upon, but everything other than Billy was out of focus. It was just me, staring up at him, with a rope around his neck. He looked down at me, but there didn't seem any recognition on his face, no appreciation of who I was. I was crying for him, terrified. I could sense the fear in anticipation of his plummeting, attached to that rope by his neck. But still, he just stood there, idle, seeming to not have a care in the world. I fidgeted where I stood looking at him, fretting over the fact that I must do something, but what? My feet were rooted there to the ground, my eyes stuck in ascension as I watched and waited.

Finally, I heard the snap of a trap door and knew nothing more afterwards as I was woken by the sound of my own screaming, my arms flailing. My left arm hit the glass kerosene lamp on the table next to the bed. It fell over and broke against the table, lighting my arm up, and I squealed in shock. Luckily, by this time, Jimmy had come to bed and was dozing in a chair, already woken by the sounds I made in my sleep as I watched Billy prepare to drop.

He moved quickly and grabbed for a woolen blanket that lie at the bottom of the bed, using it to put me and the rest of the flames out. I didn't realize the stinging singe at first. I was only upset by the shock of it all.

"Lucy, Jesus!"

With the light extinguished, Jimmy couldn't see and so he felt around for matches, finding a box in his shirt pocket. He struck one and peered at what I'd done to myself. The sleeve on my forearm was burnt away, and the skin there was red and angry.

"I'm going for the doctor, you stay put, do you hear me?"

I nodded, still in shock and confused.

ᴏᴏᴏᴏᴏᴏᴏᴏᴏᴏᴏᴏᴏ

On his way out, Jimmy bumped into Henry Brown.

"Get Billy!" he commanded.

"What is it?" Henry wanted to know.

"Just get him. Tell him it's Lucy, she's hurt..."

Jimmy moved to go by but Henry grabbed him by the arm.

"What do you mean she's hurt?

"Goddammit, she's *hurt*! She burnt herself, tell Billy—he'll want to know!"

"Is she gonna be all right?" Henry inquired.

Irritated by being caught up with these senseless questions, Jimmy hastily replied, "Yeah, she'll be fine, but all the same...I gotta go for the doctor, now let me alone and get Billy!"

Henry did as Jimmy instructed, tracking Billy down in his room. Knocking on the door he heard muffled sounds and a *Who is it?* It was Billy's voice.

"It's Henry, Billy! Open up, it's important!"

After a few seconds, Henry heard footsteps grow louder as they approached the other side of the door. Finally, it opened, revealing Billy there, half dressed. He was wearing his pants, but his shirt was off. Henry took note of someone else in the room with him, a girl he'd been enamored with all evening.

"What the hell is it, Henry?" Billy demanded, irritated.

"It's Lucy, she's hurt."

Henry turned to run but Billy caught him by the arm and pulled him back.

"What do you mean she's hurt?"

"She got burnt's what I heard."

Henry could see the concern on Billy's face, and so to calm him he relayed what Jimmy had said. "She'll be all right, it's just her arm. But Jimmy's going for the doctor."

With that, Billy let Henry go back off into the night and just stood there in thought. Lucy was hurt, but she'd be all right, he'd said. Billy wanted to go to her, knew that she'd want him, too, but he stopped himself. He would send her a message by not going, reminding her that things were done. Spending such a pleasant afternoon with her had been a mistake and he'd have to correct the step by going backwards.

But his darling girl was hurt, whether she'd be all right or not. Wasn't that a decent enough exception? He was torn, but still shut the door and went back inside. He sat on the bed, lost in thought over what was happening, thinking more about what he should do.

The girl he was with, a girl by the name of Ellie, crept up behind him on the bed and put her arms around him.

"Lucy's been hurt?" she asked.

Billy nodded.

"Don't you want to see to her?"

Billy sat very still, staring out into space.

Ellie moved around to his side.

"Billy...I know how much you care for her. Everybody does. Go to her, see for yourself that she's okay. It's the only thing to do—"

"I know it," he snapped.

Ellie, taken aback, recoiled from him, not out of fear, but uneasiness. She didn't want to press him on a position that obviously sat very delicate with him.

He turned a bit and reached his arm out to her, rubbing hers to comfort her.

"Perdón, lo siento...I'm sorry. I didn't mean to seem angry with you.

Ellie leaned forward again and placed her hand on his shoulder.

"It's okay, dear heart, I know you're upset. I remember what you've confided in me. I just think that in this instant you should check on her. I think it's important." Then she smiled. "You can come back to me when you're satisfied."

Billy shook his head. "No, I won't go. Better if I don't. If I don't go it'll be the last straw— she'll never forgive me, and that's how it should be."

"Why, Billy?"

"Because...if she never forgives me, I can't wager a way back into her good graces when I falter and can't help myself but to give in. She makes me want to do that, and I have to make it so that can never happen. She's better off being distant."

"Well...that's quite a thing to say about someone who you care so much about."

Billy scoffed at that. "Care for her? I love her! It's because I love her so much that I know she's better off, and she knows it, too, she just refuses to accept it and go away."

"Billy," Ellie leaned intimately close and spoke into his ear. "You'd better be sure you're ready to deal with the regret of your actions."

"Christ, don't you get it? That's exactly what I'm telling you. I already regret it, but it won't matter because my not going to her over this will be it for her. If I beg her for forgiveness, there's no danger of getting it. She'll realize there's nothing here for her. I can't get in the way of that if I fix it so she refuses me forever."

He turned to look Ellie in the face. "If you were Lucy, so it was you in her shoes, would you forgive me for disregarding your wellbeing? Would you forgive me if I made it so you should think I didn't care if you was okay?"

Ellie answered honestly, "No. No I would not."

ooooooooooooooo

He didn't come! Billy didn't come! Henry and Jimmy were there, and Tom, showing their concern. Minxie came to check on me when the news got to him, as did Big Jim. But the one who should have been the first through the door was nowhere to be found.

The doctor layered cotton gauze covered with linseed oil over my arm. The burn wasn't too bad, he said, but it felt awful enough to me. My arm felt hot and uncomfortable, and stung me over and over again. The treated gauze relieved my pain somewhat, but I was left with a small amount of laudanum to help me sleep.

I looked at the bottle knowing that Billy wouldn't approve, but Billy wasn't here, and hang him if it mattered to him at all. Jimmy gave me a small dose and lay down with me to help comfort me as I fell asleep.

We had been given new bedding to replace the sheets and blanket that had been scorched, and the side table that held the lamp was removed entirely, but the smell of burnt wood and such still lingered about. I floated to sleep nonetheless, with thoughts of Billy far and away.

One may think I was angry with Billy. I would be lying if I said I wasn't upset. But I understood, and I hate to admit that as a fact. I felt he should have come for such a thing, but he wanted to make his point very clear, and what better way to do so than to ignore me at a time of such an accident as mine? I was stunned that he could stay away, but if I'm fair, I'd just bet it wasn't easy for him.

No matter, I was finished. The Ladies had taken off north, and I asked Jimmy if he would leave with me and follow after them. He expressed censure, but said he would, and we both prepared our things to leave immediately. He was to tell no one of our planned departure, and he was only too happy to keep the secret.

21

December, 1879

A few of the men stood along the boardwalk outside of The Keeper's Inn and had spied Lucy walking alone along the other side of the street. She was wearing her winter coat, hugging it close to herself as the day was bitter and the wind unsettling.

Billy watched intently as she made her way down to the Sundry store and entered, even as Jimmy watched him with a superior intensity.

Spitefully, Jimmy asked, "Ain't you even gonna ask how she's doing?"

Billy turned to look at him, the keenness of his eyes unchanging as they shifted from Lucy's direction to his.

"Well?" Jimmy demanded.

Tom stepped in and put his hand to Jimmy's chest, pushing him back lightly, but Jimmy, taking offense, dug his heels in and pushed back at Tom.

"You can't talk to him in that a'way," Tom insisted.

"You ain't his keeper, Tom, and I can talk to him any way I damn well please!" Then, looking at Billy, he said, "You're a goddamned son of a bitch, ain't'cha?"

Tom stepped to Jimmy again, but Billy held him back.

"No," he insisted. "Let 'im have his say."

Tom looked at Billy, perplexed. He was going to let this idjit talk to him like that? Tom shrugged, letting Jimmy be his guest in getting himself into a bad situation.

"Go on, Jimmy," Billy said.

Jimmy looked on at Billy a moment, unsure of what he was playing at, allowing him to talk down to him in front of the others, but Billy's face looked in some way interested, and in some way ashamed. Jimmy had the distinct feeling that Billy wanted to take the punishment.

"Where were you when she got hurt?" Jimmy asked.

Billy only stared, full-on shame dimming his naturally bright face. He couldn't blame Jimmy for this, for being so upset. He knew, after all, that he cared about Lucy, too. Very much. Billy knew he deserved this punishment, allowing Jimmy to chastise him in front of the others.

"I heard you was with yet another girl, in fact. Lucy could have gone up in flames! Lucky enough I was there. *I* was there,"—Jimmy pointed to himself, then to Billy—"not you!"

"Moffey—"

"You gonna give me some excuse now, about how you're trying to show her you're done with her? She gets it—we all do. It doesn't excuse you from being such a poor excuse for a man. Out of any of us, it's *you* should have been there!"

"Maybe things are a little more complicated than all that," Billy suggested.

"What could be more complicated than simply showing somebody you care about that you give a damn?"

"All right, Jimmy. You said your piece—"

"No. No, I ain't finished yet." Jimmy took in a deep breath to quell the anger welling inside of his chest. "The entire town out there in Picacho knows what happened to her. Knows that she was with child, and unwed. Word's made it way around here, too. You turned her into a whore. You shamed her while you walked away and screwed around with your dirty little camp girls. You ain't nothin' but a goddamned pimp!"

Tom stepped up. "All right, that's it! That's enough—"

Billy pushed him back and told him to stay out of it.

Billy closed his eyes tightly and dropped his head. It had never occurred to him that Lucy's reputation had been damaged even further in such a way. He was too busy being selfish in a way he thought would be best for her.

"You're a real bastard for that, Billy. You let her bleed it out and then turned your back!"

Billy's head remained down, tucked in shame.

"Did you think she was going to survive that without any consequences?"

"No," Billy whispered. "I didn't think nothing of it, truth be told."

"No, you didn't. You thought about yourself—"

"I thought about her! I thought everything about her, except that! I walked away from her for her own good, and it wasn't easy! It still ain't. Say what you want to me about being a real piece of shit, I deserve it, but don't you never tell me that she was never a thought in my mind!"

Jimmy only stood as the two of them stared at one another, their eyes locked in battle, until finally Jimmy said, "Aw hell, this ain't worth it. What's done is done, and you did it..."

Jimmy walked away from him, crossing the street to meet Lucy on her way back from the store. He met with her and they walked together back to the room that they now shared. Billy looked on, his wretched soul crushed more than it had been.

oooooooooooooooo

I had my saddle bag in the room and was placing my things inside. I didn't have so much and it didn't take me long.

"My things are set to go," Jimmy remarked.

"Good."

"You sure you wanna do this? Leave him, I mean."

I thought a moment. *No,* I thought. *No, I don't want to leave him. Never. Not ever.*

"Yes," I bravely replied.

A knock sounded from the door and Jimmy asked who was on the other side. When Billy declared himself, Jimmy looked to me for an answer.

"Come in," I hollered.

The door opened and Billy peeked around it before entering. I looked at Jimmy and cocked my head, indicating for him to let us alone. He nodded then shifted his eyes warily to Billy before walking past him and out the door. I went about my business, but slowly, feeling both awkward and thrilled. Things were strange between us but Billy always gave me a pleasant charge.

"What's it you're doing there?" he wondered.

I didn't answer. I just went about my business. I didn't want to lose it, no matter what he came here for, to apologize, say he was sorry. Didn't matter. I couldn't let it matter.

He hooked his thumbs in his gun belt and stood there thinking on what to say when it occurred to him. "How're you feeling? You know...your arm."

I felt my face flush in anger at that, but I needed to remain calm.

"It stings, but it's well, I can assure you. At least that's what the doctor says."

His eyes squinted, trying to smell the proverbial rat in the room.

"Just what *is* it you're doing there?"

He walked toward me and grabbed onto my good arm as I had my hands in my bag.

"What does it matter to you what I'm doing?"

"Because it looks like you're getting your things together—"

"So?"

"So what do you think you're doing?"

I thought to shift his mind from my task by turning things around on him in order to divert him.

"Just who were you with that you were unable to get away to visit with me, to make sure I was all right?"

He stared at me wide-eyed, confusion creeping onto his face, not sure which argument to pursue. He peered back to my bag, then into my eyes.

"What...what are you talking about?"

"The whore that you again soiled my bed with. Who was she that she kept you from me?"

"Hey..." Lightly, he yanked my arm and made me look into his face. "What do you know about it?"

I looked at him in disbelief.

"Tell me you were alone. Tell me you were alone right now and I'll believe you."

He remained silent and put his head down.

"What is it?" I asked him. "You don't want to lie to me? Is that it?"

"Lucy, please, not this, not now. I came to see how you're fairing—"

"Yes, I know that, Billy, but you'd have known how I was fairing if you'd have come to my side instead of lying by that of another."

I had stung him. The look on his face told me so. I could see how his countenance grew angry before my eyes. He had come here looking conquered and humbled, and perhaps I should have let that decide how this would go. But I was angrier than I could have imagined, whether I understood him or not, whether I believed in him or not. He wasn't there. He wasn't there. *He wasn't there!*

He squeezed my arm again and his face seemed to fall in on itself as his brow creased in anger and his eyes pierced mine. I yanked myself from him and pushed him away. I felt he was too close to me—closer than I wanted him to be, a feeling I was unfamiliar with.

"I can't go through this with you anymore. You know how it is, don't play this game with me just to pique me!" he barked. "If nothing else, I want for us to get along—"

"Yes, I know you're tired of the game you started, and I'm finished with it, too. I never cared for it in the first place. If you love me the most, then it's me you should be with and no one else."

"I'm tired of this argument with you—"

"You ain't any more tired than I am, Billy. I'm tired of never getting a say. I gave myself to you, and you took what I gave you. And you have the nerve to humiliate me and put me out the door like some private whore."

"You gave it up willingly, so don't you get high and mighty and act like you had no choice in the matter."

"That's right, I gave it willingly. You loved me, and I loved you. Is that what it's like for you and the others. Do you love them? Do they love you back?"

"It doesn't matter if they do or not."

"Did it matter if I did? I trusted myself to you and you treat me like nothing more than a common harlot."

His eyes blazed and his cheeks grew hot. His breathing grew loud and forced as he tried to control the anger he was feeling. I empathized, but apathetically, as I was in my own angry little hell. There was nothing I was about to do to comfort him. Not anymore.

"We've been through this several times. I've never made you any promises. From day one I made damn sure you knew it wasn't going anywhere with us."

"Then why did you take me to bed and lay with me and tell me things like you wanted only me?"

Hands on his hips, he threw his head back and let out a breath, smiling mockingly before looking back at me. "I see. I broke you, so you think that means I oughta be stuck with you. It ain't much of a riddle. I knew you was willing and I took advantage. I don't remember you trying to stop me, neither. You ain't no different from those other girls who fall on their backs when I want them to..."

I looked at him, my face severe. As his allocution wound down, his last words trailing almost to a whisper, I saw from the look on his face that he had forced himself to go through with those awful words, like a sick child who forces himself to swallow awful medicine because he knows it will make him better. He'd said those things because he felt that meanness was the best trick to push me away again, and pushing me away, as always, is what he felt was best.

But, he knew he'd made a grave mistake and gone too far, and he lowered his face to me, turning it to the right slightly, giving me his full permission to punish him, as if his permission would have mattered at all.

I walked to him, my eyes unblinking, and I doled out the first slap. I hit him as hard as my good arm would allow, leaving an angry red mark in the shape of my hand.

But I wasn't finished, and he knew this, holding steady to allow the second strike to hit home. After I'd struck him again, I grabbed my bag and pushed past him and out the door where Jimmy had our horses waiting. Behind me I could hear him curse and yell that he was sorry. I heard him come after me.

When he'd caught up to me he again put his hand gently around my good arm and tried to swing me around to face him, but I fought against this. Tears began to spill, and I hated every one of them. I hated that he could hurt me so badly, and knowing that he didn't mean it, what he'd said, made it all the more worse. If he could love me beyond words, yet still manage such awful, deliberate words and fell me with such ease, what did that mean? I didn't know, and I didn't want to consider it.

"Lucy, please, stop. Stop! Look at me, please!"

I didn't want to look. I didn't want him to see that he had gotten to me, but I knew I had no choice. I wouldn't get away from him without allowing him his chance to apologize, if it were even possible to apologize for what he'd done and said. I turned around and looked at him. When he saw my face his own fell.

"Mi Dios, mi amor. No..."

He put his hands to my arms softly, staring intently into my face. I swiped his arms from mine, angering my wound, and turned back around, but he was quick and grabbed me again, turning me to face him with such fluidity.

"You're leaving, aren't you? Don't do that."

"Why? Isn't that what you wanted? You've been making it a point to ensure I knew that's what you wanted. You go around with them other...those other, *girls* to discourage me. You say awful things to me! Well, now you're getting what you want!"

It was almost hard to get the words out—I was so frighteningly upset. I tried to turn away from him again but he wouldn't allow it.

"No, I don't want you to go. I never wanted you to go. I know you know that—"

"—Right. I knew that, but you could still pretend, couldn't you? Under the pretense, you could fuck whomever you wanted. I'm gone, Billy. Gone! There's nothing you can do, or say, that will make me stay. You won't hurt me again, not ever."

He crumbled to the ground like a broken man and kneeled before me in the dust, pleading, but I turned around and walked toward my horse. A crowd had gathered around, quietly watching the display, including our friends, but we barely noticed, and either way, I couldn't have cared less. I was more than happy to stomp their hero to the ground after the way he'd treated me in front of them all.

When he saw I kept walking, refusing to stop, even for his sorry display of repentance, he got up and ran around me, standing in front of me and blocking my way. Putting his hands to my arms again, he plead, "I'm begging you...don't leave. I came here today to make amends with you—to fix our friendship."

"You were too late. Far too late! And I never wanted to be your 'friend'."

I stepped around him and handed my bag off to Jimmy, who had the rest of my belongings strapped to my horse.

"Where are you going?" he asked.

"It doesn't matter—not to you, anyway."

I mounted my horse and looked down at him. "And don't you come looking for me, neither!"

"You're going off with them girls, ain't ya?"

Fear shown in his face, and I couldn't decide if I enjoyed this or felt badly. I was still consumed with love for him—I was very madly in love with him. But I wanted to see him feel as lowly as he had made me feel. I wanted him to suffer, even if only for now.

"Please stay away from them girls, Lucy. If you gotta leave, then go, but please don't go near them girls—they ain't right and—"

"And you are? And I got my own money, Billy. I don't need to make any off your name giving it up like I gave it up for you."

This stung him and he started at me, placing his hands around my boots, trying to hold on, his glassy eyes blinking in disbelief and his mouth open in shock.

"I didn't mean that, and you know it!"

I sniffed, but an evil place in my heart truly began to enjoy this.

"I don't know what I know about you anymore. I had put all my faith in you, and it brought me to this."

I spurred my horse and he stood back, looking up at me, still in shock. Jimmy followed me along and I left Billy in my wake as I looked forward at the wide open spaces before me.

I once knew a boy named William, and I was proud to know him. But this boy I was leaving behind I couldn't get away from fast enough. And I knew he wouldn't let me run off for long without coming for me, but I didn't care about that now. I trotted along the street until we reached the town limits. I brought my horse to a gallop and I didn't look back.

Readers Guide

1. Early in the novel, Lucy tries to talk sense to Billy after their defeat in Lincoln. She tries to get him to see the error in pressing on with the war, but Billy refuses to listen to her. What are your thoughts concerning Billy's view?

2. Billy dislikes Lucy associating with the Painted Ladies who are wandering whores. Billy forbids Lucy from having anything to do with them, but Lucy discounts his concern as she is in need of female company. Is it understandable that he should feel this way given the reputation of the Painted Ladies. Do you feel Billy is right in trying to protect Lucy from their bad influence?

3. During the Día de Los Muertos celebration, Lucy sees the bright lights of the fireworks display, letting go of Billy's hand as she runs toward the colorful display. Could this be seen as Lucy finding her own bearings in a savage new world?

4. Lucy is summoned to testify against Finnegan Flynn in a court of law. Lucy's first strategy is to lie as she believes it could mean sending a crooked man and cold-blooded killer to the gallows. Billy advises against this, telling Lucy to save her soul by telling the truth. He reminds her that by lying under oath for Flynn may mean the same as one lying under oath against Billy. Do you think Billy is in the right to reprimand her for this?

5. James Moffey is caught between Lucy and his old friend, Finnegan Flynn, when Finn is on trial for murder. Lucy expects Jimmy to tell the truth, that he saw Finn cause trouble against the Chinaman, and stand over his corpse with his gun out. Jimmy lies in court out of loyalty toward his friend, and Lucy is furious. Is it understandable that Lucy should be angry with him?

6. When Lucy is caught in an opium den and is under the severe effects of the drug, Billy becomes angered and handles this by treating Lucy roughly, dunking her in a trough of water nearly drowning her before locking her, cold and wet, in a room in order to teach her a lesson. It is made clear that he is sorry for his actions, but under the circumstances and his feeling responsible for her, would you say he treated the situation unfairly?

7. Billy attempts to make peace between the remaining Regulators and Dolan/Evans Boys. Meeting in Lincoln, they celebrate until one of Evan's men murders an innocent man. In order to make the death look as though the murdered man instigated it, Dolan instructs one of the men to place a gun in the corpse's hand. Billy, desperate to get out of town and away from the crowd of outlaws and trouble, offers to place the gun in the dead man's hand as an excuse to leave, which he of course does not do. Do you agree with Billy's reasoning and quick thinking?

8. Billy receives what he believes is an excellent opportunity to have his name cleared by Governor Lew Wallace, the terms of which include Billy turning state's evidence of the Dolan/Evans Gang. Governor Lew Wallace promises if Billy does this, he'll clear his name of all considered wrong doing during the Lincoln County War. Billy jumps at the opportunity, but Lucy has reservations which she proclaims to Billy, telling him Wallace is merely using him and will say anything to get what he needs. Billy refuses to heed Lucy's advice, desperate to have his name cleared. What are your thoughts? Is Lucy right in warning Billy? Or is it understandable that Billy should ignore Lucy's warning?

9. Lucy is angered at the site of seeing Billy and one of his admirers, Celsa Jaramillo. Celsa taunts Lucy, and because of this, Lucy acts out, embarrassing the girl in public and upsetting Billy. How do you feel about Lucy's reaction to the girl, and do you feel Lucy was justified in her actions?

10. After Lucy is shot by Adriana and nearly dies, also suffering a miscarriage, Billy distances himself from her in some seemingly unforgivable ways. Once it is understood that he is attempting to force Lucy away for her own good, believing himself to be the only true reason she stays, can he be redeemed in the Reader's mind though he is misguided in this action?

11. As with the previous question: When Lucy burns her arm, Billy refuses to go, giving the explanation that there will be no chance for Lucy to forgive him if he doesn't go to her. In Billy's mind, he believes he is making a great sacrifice for true love. Is this understandable? Can the Reader identify this as a selfless act?

12. Despite knowing that Billy is cruel to her for her own good, is Lucy choosing to leave Billy the right thing for her to despite the dangers of crossing uninhabited land? Is this the best way to teach him a lesson, and for him to understand that he is not in charge of their relationship?

www.ingramcontent.com/pod-product-compliance
Lightning Source LLC
Chambersburg PA
CBHW060244030726
47493CB00025B/2148